# A Thousand Glittering Lights

Jennie Lynn Roberts

First paperback edition June 2024

Editor: Olivia Ventura at Hot Tree Editing
Cover design by Sarah Hansen at Okay Creations

ISBN 978-1-7399518-8-7 (paperback)
978-1-7399518-9-4 (e-book)

www.jennielynnroberts.com

*For Gayle*

**"We can do hard things."**
*Glennon Doyle*

*And for all the writers, creators, and people who imagine
magical things. Our world is more beautiful because of you.*

# Acknowledgments

A huge thank you to Olivia Ventura at Hot Tree Editing for all her help. I owe a great deal of my journey as a writer and author to her insightful challenges and thoughtful guidance.

Thank you to my amazing beta readers—Jennifer, Andrea, and Kim—for their careful observations and all their support.

Thank you also to Sarah Hansen of Okay Creations for this gorgeous cover. I love it!

As always, thank you to my family. I love you, Mark, Alethea, and Michael. You make the magic possible, and you mean the world to me.

# A THOUSAND GLITTERING LIGHTS

JENNIE LYNN ROBERTS

# Chapter One

S‍HE COULD DO IT. She could walk across the paving and climb into her shiny black mini. She could drive down to the sea, dig her feet into the sand, and enjoy the pale spring sunshine. There would be freedom and movement. Salt in the air. People to talk to.

*Light flashed on metal. Diesel fumes and the stink of hot tires on tarmac burned her nostrils. She screamed as she flew over the handlebars, the merciless road hurtling toward her. Pain exploded.*

Ellie stepped back unconsciously before bumping into the door behind her and realizing she was going the wrong way. She stopped. Took a breath. And made herself move forward once more. One foot after the other.

Sunshine filtered through the spring leaves, dappling the neat paving, but the splashes of light and dark churned uneasily. She kept going. Her keys were still in her hand. Her breaths were shallow and aching, but she took them. Every day, she took a few more steps. Today would be no different.

If only she didn't have to do it all alone.

Maybe she should bring Nissy with her? Ellie glanced back at her cottage. Nissy was sitting in her usual window, daintily washing her ginger-and-cream striped paw and enjoying her favorite sunbeam. She definitely didn't want to be bundled into her cat carrier and put in the car. She wouldn't approve, even if she was free to ride shotgun up front with Ellie.

A vision of Nissy wearing driving goggles and a short scarf that flapped in the wind as she sat primly on the passenger seat rose in Ellie's mind. She snorted a little hysterically; Nissy would *not* be impressed. And she'd only just forgiven Ellie for abandoning her at the cat-sitter while she was in hospital.

Still, a spark of warmth rekindled in Ellie's chest. She wasn't alone. She had Nissy. She had friends. She had the glorious, creative, inspiring community she was slowly building. She could do this.

Ellie opened the car door, climbed inside, and pressed the Start button. The car turned on immediately, the electric engine turning over almost silently—too silently. She turned on the radio, but the upbeat indie rock of her favorite station grated, and she turned it back off.

Opening the window helped. The sound of birds singing and an airplane buzzing in the distance filtered in to keep her company as she rolled forward.

She paused at her gate to check her narrow country lane. It was empty as usual. Her little lane wasn't the problem. The problem was the much busier road she'd reach in a few minutes. Crowded and twisting, it took its travelers—commuters and tourists from the seaside towns— back and forth to London.

Yesterday she'd made it to the gate. Today, she would go farther.

Movement in her rearview mirror caught her attention, and she paused to check behind her. What had she seen? A shadow had moved. Hadn't it?

She scanned the area carefully before huffing at herself. There was nothing out of place. God, she was jumpy.

Ellie crawled along the dirt lane, reached the main road, and stopped. She took a breath. She was ready to face this demon. She wiped her damp palms on her thighs before taking hold of the wheel once more, and then moved her foot to the accelerator. It was time—

A cyclist came around the forested corner. The rider flew down the hill, hurtling too fast down the center of the narrow road. Light glinted off their bicycle, and their short hair blew wildly. They weren't wearing a helmet. God.

Ellie froze, nausea rising swiftly. She could still feel the crunch of metal. The uncontrolled horror of knowing she was in the air. The sickening thud. And something about the helmet. Something scratched at her brain. Something terrible. Something important.

She clung to the steering wheel, trembling, eyes hot and prickling, swallowing acid and battling with herself. It was just one cyclist. They were gone. She'd made it farther than ever before. She could keep going. Panic attacks weren't new to her. She'd had them before. She'd survived them before.

She rested her forehead on the wheel and concentrated on finding the safe place in her mind. Pausing there, trying to be kind to herself. Did she have to face all her terror today? Or could she take the win?

Yes. She could take this win. Tomorrow, she would try again.

The nausea receded as the heavy weight of fear lifted. Ellie reversed until she could safely turn and drive slowly back to her driveway. Her breathing settled as she parked and climbed out of the car. Now, with her back to the gate, she could focus on the roses and clematis sprawling up the cottage walls and appreciate the forest spreading around her property. She could take another, slower, deeper breath. The earth smelled of growing things, of sweet pea flowers and sunshine on green leaves.

Nissy had finished grooming and was dozing, amber eyes half shut. She looked warm and content. Of course, she'd chosen to sit exactly two inches to the side of the special floating cat bed Ellie had spent an entire day watching YouTube videos to build for her.

When Ellie first brought her home from the shelter two years ago, she'd been scrawny and skittish, meowing, yowling, and complaining all day. Now that she was happily settled, she preferred chirping her demands, and mostly expected to be treated like a princess without stooping to make requests in the first place. She was taking her time to decide whether the new bed was worthy of her, but she'd always adored that sunbeam.

They had that in common. They both loved curling up in a sunbeam. But somehow, unlike Nissy, Ellie'd found herself caught up in more and more obligations and responsibilities, and fewer and fewer sunbeams. There was always just one more thing to do. Something she might miss or get wrong. So she'd worked harder.

And then she'd nearly died and lost it all.

Ellie lifted her hand to rest it on the solid wood of the door. It was smooth and warm from the sunshine. The cottage was still here. Nissy was still here. *She* was still here. And tomorrow, she would go just a little farther.

She made her way inside closing the door behind her,

dropped her keys in the bowl on the hallway table and, as she did, she raised her eyes to the large mirror on the wall.

A huge, scowling man stood behind her.

Her body flooded with fear. A rough scream caught in her throat. There was no time to run. Nowhere to escape—he was right behind her. He was between her and the door.

Panic returned in a rush as shock and dread coiled around her. Could she reach for her keys? Could she use them as a weapon? Should she fight? God.

She froze, caught by the churning terror, with no idea of how to save herself.

But he didn't move. He stood as still as she did, and even more silently. Watching her in the mirror as she watched him.

He was tall, several inches taller than her, and his dark hair was tousled, as if he'd been out in the wind or run his hand through it many times. A rough beard covered his jaw, with a small gap where a scar cut through the top of his lip.

Her gaze traveled over his face until their reflected eyes met. His were a clear ocean blue, bracketed by tiny lines, full of some unreadable emotion... and utterly focused on her.

Ellie jolted. She didn't know him at all. But somehow, they were connected. Awareness thrummed between them, twisting and curling in the space between their bodies. And she would have sworn he felt it too. His frown grew deeper, his eyes darker. His gaze held her locked in place.

He saw her. And she saw him. She saw his brooding intensity. His look of grim severity—as if he had swallowed all his pain and grief and longing and turned it into flinty defiance—him against the world.

Her hand reached out toward the mirror as if she could

touch him there. Insanely, stupidly, somehow without her thought or control. "Who are you?" she whispered.

He shook his head. Just one tiny motion. But then he lifted his hand toward her and took a deliberate step closer. It was enough to release her from her strange captivity, and she spun to face him. To face the danger head on. But her hallway was empty.

He was gone.

# Chapter Two

Ellie did another lap of the house, checking the locks on doors and windows with one hand while holding her phone against her ear with the other. Nissy was sleeping in her plush cat cave in Ellie's home office, entirely disinterested in helping to secure the house.

Night had fallen and, out here, miles from the nearest village, it was *dark*. It was comforting to have her best friend on the other end of the line. "How are you, Vic?" Ellie asked, testing the window bolts in her office. It was the only room in the house that held anything of real value: Nissy, and Ellie's tech. "We haven't caught up since I saw you in the hospital," she continued, not adding that they'd mostly discussed physiotherapy programs and the tepid rice pudding. And that weeks had passed since then. Weeks of rehab and recuperation.

"Yeah, I'm... I'm good," Vic replied. "Just busy, you know."

Vic *was* busy. And she'd picked up a lot of work for Ellie while she was recovering, which she was very grateful for. But Ellie was back now. More or less. And Vic had been "busy" for months. "You're not alone. If you need something, let me know," Ellie said, moving to the next room.

"I will." Vic's tone was firm and friendly enough, but it still lacked the warmth it used to have. And Ellie was starting to wonder how long it would take before they felt like sisters—not by blood, but by choice—once more.

She shivered and pulled her gown closer. It was a velvety soft black fleece embroidered with tiny silver stars, and she loved it. It was a kind of armor. Protection against the darkness. Warmth when she felt alone.

"How long are you planning to work from home?" Victoria asked in her ear.

"I don't know," she admitted. "I'm not ready to come back to London yet. Hopefully in a week or two." It was the truth... but not the whole truth.

Ellie trusted Victoria with her life, her business, *everything*.

They'd met in preschool and quickly become best friends. When Ellie's mother died of cancer when Ellie was ten, it was Vic's shoulder she cried on. When her father buried himself in work, distancing himself from the daughter who looked just like his lost wife, Vic became her family.

Neither of them questioned whether they would go to college together, they both simply assumed they would. They studied computer science together and they shared a house, sometimes bickering, sometimes arguing, but always as close as sisters.

They were both driven. Both determined to work hard and play harder—online for Ellie, IRL for Vi—and they brought out the best in each other. Ellie gave Vic the stability and freedom from drama she never seemed to get at home, and Vic was Ellie's champion; cheering her on and dragging her away from worrying about her to-do list. They'd been best friends for most of their lives, staying close even when Ellie was working eighteen-hour days and Vic was off traveling the world with a backpack.

But things had changed between them and now Ellie didn't want to admit how difficult getting back onto the road was proving. Telling Vic about her panic attacks felt like adding weight to an already floundering raft. It was easier to stay positive, and hopefully find a way back to the comfortable—and comforting—friendship they used to have.

"You don't want to come to London?" Vic asked, a hint of *something* in her voice. Victoria loved the city. She loved the bright lights, the vibrant clubs and restaurants. All the glamor. But Ellie didn't miss it—not that she'd seen much of it in the last few years, anyway.

After she'd set up Dangerous Business Games, she'd spent most of her time in London. Getting her business off the ground took every hour of every day and she'd needed to be there. But she wasn't at parties, she was working.

Eventually she'd found her feet. Vic had joined her, taking some of the weight from her shoulders. She'd recruited great people and developed an amazing team. And she'd bought her dream home near the sea... and then she'd spent even less time enjoying London's amusements. Property was much cheaper so far out of the city, and she used all the money she saved—and the hours of travel time— to write storylines and develop her code.

After she brought Nissy home, she'd moved to working remotely three days a week and only going up to London on Tuesdays and Thursdays unless she was really needed. Nissy was happier—they both were—surrounded by trees and open skies.

But it was more isolating, too.

Ellie rattled the kitchen door, checking it was firmly locked, and peered through the glass to her vegetable garden. It was a mass of shadows and darkness, impossible to see even if someone had been standing right in the middle.

She shivered and rubbed her arms, trying to soothe the goose bumps. To warm the chill she couldn't quite shake—the chill she hadn't been able to shake for weeks. She needed to do something. Change something. But she'd been caught in a holding pattern, some strange gray purgatory. As if something deep inside her had been waiting.

*Waiting for him.*

No. That was insane. She'd spent too long creating imaginary worlds, and now she'd started to believe her own fantasies. Ellie pushed the thought away and focused on Vic. "I'm much more productive down here without all the distractions of the office. Would you believe that I got over three thousand e-mails while I was in hospital?" She grimaced to herself, wishing she could quietly delete them all without anybody noticing. "I'm working through them in between speccing some of the later game dynamics for after Luke and Sienna find the fae lord's mountain citadel."

It was going to be *gorgeous*. The citadel was a magnificent hybrid of Minas Tirith and the Goblin King's labyrinth. "They have to work their way through the maze for hours before they find the entrance to the sky bridge. There are so many puzzles we can incorporate. And the shadows make it so much edgier. The mist is everywhere—corrupting the earth as it spreads—so the creatures they meet can be just that little bit twisted. The best kind of sexy, diabolical fae." A moment of lightness bubbled through her; this was what she had always loved.

"You don't need to do any of that," Vic replied sharply, and Ellie's bubbles of joy popped and faded. "Don't you think maybe it would be better to take a break for a week or two and leave it to... ah, let yourself heal?"

Well. Clearly. Since now she was seeing people. She remembered his face so clearly, like it was etched into her brain. Those eyes, looking straight into hers. Except... he wasn't real. No one had been in her house. Nissy had been asleep on the windowsill in the dining room the entire time. Ellie's office was empty, her firewall untouched. All the windows were closed, just as she left them. Her front door was locked. She'd tried it four times. And she'd just checked it all again.

But... why was Vic suggesting a break? Hadn't she just said she was too busy? Had Ellie misunderstood the question about London? It didn't sound like Victoria was asking how soon she could come back—it sounded like Vic wanted her to stay away.

No, that didn't make sense. Vic was looking out for her. "I can't take a break," Ellie said slowly. "Then you'd be even busier. And it's not a good time to take my eye off development."

She pressed her face into the glass of the wide folding doors that led from her living room to her deck and peered into the dark garden. Maybe she should get some security lights? Maybe some cameras? Having the forest nearby hadn't bothered her before, but now it seemed menacingly dark. An ominous presence of deep purple and pitch black, creeping toward the house.

Nissy sauntered into the living room behind her. The darkness didn't bother *her* at all. Ellie reached down and scratched gently behind her silky ears, letting Nissy's gentle purr soothe her.

"Don't you think?" Vic asked. And judging by the hint of impatience creeping into her tone, probably not for the first time. Damn. Ellie'd left her hanging. She wrinkled her nose, frustrated. Somehow conversations with Vic kept going wrong.

"Sorry, Vic, what did you say?"

"I said that if you're determined to work, maybe you could leave the game dynamics to my team and focus on the marketing package. We need a brief for the agency that brings some storylines to life. You've always been the best at that."

Best at briefing an ad agency? Better at a junior marketing role than the essential systems for her own game?

Ellie sank into the closest sofa. Victoria was her head of Development. It made sense that she wanted some autonomy, but that didn't change Ellie's ultimate responsibility.

When she'd launched the first game, there'd been plenty of people who mocked her. More than one nasty troll came crawling out from under their social media bridge. But she'd believed in her idea. She still did. A lot of people underestimated the number of female gamers, and adding a sexy storyline with a fulfilling HEA tapped into a severely underrepresented market. The fantasy world she'd created —underpinned by the romance between Luke and Sienna— was a thrilling, beautiful escape for her family of players. And she took that seriously.

"There's no point in starting work on an advertising brief yet," Ellie argued. "The people who loved *The Shadowbound Rift* are already desperate for *Part 2: The Binding*. We need to make sure it's absolutely perfect before it goes out into the world. Once we know what we're doing, we can start pulling together a teaser campaign and looking at advertising."

Victoria huffed. "Having a clear premise now won't hurt."

"We already have a clear premise—Luke and Sienna battling more sexy fae—and we're sharing it across all our social media. But spending money and time on advertising when we don't have a finished game doesn't make sense."

"But if we want to sell—"

"I *don't* want to sell." Ellie cut Vic off more sharply than she intended. But she was tired of this discussion.

Vic was her family, she had been one of her earliest employees—she had the stock options to prove it—and she would take a hefty payday if Ellie sold... they both would. But Ellie wasn't ready. She didn't think she ever would be.

The whole idea of the sale had blindsided her. And with her accident only a week later, she hadn't had a chance to deal with it before her world upended. And then when she'd come home, she'd put it off. Partly because she was hurting and tired. But mostly because Vic was so keen on it... and it was her father's brainchild.

He had found the buyer and come to her with the deal. He'd been full of excitement and joy, talking about her game and the world she'd created with interest and respect for the first time ever.

The little girl in her had been looking for that approval —that acceptance and encouragement—for so long, she'd hardly known how to respond. And so, instead of shutting it down immediately, she'd promised to think about it. And then Vic had leaped at the idea, and suddenly she was stuck. Her father and her best friend stood on one side; what she wanted—what she knew was right—was on the other. She didn't want to hurt them. Or lose them. And so she'd delayed.

Ellie softened her voice and tried to close the gap between them. "We don't need to sell, Vic. *The Shadowbound Rift* means something to people. You know that."

Ellie let her gaze travel away from the window, back to the framed character art spread over her living room walls. Some of it was from the game, but a lot of it had been sent in by fans. People so in love with the story that they wanted to build on it, wanted to add their own creativity and imagination... and a whole lot of spice. "Our players love Sienna and Luke. They want to take them through the next chapter in their story." She paused for a second, looking for the right words. "I don't want to put that in the hands of someone whose only focus is how much money they can make."

Vic blew out a rough breath, but she was listening. She also loved Sienna and Luke. And Vic wanted what was best for her, Ellie knew it, just like she wanted the best for Vic.

She tried to find an olive branch. "Send me whatever you feel I can help with the most—whatever will take some of the load off your shoulders—and I'll look at it tomorrow. And maybe you could come down and visit sometime. Let's take that break together. It's still a bit cold to swim in the sea, but we could eat fish-and-chips on the beach. What do you think?"

"Fine." Vic didn't sound especially excited about the idea. "But you are at least thinking about selling, aren't you?"

Ellie curled her feet under her and leaned back tiredly as Nissy jumped up to sit on the arm of the sofa and kneaded it with her paws. She had already thought... and thought and thought. "I've been over this a hundred times now. I think it would be best to turn it down."

"No!" Vic's response was instant and grating.

"No?"

"I mean—" Vic took in a breath, loud enough to hear down the phoneline. "—Please just think about it. For me. For all these years, I'm asking you."

"Vic—"

"It would be your due diligence anyway. You wouldn't want to make a mistake because of a knee-jerk reaction. You need to think it through properly."

That stung. God. Vic got her right in the soft, perfectionist part of her heart. "Okay," she agreed tiredly, "I'll give it one more look. We still have a few weeks to consider the offer anyway."

"A few weeks. I didn't realize we still had that long to wait," Vic muttered.

"Yeah, we got an extension because of my accident, but honestly—" Ellie swallowed the rest. Muffled in the background of Vic's call, almost too quiet to hear, and presumably not intended for her to hear at all, a masculine voice said something that sounded a lot like, "Too fucking long."

Ellie dropped her feet to the floor and sat up straight. What was too long? Was it the sale? Who was with Victoria during their conversation? No one else was supposed to know about the offer. And, even more worrying, she thought she'd recognized the voice. "Is Warren there?" Ellie asked.

She'd never liked Vic's on-again-off-again ex. He was always quick with a backhanded compliment, showering Victoria with attention one minute, then cold and jealous the next. He put Ellie down whenever he could: if she ever had to hear him call her Ellie-belly again, she wouldn't be held responsible for her actions. And Nissy had hated him —which was enough of a veto for Ellie. But, even worse, he had definitely cheated.

She'd been glad when they had finally broken up for good. At the time, it had been awful. She'd told Vic what she'd seen, and it had devastated her friend. But their friendship had survived—intact, if a little cooler—and Vic had let Warren go. Thank God. It was worth the time it took to get their friendship back on track if it meant Vic was safely away from Warren.

"No," Vic answered quickly.

That was weird. "I thought I heard him...."

There was a second of silence before Vic chuckled a little too loudly. "You didn't. I... I leaned back and accidentally turned the telly on. Don't worry; it's off now."

Ellie paused uncertainly, trying to listen, but there was no other background noise. Just Victoria's voice as she moved on to talking about plans for the next day.

Vic had visited her in the hospital. She had stood beside her when her family was nowhere to be found. Vic held her hand when her heart was broken by her first serious boyfriend, and Vic bought the champagne when *The Shadowbound Rift* went live. Ellie trusted her. Hell, Vic was in her will as principal beneficiary. If Ellie died, Vic would get everything.

But she still felt strangely unsettled. As if she had to choose her words carefully as she navigated the rest of their conversation. By the time they said goodbye, Ellie was exhausted. Her ribs ached, and so did her heart.

She put down her phone and picked at a loose thread on the sleeve of her gown, listening to the wind. Then she pulled out the television remote and flicked through channels, scrolling listlessly. But nothing held her interest, and she turned it off again in disgust.

Nissy walked over to her and put a foot on her lap. But before she decided to sit, she sneezed delicately, whiskers twitching. Then she shook her furry head and sneezed again.

"Bless you," Ellie murmured, kissing her on the head. But Nissy narrowed her eyes and glared at Ellie as if she was responsible for her sneezes *and* all the ills in the world, and then stalked away to sit with her back pointedly turned.

The rejection stung, and Ellie picked up her book, trying not to feel abandoned. She read two pages. And then realized she hadn't concentrated enough to understand the words, and put it back down rather than starting again.

She was agitated and unsettled and she wanted... something. Someone. *Him.*

No. That was mad.

She stood, pacing restlessly before giving up and striding back into the hallway. She stepped up to the mirror. Closer and closer. Until she could rest her fingers on the smooth surface. Her eyes locked on the reflected hallway behind her and she bit her lip, half afraid that he would be there, half afraid that he would not.

The mirror was cold beneath her fingertips. The tiles in the hall chilled her feet through her socks. A door rattled as the wind moaned softly through the nearby woods.

And the hall stayed empty.

# Chapter Three

There was darkness. And there was a voice.

The voice spoke sometimes, a rambling dialogue interspersed with the occasional huff of irritation or snort of quiet laughter, as if the speaker were talking to herself. The melody rising and falling soothed him. It held him. Kept him company in the darkness.

Sometimes she cried. It was rare. But those were the worst times. He could hear her grief, but he couldn't see her or touch her. And if she heard him calling to her, she certainly never responded.

And sometimes... sometimes he heard the rustle of limbs moving against the sheets. Sometimes she would moan. He couldn't see her. Could only hear her. Could only wish that he knew what she looked like, so he could imagine her soft and warm and languid.

And he had to remind himself that she was a dream. A fantasy that his brain had offered to soothe him, drifting alone in the darkness.

But then he saw her. The darkness faded, just for a moment, and he found himself standing in an unfamiliar hallway in an unfamiliar house. He looked up, into a mirror he'd never seen before, and there she was.

She had shoulder-length blonde hair, fine strands framing her face. Big green eyes that looked right into his. She called to him like a siren, as unknown and dangerous, but just as beguiling.

Somehow, she brought back memories of pain. Of fear. Memories that he pushed down and away.

She asked him his name, and he recognized her voice immediately. But deep in his bones, he knew those weren't the right words.

"Please don't leave me," echoed through his mind, but he couldn't form the sounds.

She stretched her fingertips toward the mirror, almost as if she felt his presence like he felt hers. He lifted his own hand in response, reaching for her as he stepped closer. He needed to wrap his arms around her. To hold her. To save her. She was in danger... but he had no idea what threatened her.

He only knew that they were connected. And that was terrifying. How could he hold a dream? How terrible would the darkness be after he had glimpsed the light? What if something happened to her while he was lost in the darkness? The thought filled him with dread as the shadows washed over him once more and the world faded.

The next time he awoke, it was light. The first thing he noticed was the sunshine spilling over his surroundings as the foggy darkness retreated. And the second was the sound of her voice coming from deeper in the house. Calling to him.

He drifted into a cottage-style living room, slowly becoming more aware. The room was spacious, full of light and air and bunches of cut wildflowers. Curtains drifted in the slow breeze coming in through an open folding door. Art covered the walls—a variety of styles and colors, but all of the same couple. A man and a woman, carrying swords, dressed in leather armor, fighting shadowy enemies.... No, not always fighting. Sometimes they were doing something else entirely. Something involving significantly less armor.

Where the hell was he?

He wandered back into the hallway and caught sight of himself in a rustic-style framed mirror on the wall. The mirror from his dream.

It was weirdly dissociating. He could see himself, see the hall, see himself *in* the hall. But it didn't make any sense.

He blinked, and the swirling vision settled. His face stared back at him. Familiar blue eyes. The white line of a small scar on his upper lip. He ran his fingers over the slight ridge, his mouth twitching into a smile. It was a funny story. He'd...

He froze. He couldn't remember.

His eyes widened in the mirror, fear written over his reflection before he got control and pushed it away, composing his features. Where the fuck was he? Why was he in this place?

Something was profoundly wrong, but he couldn't solve it until he knew where he was. That was what he needed. Concrete steps. A rational action plan.

But then an even worse question filled his mind. One he had no answer to. One he'd never imagined ever asking.

*Who* was he?

He leaned a hand on the wall, bowing his head, and sucked in a ragged breath. He had to do something. He needed answers. He needed *her*.

# Chapter Four

Ellie rubbed her eyes tiredly before turning yet another terrible page. Half of her couldn't quite believe that their lead writer had even looked at the storylines. Duane should know better; he was her most senior manager after Vic... and Vic definitely should know better.

Ellie read another few paragraphs, groaning at yet another narrative branch that led to a main character's certain death. Sure, they had to put Luke and Sienna through hell. *The Binding* was the sequel. There had to be suffering. The fissure between the two worlds that the characters were sucked into in the first game had fully opened, releasing the ancient fae to cover the earth in mist and growing darkness. The fae lord had built a citadel right on top of the fissure, guarding it with every kind of dark and deadly beast imaginable. Of course there would be danger, destruction, tension, and poor decisions. And of course Sienna and Luke would challenge each other. But they had to have a *chance*. There had to be hope.

She folded her arms on the kitchen table and let her head rest on her forearms. She'd chosen to print the storylines and work through them on paper, sitting in the sunshine that poured in from the wide windows. Sometimes it helped to see the words on paper, and her gaming room—ahem, office—was in the darkest corner of the house, well away from any irritating glare. But the sunshine wasn't helping. The storylines stayed miserable.

She sighed into the table. Her Dangerous Business team was the best. Duane just needed some direction. But Vic... damn it. She'd let Vic get away with more and more. Ellie had been so worried for her friend—and their friendship—that she'd made allowances. But there was a limit to how far she could let this go.

The storyline had to be fixed; she would start there. She pulled her notebook closer, maybe there was something she could save. Perhaps if she—

"Fuck," a masculine voice muttered quietly from the direction of the hallway.

Ellie startled.

Someone was in her house. A man. A man who sounded... enraged. No. Tormented? She couldn't tell. But the intensity of the emotion was clear.

Was it *him*?

She rose quietly to her feet, wincing as the chair legs scraped along the tiles. Had he heard her move? Thank God she'd chosen to work in the kitchen—just a few steps from the back door.

She grabbed her phone, tucked it into her pocket, and then crept toward the door, keeping her movements stealthy and silent.

Fear and worry churned through her mind. What if it was him? Should she try to look? No. Absolutely not. Every too-dumb-to-live decision started with checking on a strange noise. She should get out.

Even if it was him. *Especially* if it was him.

The back garden was surrounded by sheltering trees. She could hide. Or run. She could call the police. All she had to do was make it outside, through the vegetable garden, across the lawn, and out to the woods.

She held her breath as she flicked the lock and then slowly turned the handle, praying that it didn't squeak. It opened silently. She was almost there. But then she froze. What about Nissy? God. Ellie had opened the living room door to the deck for her an hour ago. Was she still outside? What if she came in? Would he hurt her?

Ellie couldn't leave without her. She hesitated, racked with uncertainty.

And then she heard it. A low, strangled noise. A noise that sounded like despair. Like unadulterated grief, quickly stifled.

No. That was ridiculous. That rough moan could just as easily mean he was furious. It wasn't safe for her there. She had to get out, circle around the outside and look for Nissy. She could call the police while she did it.

She pushed the door open and snuck onto the first low concrete step. She was almost there. Almost free. But before she could move, she heard him.

"Please." His voice was guttural. Hoarse, even. As if he hadn't spoken in hours. But it held her.

She spun back, drawn to the sound. There, standing in the entrance to the kitchen, was the man from yesterday. It *was* him.

She almost stepped toward him, almost got drawn in, but she forced herself to stay away.

She grabbed the door, ready to slam it shut between them and run, but he did the last thing she expected. He stepped back—away from her—his arms coming up, palms open, and she stopped once more.

"Please don't," he repeated.

"Don't what?" she whispered, standing on the concrete step with the door handle gripped in her sweating fist.

He held out his hand. "Please don't leave me." He cleared his throat, blinking as if he'd surprised himself. As if he'd said more than he intended. "Please stay."

Something about the words gripped her. She had heard them before. They meant something to her. To them. They bound them together somehow. Although she had no idea how. A chill drifted over her skin; the breeze raising the hairs on her arms.

She stayed there, just outside the door, watching him, telling herself she could still run. Telling herself she could slam the door and be gone in an instant if she needed to.

He was wearing a plain black T-shirt that highlighted the tanned bulk of his arms and the lines of ink that traveled up his right bicep to disappear under the fabric. His jeans were worn and faded, clinging to the bulk of his thighs. His hair was even more tangled and his beard thicker today, as if he still hadn't bothered to shave. He was taller than her. A heavy, muscular man. She should have been frightened.

She swallowed. Honestly, she was frightened. But she should have been *more* frightened.

She stood, captured in the doorway, adrenaline pumping through her veins in heavy beats. "Why are you in my house?"

He stared at her, lips drawn into a tight line. But he didn't answer.

"I don't have anything of value here," she insisted.

He stepped back, another big step, almost taking him

out of sight, shocked offense flashing across his face before he blanked it once more. "I'm not here to rob you."

"Why are you here then?"

"I don't know. I can't—" He shook his head slowly.

Ellie pulled out her phone, holding it between them. As if it would protect her somehow. "I'll call the police."

He raised his hands further, his serious blue eyes locked on hers. "I'm not going to hurt you. I promise."

She snorted softly. How stupid did he think she was? "You're in my house, and I don't know you."

"Don't you?" His voice was low, but she could still hear the hint of disappointment and confusion. Something about that look of bewildered disorientation, swiftly replaced with a practiced stoicism, settled her.

Nissy chose that moment to step into the kitchen, nose in the air, the tip of her tail flicking gently. She looked up at the man, considered him, and then brushed against his leg, nuzzling her cheek against his jean-covered shin.

Ellie started moving without stopping to think. She needed to get Nissy. She had to protect her. Save her. But then, too quickly to be anything but automatic reflex, the stranger lowered his hands and reached down to gently stroke Nissy's head, massaging the sensitive spot behind her ears. "Aren't you gorgeous?" he asked.

His words—low and rumbling, but friendly—caught Ellie and brought her to a stop. Somehow back in the kitchen. Far closer to the intruder than she'd ever planned.

The man looked up and straightened quickly, as if embarrassed to be showing any kind of emotion. Nissy gave him a cool look at having been abandoned and tapped gently over to Ellie instead.

Somehow having her cat beside her, and having seen that brief unguarded tenderness, reassured her far more than anything he'd said. "Should I know you?" she asked softly.

"I'd hoped..." He leaned heavily against the doorframe. "I thought you could tell me—" he shook his head, voice fading.

"Tell you what?"

For the first time since she'd locked eyes with him in the mirror, a clear emotion stood stark on his face: sadness. "Who I am."

Ellie took another unconscious step forward, drawn by the bleak look in his eyes. "What do you mean?"

His face was pale beneath his beard as his lips twitched into the tiniest, most self-deprecating smile she'd ever seen. "I don't remember anything."

"You don't remember *anything*?"

"No. I don't know where we are. Or how I got here. Or even"—his chest rose and fell on a rough breath—"who I am."

Ellie put her hand out to rest on the kitchen table, needing its stability, hardly noticing that she had come fully into the room. Her attention was held by the rigid tension in the muscles of his neck and the deep lines scoring his forehead. And her growing awareness that he must be under some immense weight, some terrible pressure, that made him hold himself so stiffly.

"Maybe we should call someone," she offered. "Emergency services. A doctor. Someone who knows what to do."

"Yeah. Okay. That makes sense."

They stared at each other for a long moment, neither of them moving. But then he swayed, ever so slightly, and leaned even more heavily against the doorframe, one hand coming up to brace himself.

He looked as if he'd been through a battle. As if he was only staying on his feet by sheer stubbornness. It was a look she'd seen on her own face, and she wanted to wipe it away. She wanted to smooth her fingers down that look of painfully stoic acceptance and see those full lips twitch into a smile once more—a real one.

But that was madness. "Do you want to sit?" she asked instead, gesturing toward the chair nearest to him, on the opposite side of the table.

"Thank you." He crossed the kitchen slowly and settled his hands on the backrest of the chair, but he didn't pull it out.

His lips looked dry and cracked, and she couldn't stop herself from asking, "Do you want a glass of water while I call?"

He nodded. "Yes, please."

"I'll just—" she turned to grab two glasses, darting glances at him over her shoulder.

He never moved.

She looked away, just for a second, to fill the glass. "Who do you think we should call first?" she asked, turning back.

But he was gone.

Nissy sat at her feet. The fridge ticked quietly in the corner. But nothing else had moved. The room was empty.

Ellie dropped the glass to the table, ignoring the water as it sloshed over the rim, and strode around to his chair. She dragged her fingers over the smooth grain of the wood. Was it warm? Was she imagining it? Was she going completely insane?

She would have heard him leave. Wouldn't she?

She strode through the house; the hallway, the living room, the downstairs toilet. All empty. She ran upstairs.

Checked behind curtains, under beds, inside wardrobes. He wasn't there.

She grabbed her phone and pulled up the app that connected to her doorbell camera, pulled up the video, and watched it through. Twice. The door had not been opened. Not for hours.

Was this what a hallucination felt like? It had been so real. God. Was this the pain meds? The stress? Too many years of working day and night without a break? She lifted her hand to her mouth and realized that her fingers were trembling and her lips were freezing cold.

She stumbled into her living room and sank onto a sofa, pulled a blanket up to her chin, and opened her phone. She was right, she desperately needed to call a doctor.

For herself.

# Chapter Five

Ellie heaved herself off the sofa and through the house to answer the doorbell in her slippers. After spending the day feeling like she was being dragged through a hedge backward, making her get off her sofa was just mean. Especially since Nissy had finally deigned to come and sit on her lap and was purring gently when the bell rang. Still, if they'd come all the way down her narrow lane, the least she could do was give them directions to wherever they were really supposed to be.

She swung open the door, already wondering if she was going to need her phone so she could use the maps, only to find Victoria balancing two tubs of ice cream, a large apple pie, and a bottle of wine... and trying to press the doorbell again with her elbow.

Ellie chuckled, reaching to help with the pie and bottle, warmth filling her. "Vic! I'm so glad to see you! I didn't know you were coming."

Vic gave her a half-hug over their full arms. "You didn't think I would let you spend all day in hospital and not check up on you, did you?"

In the past, she wouldn't have doubted it. No matter what else was happening in their lives, they'd always looked out for each other. But lately they'd seen less and less of each other. Ellie had invited Victoria out multiple times, only to be met with excuses—Vic was too busy, too tired, had a headache, was still at work—until Ellie had stopped asking. But she couldn't say any of that. Not with Vic standing in her hallway, having come all the way to see her.

She smiled instead, leading the way indoors, and spoke over her shoulder, "You're the best." She meant it. Her best friend was with her, the pie was still warm, and the scent of rich butter and cinnamon-sugar rose through the air. It meant the world.

"So." Vic grinned at her. It was a genuine smile, although she looked a little more brittle than usual. "Did they find a brain then?"

Ellie snorted as she grabbed a pair of bowls and started serving. "Probably would be more worrying if they did, right?"

"I don't know." Vic took out two glasses and poured the wine, moving around the kitchen with the comfort of long familiarity. "First time for everything."

They both laughed as they carried their bowls and glasses through to the living room to settle into their usual places on the sofa.

They sat quietly, enjoying the hot pie and cold ice cream, before Vic met Ellie's eyes, her expression serious. "How did it really go?"

Ellie swallowed a spoonful of choc-chip cookie dough ice cream and lifted a shoulder. "It wasn't so bad."

It had been *quite* bad. Just the smell of the hospital made her start to sweat; she only had unpleasant memories associated with that sharp, antiseptic scent. Never mind spending the entire day there—alone—being jabbed with needles, poked and prodded, and even having to lie still in the claustrophobic MRI machine while it thudded and whirred. All while wondering whether they were going to find something deeply wrong with her. And she'd caught a cab there and back, which meant she'd felt completely out of control during the journey. It was difficult to see past the driver's head, and he was singing along with the radio instead of concentrating. She'd almost asked him to bring her home so she could just drive her own damn car, panic attack or not.

Vic frowned at her, her gaze full of concerned understanding. "It was horrible then."

"Yeah, it was horrible," Ellie admitted before doing her best to lighten her tone. "But at least it was only for the day." Unlike the last time she'd woken up in hospital—with two broken ribs, a punctured lung, and badly lacerated legs and arms. "And I didn't have to stay the night."

Vic huffed a rough agreement. "Why did you need to go back? Your message didn't say, and I thought you were doing much better."

Nissy stalked along the back of the sofa, bright eyes focused on the bowls of ice cream, and Ellie lifted her to sit on the cushion beside her, using the time to find the right explanation. One that didn't give Vic any more reason to suggest she should sell her game. "I had some... visual disturbances," she hedged.

Vic tilted her head to her side, chewing slowly. "Like a migraine?"

Not even vaguely. Unless a migraine looked like hot, brooding intruder who didn't know his own name. She shook her head while she tried to work out what to say.

"More like a weird kind of mirage." That was a better word than hallucination, right?

Vic winced. "Sounds worrying. Do you have any ideas what caused it?"

"Not yet." Who knew? Maybe something was very wrong. Or maybe it was stress, or a delayed response to the trauma. Or maybe she'd just lived in her own made-up world for too long. Or maybe it was real.... But she didn't begin to know how to feel about that.

Vic patted her leg. "Are you better now, though? That's the main thing."

"It went away," Ellie said quietly, instead of admitting the truth. She didn't feel better. She wished he *hadn't* gone away. She wanted him to have been real.

And that worried her more than anything. She shoved the thought as far away as possible. "I'd rather hear about you. I'm sure you had a much more interesting day."

Vic hummed noncommittally before taking another bite of pie. "It was fine."

"How are you getting on with the designs for the bathroom upgrade you were looking at?" Ellie asked with a smile. Vic had inherited her stunning Georgian townhouse near Hampstead Heath from her granny, and she adored it. The last time Ellie had visited her there, she'd had big plans for a freestanding claw-foot bath.

"It's on hold for now."

"Really? I thought—"

"It's not the right time," Vic said firmly, cutting off that conversation. "I'm focusing on other things."

"Oh. Right." There was a lot to do in a house that old. "If you want help—"

"No, thanks."

Okay.... Ellie searched for something else to ask. She

was tired and her body ached, and somehow this conversation was way harder than she'd expected. She'd been so glad to see Vic, but now she just wanted to go back to her comfy sofa. Luckily, there was always work. "Did you get those storyline notes I sent through? Has Duane got the team making the changes?"

Victoria stiffened, just a fraction, but Ellie knew her too well for her to hide it. "They're doing what you asked," Vic said, although she didn't sound thrilled. "I agree the first drafts weren't perfect, but I think there's something in those original outlines. I think we can take the story somewhere a little darker. Add in some real threat. Real danger."

"Of course there has to be danger," Ellie agreed. "But this is a romance. There has to be some hope."

"Players will think it's more realistic—"

Ellie shook her head. "Not our players. There's enough reality in the world. This is about creating an escape. Somewhere deadly but also beautiful. Somewhere there's a chance to make it out alive with the person you love at your side."

"Mm-hmm." Vic swirled her spoon through her bowl, watching it move as if the melting ice cream was deeply fascinating, before looking up once more. "Hey, did your father call?"

Ellie blinked. The complete change in subject was disorienting. But also... it made her think perhaps the more combat-based storylines hadn't been quite as unintentional as she'd thought.

She focused on Vic's question and forced herself to smile, aiming for casual, even while knowing she couldn't completely hide her response. Vic almost certainly already knew her father hadn't called—and she'd know how much it hurt.

Ellie had spent years trying—and failing—to be the perfect daughter. A daughter worthy of attention.

But her dad hadn't come to visit her when she lay in A&E, the heartbeat monitor beeps discordant in her ears, wading through a sea of pain after her accident. He sent a note saying that hospitals were too difficult for him, and he hoped she felt better soon. It hadn't helped her feel better in any way, and she didn't bother telling him she was going back in for more tests today. There was only one reason for Vic to bring him up now. "Did he come to the office?"

Vic nodded slowly.

"I guess he was disappointed I wasn't there, working to sell the game," Ellie said quietly.

"Yes, he came to talk to you about Silver Wolff," Vic said, studiously avoiding her eyes.

Of course he did. After all these years of Ellie trying to be the daughter he needed, he'd finally shown an interest in her... and it wasn't even an interest in *her*. And then another terrible thought occurred to her. "Vic, is that why you're here? After I spent the day in hospital? To try to convince me to sell?"

"No!" Vic dumped her bowl on the table and stood. "No. I was worried about you! I wanted to check on you. I didn't want you here all alone. I just thought—" She let out an exasperated grunt and strode toward the folding doors to look out at the dark garden.

Ellie blinked against the tears in her eyes. Hell. She was too tired to deal with any of this. Just thinking about selling made her want to go back to bed and pull the covers over her head.

She wiped her eyes with the back of her hand and looked up at her precious fan art. She wanted to keep the community she'd been building, not give it all away. "I really don't think this sale would be good for us. I think it would be better—"

Vic spun back roughly enough to cut off Ellie's words. "The sale has to go ahead."

Ellie looked across at her, the space between them wider than it had ever been. "What does that mean? Has to?"

Vic cleared her throat. "Everyone has worked too hard to lose this opportunity. Don't you think it's time to take the reward for all that work? Don't you think it's time to really live, not just slowly die chained to a desk?"

Ellie rubbed at the building ache in her chest. Of course she'd thought about the things Vic was saying. She needed a better balance in her life. But she needed to make this decision for the right reasons.

A memory rose. Of flying down the steep road with the wind in her face, the thrill of speed and freedom sending joyful adrenaline sparkling through her blood. The group of cyclists around her—some she knew, some down from London for the day—mirrored her joy. Their faces were half hidden by helmets and sunglasses, any exposed skin flushed with hard exercise and exhilaration. She was in the lead. Usually she was content cycling somewhere in the middle of the pack, but somehow she'd found herself in the front that day. She was pulling away, pushing herself even faster. And then, without warning, there was a huge SUV beside her. Dark windows. Dark paint. Too close. Real threat. Real danger. The smell of hot rubber. The sounds of the engine. Too loud. And then—

"Ellie? Are you okay?" Vic stepped closer. "You went pale."

Ellie swallowed. The aftertaste of the ice cream in her mouth was too sweet. Her lips were cold, and her head throbbed. "Yeah, sorry. I just..." She shook her head and then winced when it hurt even more.

"I lost you for a moment there, El." Vic sighed, looking guilty. "Sorry. I shouldn't have said anything about dying."

"It wasn't your fault." Ellie gave Vic the best smile she could, fighting to speak through the tightness in her throat. "I guess it just takes a while." And the tension between them wasn't helping. God, she hated conflict.

Nissy stood from her cushion and stalked onto her lap, nosing around her chin. Her soft whiskers tickled gently, and Ellie held on to her small warm body.

"I wish it had never happened." Vic stood, looking at her with concern. "Here, let me tidy up so you can get some rest." She stacked the empty bowls and carried them into the kitchen.

Ellie gave Nissy a last cuddle and then put her back on her cushion, then pushed herself up to follow. She found Vic rinsing bowls at the sink. "You don't have to do that."

Vic threw a smile at her over her shoulder. "I don't mind. I hate seeing you look so pale."

Ellie leaned against the doorframe, suddenly even more tired than before. She was standing precisely where her hallucination had stood. His big shoulder pressed against this exact doorframe.

If only he was real.

"Shall I get the guest room ready for you?" Ellie asked. "We can have leftover apple pie for breakfast like we used to."

Vic chuckled, but her back was still to Ellie. "Thanks, El, but I need to get back."

"Tonight? Really?" It was a long way back. But maybe they needed the space.

"Yes, I promised—" Vic turned away to stack the bowls

in the drying rack, cleared her throat, and then started again. "I've got a lot to do tomorrow. Easier to drive back now than face the morning rush."

Ellie watched her friend, taking in Vic's stiff shoulders as she fussed with the crockery. "Okay, if you're comfortable with the drive.... Hang on. Who did you promise?"

Vic shrugged without turning around.

"Are you seeing someone new? That's great news." Relief welled through her. If Vic was dating again, starting to try again, perhaps she'd begun to recover from the hurt Warren caused.

Vic spun to face her, her voice sharp. "What? No! Of course I'm not seeing anyone else. Warren is..."

Hell. Ellie leaned more heavily against the frame, just as her hallucination had done. "Warren is?" she prompted.

"Nothing." Vic dried her hands with jerky movements.

Ellie moved closer, her heart thudding heavily in her ears. "Are you back with him? You can tell me, Vic. I—"

"I don't want to talk about this with you."

"Okay." Ellie took a slow breath. "Okay, that's fine. I just don't want to see you hurt again. You're my family, and Warren—" What were the right words? She didn't know anymore.

Maybe it didn't matter; Vic clearly didn't want to hear them anyway. She neatly tucked the tea towel away, smoothing it until it was perfect before stalking past Ellie and into the hall. "I have to go."

"Alright." Ellie forced a smile. "I'll be here, if you need me."

Vic grunted as she grabbed her coat and bag. They didn't hug goodbye, and Ellie stood at the door watching for long moments after she drove away.

Then she closed up the house, checked all the locks, said goodnight to Nissy—who had taken herself to her cave —and made her way upstairs for a hot shower.

And if she checked every mirror more than once, if she lay listening for a deep voice long past the time she should have gone to sleep, she was just being careful. It didn't mean anything.

And the quiet emptiness—the fact that he had disappeared and never come back—had nothing to do with how alone she felt.

# Chapter Six

Ellie opened her eyes in darkness. Her bed was soft and warm. The house was quiet. And yet, somehow, the air felt different. Heavier. Closer. Like the pressure building before a storm that wouldn't break.

She turned on her bedside lamp, already suspecting what she would find. He was there.

He stood in her doorway. Arms stretched out, gripping the frame. His face was gold and shadow in the soft light, while a chasm of darkness loomed behind him. As if he had emerged from some grimly veiled place. Like a fallen angel. Beautiful and fierce and separated from the world.

His eyes met hers, filled with emotions she couldn't name. Perhaps he didn't know them himself—lost along with his memories. Perhaps that was the curse of a fallen angel: their past was torn from them as they tumbled.

Perhaps she should be more careful about what she read before trying to sleep.

She sat up in her bed, dragging the covers up to her chin. Her cotton pajama bottoms and worn gamer T-shirt were somehow far too flimsy a defense against the weight of his presence.

Her pulse picked up, butterflies stirring in her belly. Could it really all be in her mind? Could he really be nothing more than a fantasy?

Her covers were warm and heavy, smelling of fabric softener. They were tangible. Solid. She had to remember that he was not. "You aren't real," she whispered.

His forehead furrowed, eyes dark in the low light. "I *feel* real," he said.

Ellie huffed. God only knew what real felt like. The most real she felt was when she was imagining herself as someone else. A character in a world she'd invented. She didn't have an answer, so she stayed silent. Watching him as he watched her.

He hung more heavily on the doorframe, the muscles of his arms bunching in the warm light, but the shadows under his eyes looked even darker than before.

"What are you doing here?" Ellie asked eventually.

"I'm... I thought you'd prefer me to stay out of your room."

She wrinkled her nose. That wasn't a real answer. "But watching me sleep is alright?"

"I wasn't."

She let out a bark of incredulous laughter, and he let go of the frame to scrub a hand through his hair, mussing it further. "Okay. I was. But only for a second. I... woke up here."

"You woke up in my room?"

"Apparently."

"Where were you before that?"

"I don't know."

Hell. What would that be like? To wake up somewhere,

not knowing where you were or why you were there, or even who you were. Every time she saw him, he looked more drained, more exhausted.

The thought made her pause. Would her subconscious create such a nuanced hallucination? Would a fantasy gradually grow more tired? It didn't seem likely. But then, was it more likely that she had developed a brain injury sometime *after* she was released from the hospital? And she hadn't taken any painkillers since she first saw him, just in case—even though her ribs ached and the healing scars on her legs still burned and itched—so it wasn't that either. But if he wasn't a figment of her mind, what was he? Some kind of spirit? A phantom?

"Are you haunting me?" she asked.

He stepped forward, seeming not to notice that he'd crossed the invisible boundary into her bedroom. "I think *you* are haunting me," he admitted roughly. "Why do I keep coming here? Why do I hear your voice? How did I... Shit." He bowed his head, hiding his expression, tension written over the tight lines of his shoulders. "None of this makes sense."

He could be lying, but the look on his face before he turned away, the combination of horror and grief and exhaustion... that would be hard to fake. And she knew— she *knew*—exactly how it felt to be horrified and grieving and exhausted. She knew how hard it was to be alone.

"Are you going to hurt me?" she asked quietly.

"No." His eyes flew to hers. That intense gaze locked on hers. "Fuck, no."

"Okay." Somehow she believed him. Despite the darkness curled around him, he sounded sincere. She watched him for a long, silent moment, both of them caught in a strange stalemate. He wasn't going to take another step without her invitation, she knew it deep in her bones. It was up to her.

She could tell him to leave, and he would. She could roll over and pretend he didn't exist—and perhaps he didn't. Or she could stop trying to think through every possible consequence for every possible action, stop tying herself up in knots, and do what felt right.

Ellie pushed away her blankets and slowly stood. The thick carpet was soft under her feet. Cold air whispered in from the open window over her suddenly too-exposed skin. But she was committed to this path now.

She walked across the room and stood in front of him. Up close, he was even taller. Even more solid. She held out her hand. "I'm Ellie."

She didn't know what to expect. Perhaps he would disappear, fade from her world never to return, exorcised by her acceptance. Or perhaps his hand would pass through hers, as insubstantial as mist.

She didn't expect his fingers to close over hers, big enough to engulf hers completely. His hand was strong and firm, but icy cold. She couldn't help her gasp, or the way her hand twitched in his, wanting to hold him tight. Wanting to pull him closer and wrap him in her arms and breathe heat back into his body. But he let her go immediately.

"You're so warm," he said, forehead creasing. "I didn't realize how cold I was until now." He swayed fractionally closer, as if he might take her hand once more. Or bring her in against his body. But then he retreated again, as if suddenly realizing how close he was to touching her.

Her hand still tingled, and she almost swayed with him. Almost. But she made herself stand still, looking up at him. "What shall I call you?" she asked.

He shrugged. "I have no idea."

Ellie stepped back, breaking the unspoken dance. Freeing them both. She wrapped her arms around her stomach, suddenly colder than she was before. "We should give you a name."

He leaned against the doorframe and crossed his arms over his chest. "What name?"

Hell. She racked her brain for inspiration. "Ah... Jonathan? Billy? Or how about Jim or Steve?"

He let out a gruff chuckle as his expression lightened for the first time. "Are we in a supernatural horror?"

Ellie snorted. He'd caught her. But then she realized what he'd just said. "You remember *Stranger Things*?" Her smile spread. "That's good, right?"

He started to nod, but it turned into a slow shake of denial. "I remember some things. I remember pizza. I remember swimming in the sea. I know that I like red wine better than white. It's the other stuff—the important stuff— that I don't know." His expression grew grim once more. "Who am I? Where do I come from? All of that is gone." His voice lowered to a rumble. "And sometimes I'm not even here. Sometimes, all I know is darkness."

Her hand itched to reach out. To press against his face and take away the pain she saw flickering there before he could hide it. But there was so little she could offer him. This stranger. She couldn't give him answers. She didn't even know where to start. But maybe she could help him feel that she had heard him. "I probably have some frozen pizza if you like. Definitely some red wine."

His lips twitched, and he almost smiled. Almost, but not quite. "Thank you but... it's hard to explain. I don't feel hungry. I haven't wanted anything to eat since I woke up here the first time."

She bit her lip, thinking. She couldn't call emergency

services when there really wasn't an emergency and he might disappear any moment. "We could look online. Maybe someone will have posted something? Or perhaps there's a forum for missing people?"

He seemed to hesitate for a second before replying. "Yeah." He looked away for a second, and then back to her. When he spoke again, he was more certain. "Yes, we should do that. But could we... I'd rather face it in the morning."

The rational part of her thought they should be trying to work out who he was. They should do the work. And the work should come first. But another part of her—the part that had spent hours looking for him when he'd gone—wanted to spend just a little longer with him before they found where he should be. Or worse, discovered that he didn't really exist.

She'd already decided it was time to live more. Listen to her heart more. "Okay," she agreed. "Let's look in the morning."

He glanced over her shoulder into her room. "Shall we sit for a bit? Downstairs maybe?"

Was that what she wanted? There wasn't much furniture in her bedroom. The super king bed with its forest-green and cream covers dominated the room. Beside it, side tables held small ceramic lamps, while the far wall was covered almost entirely by a heavy, ceiling-to-floor mirror, positioned to give her a view through the window no matter which way she lay. She liked her sleeping space uncluttered, but now it didn't offer a lot of seating options unless he sat on the bed with her. Would that be a mistake?

She hesitated for a second and then let her worries go. She didn't want to have to go downstairs. She didn't want to break this strange truce, or put more space between them. He was in her room already; he might as well stay.

She waved him awkwardly to the end of the bed and then climbed in herself. The covers warmed her chilled skin. Gave her a shield against the constant awareness of being with him. Although, now that she had it, it felt more like a barrier than a shield. A barrier she didn't want.

He sank down. Not onto the foot of the bed as she'd expected, but onto the floor. He leaned his back against the mattress, bent one knee, and rested his arm on it. He looked tired, like she felt, and she almost invited him into the bed. Almost threw caution away entirely. But then she would want to hold him. She would want to smooth the lines on his face with her fingers. To curl her body into his. She would want more. So she kept silent.

Neither of them spoke. They just sat quietly, two people surrounded by the night, keeping company.

She left the light on. But it was warm and hushed, and she'd been so exhausted, her body had been so battered. Her eyes grew heavy, even as she tried to fight it. Having him there, sitting with her, gave her a sense of calm. As if he would watch over her.

It didn't make any sense. But they were connected. He was—

"Jon, I think," he said quietly, and she opened her eyes again.

She blinked slowly, half asleep. "The misunderstood loner who becomes a hero."

"No. I'm not a hero." His voice was rough. He cleared his throat. "I don't want to be a hero."

She waited quietly until he finished. "It's the sound of it. It seems familiar."

"Okay, Jon. It's nice to meet you."

There was a beat of silence, and then he replied, "It's nice to meet you too, Ellie."

There was a stranger in her room, but for the first time in as long as she could remember, she felt safe. Her ribs ached, and she turned over on her pillows, finding a more comfortable position. The pain eased, and she sank further into her mattress.

"Jon?" she murmured his new name, trying it out.

He didn't answer.

"Jon?"

"Oh. Hmm?"

"What does "real" feel like anyway?"

He was silent even longer, but she could hear him shifting against the fabric of the covers where he leaned against the bed.

"This," he said eventually. "This feels real."

# Chapter Seven

Fuck, his neck hurt. He was too damn old to sleep on the floor, propped into a weird half-sitting position, head bent back at an awkward angle. He didn't know exactly how old he was, but he knew he was too old, nonetheless.

But he'd also known he couldn't just climb into bed with Ellie. No matter how deliciously warm and rumpled she'd been. No matter how their bodies had swayed closer and closer before she broke the spell. Because then he would have wanted to hold her. Wanted to dip his nose into that sensitive space just behind her ear and breathe her in. And that would be a bad idea. For both of them.

He groaned and pushed himself up to standing, then massaged his lower back for a few seconds before gripping the strained muscles of his neck in an entirely pointless attempt at softening their spasm.

Ellie was gone, her bed left in disarray as she'd slipped past him. He hadn't expected to, but somehow he'd slept. They'd dozed and chatted off and on for hours until eventually she had fallen completely asleep, and he must have followed soon after.

There was something undeniably intimate about hearing her soft murmurs in the darkness, the same rise and fall that soothed him in the other place. She'd been telling him about her game—the *Shadowbound Rift*—a world that she'd created full of magic, adventure, redemption... even love.

He could imagine her game vividly, could easily see how her players must love the chance to live those ideals when the real world fell so short. God knew he could do with some magic. He could certainly do with redemption, otherwise why was he here? And adventure was always good too, although after this—whatever this was—perhaps he'd be less interested in more adventure. The only one he didn't want was love.

He didn't need to remember his past; he knew this truth. Love wasn't for him any more than he wanted to be a hero. Even the idea made his shoulders tense right back up.

But Ellie *did* want love. It was clear in everything she'd said. Ellie believed in love. And that was why he'd been better off sleeping on the floor, no matter how stiff his neck was.

They were both better off keeping some distance.

Still. Keeping some distance didn't mean he couldn't spend time with her. He could let her warmth and kindness wash over him. Just for a moment. He could allow himself that.

He rolled out his shoulders and followed the sound of Ellie's voice down the stairs to her sunny kitchen. She was talking on the phone as he made his way to sit at the gleaming kitchen table. He didn't pay enough attention to furniture to know what kind of wood it was, but it looked solid and somehow classy.

The last time he was there, he'd been too rattled to

really look around, but now he could lean back and take it all in. The kitchen was high-end and smelled of lemon cleaner. Marble counters complemented the sleek blue-green cabinets that perfectly matched the huge abstract painting spot-lit on the opposite wall. It was done in textured oils, creating an effect of golden beams of light falling through waves. He half expected to see a fantastical siren hidden somewhere in the depths.

Everything looked as if it had been carefully chosen and coordinated, but it was also lived in. The coffee machine took pride of place beside a half-empty fruit bowl. A magnetic strip on the wall held a haphazard collection of kitchen knives and scissors, clearly washed and thrown up in no order whatsoever. A well-used novel with an oak leaf sticking out from between its pages was balanced on the edge of the counter beside a neat folder of annotated printouts and a closed laptop.

A well-fed cat was drinking water from a bowl on the floor. She was a short-haired ginger tabby—almost certainly with zero official pedigree—but her big amber eyes and supercilious air told of a cat who knew exactly who was in charge: her.

And there was Ellie herself, moving around the kitchen in worn jeans and bare feet, her hair left loose and soft, a stray curl tumbling over her shoulder toward the expanse of skin left bare by her too-big *Stranger Things* chain of lights T-shirt.

It reminded him of their conversation the night before. How she'd walked across the room to hold out her hand to him. She'd obviously been nervous—she wore her thoughts and feelings so openly—but she was so brave. And taking her hand in his had been the first warmth on his skin in all the time he'd spent in the darkness.

She grinned at him as she finished her call, and everything else faded. That smile. Sincere and joyful. It almost made him want to reach out and hold her. Almost made him wish he'd climbed into the bed with her and let her chase away the shadows still lingering in the back of his mind.

"Good news." She slid her phone into her pocket and set the coffee machine to percolate. "You're not a brain tumor."

He couldn't help but chuckle with her. "I'm not a brain tumor?"

"Nope. The doctor's office just called. MRI was completely normal. As were all the other tests."

"You went for tests?" Why did that bother him so much? He frowned across the table at her, imagining Ellie in the hospital. Imagining her hurt. And disliking the feeling.

"Hmm." She shrugged, as if to minimize the words she was about to say. "After we... met. The first time. I thought perhaps it would be worth a checkup."

When he'd gone back to drifting. To moments of harsh smells and occasional blinding lights—but mostly darkness and the never-ending cold—and left her behind. Left her troubled and alone.

He scratched a thumb through the thick stubble on his jaw, pushing away the uncomfortable realization that he felt responsible. God.

A misty, dreamlike image filtered into his mind. A young man scowled at him, a man who looked a lot like him... but not quite the same. Some relation? A brother, perhaps? "You're not the boss of me," the man spat. "I don't need you. I don't even *want* you."

The words churned through him, as barbed and painful

as if he was standing right there in front of that unknown man. He rubbed at the ache in his chest, fighting the feeling. Fuck. He didn't even know if any of that had happened.

Ellie reached into the cupboard for two mugs, thankfully oblivious to his unsettled thoughts. "Coffee?"

He shook his head, bringing his focus back to the kitchen. To this time, in this place. "No, thanks." His lips were dry, but the thought of drinking anything felt wrong somehow. "Maybe later."

Ellie took a long, closed-eyes sip of her coffee. She was so vibrant. And so beautiful. His palm still tingled at the ghost-memory of her skin on his from the previous night. The memory of her heat. Her life.

He had to remind himself that he shouldn't step into her space, walk her back to rest against the counter, sink his fingers through her tousled hair. Here in a room that felt like sunshine on water. She wasn't his—couldn't ever be his —even if something inside him wanted her to be.

Ellie put her mug down and looked at him. She had already finished her breakfast. In a minute, she was going to suggest looking for someone who knew him. She was going to suggest trying to find answers. And she would be right; he needed answers.

But whenever he tried to force himself to remember where he'd come from, the freezing darkness gathered at the corners of his vision. The cold taunted him, hungry to take him back. And he wanted to stay in Ellie's warmth just a little longer.

It was even worse now that he knew she would be worried when he left. He cast around for a sensible topic, something to divert them both. An excuse to stay. "Do you need help with anything? If you have to work, maybe I could do something useful?" he offered. "I won't pretend to know anything about game design, but I can read stories? Or if you have some more manual labor, I like being outdoors. I can... dig?"

Ellie smirked. "Dig?"

"I guess." God. What an arse. Of all the things he could have suggested, he went with *dig*. "I'm good with my hands. I think," he added and then almost groaned. He was making it worse.

Ellie's brows raised, her eyes sparkling. "That's your special skill?"

He leaned forward. "If it's special skills you want—"

The doorbell chimed, breaking into the far-too-flirtatious comment he was about to make. Thank fuck.

Ellie frowned as she turned to press a button on a screen beside her fridge. A view of the front entrance flicked to life. A middle-aged man in an expensive-looking business suit was looking at his watch outside the door.

"It's my father," Ellie said, her frown deepening as she fidgeted. "I didn't know he was coming."

It was the first time he'd seen her look quite so uncertain. But even as he watched, she seemed to settle herself. She took a breath, wiped her hands on her jeans, and then straightened. "I'll let him in. Wait here, and I'll bring him through."

Meeting Ellie's father sounded like a hideous idea. What was he going to think of an unknown man in his daughter's house for breakfast? Or when he asked questions and Jon had no answers... and no idea how long he could even stay?

He stood and walked around the table—away from the door to the front hall—to lean against the counter where Ellie had stood earlier. There was a shaft of sunlight there, a gentle beam that warmed his shoulders, even while the rest of him felt cold once more. How the hell was he going to introduce himself? "I'm Jon," didn't feel right, no matter how many times he said it to himself.

He still didn't have an answer when Ellie returned.

Her father was instantly recognizable as related to her—they shared the same honey blonde hair, the same green eyes and slightly pointed chin—but where Ellie was soft and generous and kind, this man was cold and hard. His suit was pristine, his jaw perfectly shaven, and the expression on his face as he looked over Ellie's loose hair and rumpled T-shirt was, at best, disappointment.

The cat took one look at him, stuck her nose in the air, and stalked out.

"Dad—Steven—I'd like to introduce you to Jon, he's... uh—"

Steven pulled out a chair and sat, leaning back and running his eyes over Ellie's kitchen as if surveying his territory as he interrupted. "I won't be here long. I'll take a small black coffee and then I have a meeting to get to."

Ellie glanced at Jon and then back toward Steven. "But Jon—"

"We can talk about Jon another time. Right now, I'd like to talk about you."

Ellie cast him a bewildered look before focusing back on her father. "About me?"

"Victoria said you had been back to the hospital for more tests. Why didn't you tell me?"

"I didn't think—"

"You *didn't think.*" Steven grunted, crossing his arms over his chest. "I'm your father. And now I've had to come all this way. You know how busy I am, Ellie."

Jon crossed his arms over his own chest, irritation starting to rise.

Ellie poured a small mug of black coffee and passed it across to her father before turning to him and mouthing a small, "Sorry." And damn if that apology didn't make his irritation rise further. Not with Ellie, not at all. With Steven.

Ellie walked over to lean against the counter beside him, and he very nearly took her hand.

Ellie stuck her hands in her pockets. "Why are you here, Dad?"

"Isn't it obvious?" Steven asked.

It wasn't to Jon, but from the expression on Ellie's face, it was obvious to her. And he had a horrible feeling it wasn't to check up on Ellie's health. He wanted to tug her hands from her pockets and hold them in his.

Steven took a sip of his bitter coffee. "When are you going to finalize the sale of *The Shadow-rifting Chronicles?*"

"*The* Shadowbinding *Chronicles,*" Ellie murmured, looking more weary than she had even at midnight.

"That's what I said." Steven drained the rest of his coffee and then pushed the mug away.

It wasn't, but Steven didn't appear to care.

"I don't want to sell," Ellie replied, her voice soft, but firm. "I've told you this already."

"Come now, Eleanor." Steven leaned back in his chair, eyes narrowed. "I've created an opportunity for you that anyone in the world would be grateful for. I'm trying to help you."

"It's my game, Dad. And it's doing really well where it is," Ellie replied, her arms coming up to wrap around her stomach. She'd done that before when she'd been under pressure, and he didn't like seeing it again, especially when she'd been so relaxed and happy before her father arrived.

"It's okay," Steven allowed. "But it could be a real

success. And everyone would benefit. All your employees. Victoria. Our family. Don't you want to work together on this?"

"Would we work together though?" Ellie muttered half under her breath, but Steven didn't seem to notice as he continued, "Silver Wolff would take it much higher than you ever could."

Ellie's shoulders curled, just a fraction. Jon probably wouldn't have noticed if he hadn't been standing right beside her. But she didn't back down. "Silver Wolff would turn it into a combat-based RPG."

"And what's so wrong with that? You'd reach a far wider audience."

"A younger, far more male audience, you mean," Ellie argued. "People who are constantly being told that romance is stupid. We both know Silver Wolff doesn't care about a happy ever after."

Steven dipped his chin in agreement. As if Ellie had finally said something sensible.

"But isn't the whole point of the game that it's a romance?" Jon asked. Ellie had been so passionate when she'd explained it to him. "Isn't that the essence of the story?"

Steven ignored him completely, focused only on Ellie. "I've worked hard for you all your life. Trust me to know what's best for you now. Throwing away this opportunity would be a huge misjudgment. Just think of how much money you'll lose. How much credibility."

Ellie was silent for a moment, but then her spine slowly straightened. Jon could see it was difficult for her, but she spoke clearly and calmly as she replied, "You asked me to think about this, and I did. The first game was far more successful than I'd hoped, and we have a good chance of winning New Game of the Year with part two. And, even more importantly, if I keep creative rights, I can make sure both games stay true to their values. I can keep my promises to our players." She didn't look away from her father as she continued. "We learned a lot with the first game, and part two is going to be a fantastic launch... but not if we give it away to someone who won't love it."

Ellie looked so determined. Like a knight standing up to a dragon. Perhaps a little uncertain, but still on her feet and fighting. It took everything he had not to wrap his arm around her shoulders and pull her into his side. To give her his support. To tell her that she wasn't alone.

But he didn't do it. They both knew he couldn't make promises like that.

Steven stood and straightened his already immaculate cuffs. "Now you're just being silly. You're not giving it away, you're *selling* it. This is business; it's not the place for falling in love with a product."

"I'm not being silly." Ellie's face was blotched with pink, her eyes shining just a little too bright.

"I'm not just going to let you make such a big mistake. Max at Silver Wolff said there's still time for you to sign the contract. You can call him this week and get it finalized. We'll go out together afterward and celebrate." Steven gave a sharp nod, as if it was all decided. "I realize now that I haven't spent enough time with you lately, and there's a lot I could teach you."

"But—"

"No buts. It's time to grow up."

Ellie's face twisted, but she didn't speak.

It was too much. The look on Ellie's face was unbearable. She *wasn't* alone. She had his support. And Jon was not going to wait on the sideline if she needed him. He strode forward to stand between them, a human buffer. "That's enough, Steven. If anyone's making a mistake—"

Ellie's father cut him off, stepping up close enough to touch him. "You need to do what's right, Eleanor."

Steven was far too close to be anywhere near comfortable. But that wasn't the problem. The real problem was that Steven was still speaking to Ellie. He was still looking at Ellie. And he was looking *right through* Jon.

As if he wasn't there at all.

As if he didn't even exist.

# Chapter Eight

THE PATH MEANDERED through ancient oak and ash. Past tall trunks, reaching leaves, and sunlight dappling along the sandy path. But even as the massive trees stretched for the blue sky and sunshine, Ellie was caught in the dim green shadows at their feet.

She could hardly remember the end of the conversation with her father. All she knew was her desperate need for Steven to leave and go to whatever important meeting he had planned for that day. To just go away and let Ellie process the loss of her fantasy alone.

She had seen the moment Jon realized Steven couldn't see him. Watched as his expression turned from irate and protective to grim and bleak, and finally settled on blankly stoic. And then she'd watched him walk away. A few minutes later, she'd seen him through the window as he stalked across the deck and leaned against the railing, looking out at the garden and the wood beyond. All while her father continued talking without noticing him at all. Without seeing him. At all.

The end of the conversation was a blur. She had no idea

what Steven had said, other than how annoyed he was that Ellie wasn't listening. But Ellie didn't care; she wanted Steven to leave, and thank God he finally muttered something about the time and did.

Ellie had closed the door on her father and then stalled. The empty mirror in the hallway glared back at her, taunting her while the house closed in on her. It was too uncomfortable. Too airless. Or perhaps that was her lungs, because the familiar rooms were too big and empty without Jon. She'd had to get out.

She left him brooding on the deck. She had no idea what to say to him, and before she even tried to find the right words, she needed to get her spinning emotions under control.

She pulled on a pair of boots, let herself out her back door, and strode through her vegetable garden and across her lawn to the wrought iron gate, half hidden in the overgrown hedge. From there the forest spread out in front of her, offering a choice of paths to escape down.

It had seemed like the respite she needed. But now, hours later, walking in a slow spiral back toward her cottage, she was alone with her thoughts. And she didn't like any of them.

For as long as she could remember, she'd solved her problems by working harder. Practicing and perfecting until she was certain of success. Always doing more. Giving more. Making sure everyone around her had everything they needed before she could rest.

But now she was starting to wonder if her rest would ever come. All her hard work hadn't saved her from getting hurt. And the one thing she wanted for herself wasn't even real.

"Ellie." Jon's gruff voice called from behind her,

breaking into her thoughts, and she stopped walking. She hung her head, refusing to look at him. Refusing to take part in this... whatever this was.

"Ellie!" He was right behind her now, but she still didn't look.

"I know you can hear me."

If his words had been angry or threatening she could have walked away. But he sounded tired and a little unsure.

And she *wanted* to see him.

She turned, lifting her head, and he was there. He looked like he sounded: wary. With dark rings under his eyes, his beard even more scruffy over his clenched jaw. But he also looked... perfect. Like the man who'd stood up to challenge her father for her. Who'd sat at the foot of her bed and listened to her dreams. Whose eyes sought hers again and again. Whose heavy arms and tantalizing ink she'd longed to run her fingers over. Who she honestly knew nothing about.

"Don't look at me like that," he muttered.

"Like what?"

"Like you can't decide whether to walk away."

"I *should* walk away." A loose lock of hair blew into her face, and she swiped it out of her eyes.

He stalked closer. "You shouldn't walk Ellie, you should *run*." He gestured roughly toward himself. "I might disappear at any moment to who the fuck knows where. What can I offer you except grief?"

A tendril of rage unfurled and she crossed her arms, glaring up at him. "Is that a threat?"

He leaned over her. All heavy muscles and frustration. "It can't be a threat if I'm not real, can it?"

She barked out an incredulous laugh. "You're insulted? Because I'm questioning my sanity? That's"—she stabbed toward his chest with one finger, not quite letting it land—"gah. I don't even know what that is."

He let out a long, agitated breath. "I'm real. I told you already."

"Of course you told me," Ellie snapped. "I invented you. You're in my head."

Jon growled. "*I* told you. Me."

She shook her head but didn't speak the denial. The bleak look of misery he'd quickly suppressed earlier was too painful to risk. She couldn't bear to be the one who brought it back. Who was she to refute his very existence?

He leaned closer. Close enough for her to see the ticking muscles in his jaw. The flecks of azure in the ocean blue of his eyes. "I. Am. Real."

She tilted her chin up, looking him in the eye. "Then prove it to me. Show me that you're not just a creation of my own short-circuiting brain. Because God knows, you're exactly what I would have imagined."

He grunted, pausing to watch her. "I'm what you would have imagined?"

She wasn't backing down now. "Clearly. Since—" She waved her hand in the narrow space between them, showing that his very presence proved her point.

"And you need proof?" he asked, resuming his approach.

"Yes."

"Fine." He dropped his hands to her hips and crowded her backward, guiding her over the rutted path until her back hit a tree and she gasped.

She was caught. Trapped. Adrenaline and anger swirled through her. And maybe she would have pushed him away, but as his face came toward hers, a new riot of emotions crowded through his eyes. Want, need, and heat rose with every ragged breath he took. And an answering desire spiraled through her.

His mouth was almost on hers, the air between them shared and hot. But he held himself just millimeters away, his eyes locked on hers.

He held himself still for so long that she thought he might back down. Or—worse—fade away. And suddenly she couldn't bear the thought that he could slip so easily from her grasp.

She lifted her chin and rose onto her toes, closing the gap, pressing her mouth against his. And her movement unlocked him.

He took her lips. Slowly at first, just sips. As if he was tasting her. As if he needed proof that *she* was real.

She slid her hands up, over his broad shoulders, to his nape, pulling him closer. He grunted, taking more, and their kiss grew hotter. His grip on her hips grew tighter. *He* grew hotter. The cool touch of his skin warmed against hers.

God. He *felt* real. He felt hard and heavy. His lips were firm and insistent against hers. His hair was soft where she threaded her fingers through it. He smelled of the earthy pines and sun-warmed leaves that surrounded them, with a salty, male base note that was entirely his.

She pushed even closer, needing to be pressed tight against him, giving in to the overwhelming desire to climb up his body and hold him bound against her. He dropped his hands to her outer thighs and hoisted her up higher, pressing her into the tree, pinning her with his weight. Her curves fitted into his body as if he had been made to hold her there, his thick bulk between her legs.

She wrapped her legs around his hips, pulling him even closer. Ignoring the ache in her ribs. The rest of her ached *more.*

She could feel his length even through their jeans as their kiss grew more desperate. More ferocious. Full of nipping teeth and sliding tongues and wet heat. Her hands were in his hair, his fingers gripped her thighs, tilting her to just the right angle as he rocked against her, driving her higher as she squirmed against him, needing more. Needing skin. "Jon," she whispered, "God. I need—"

"It's Josh," he muttered.

They both froze, their rough breathing too loud in her ears. She pulled back far enough to look into his eyes. "What did you say?"

"It's Josh." He let out a slow breath. And then his eyes crinkled slowly as he almost—but not quite—smiled. "I remembered."

# Chapter Nine

He was glad he'd remembered his name. He was. And deeply relieved because Ellie no longer looked quite so tormented. Or quite so keen to get away from him. But did the timing have to be so deeply frustrating? Just five more minutes, and he would have had his hands on her skin. Ten more minutes, and they would both have been naked.

On second thought, maybe it was a good thing. He'd promised himself just a moment with her. But there'd been more and more moments. Even though he knew he couldn't stay. He knew none of this was forever.

But when Ellie had doubted him—doubted his very existence—it made him want to howl. It was worse than his own doubts. Those were almost bearable when she was holding him, tethering him to the earth. But if she let go... Fuck. It made him want to cover her with his body until she knew the truth. Until she felt him everywhere. And he felt *her* everywhere.

He'd known she was dangerous from the beginning.

He should put more distance between them. Or she should. He'd meant it when he'd told her she should run.

They shouldn't start something, not when there was no way it would end well. But he couldn't stand the thought of stopping it. If these moments were the only ones they were going to have, he wanted them.

Ellie was quiet and introspective as they walked, but when he reached down to take her hand, she laced her fingers with his and held him tightly. As if she was afraid he would disappear.

Of course she was. He was afraid of the same damn thing.

"Ellie?" He broke the tension.

She turned to face him, eyes troubled. "Mm-hmm."

"I don't want to hurt you."

She stopped walking, tilting her head to the side as she watched him, completely focused. "What does that mean?"

"I'm real. I am." God. Who was he trying to convince, her or himself? He didn't know. He swallowed roughly before continuing. "But I don't think I can stay here. I feel—"

He could feel the darkness. Feel the pull. He knew nothing about himself except for his name, but he knew that this was borrowed time. And even if he could stay, they would be on borrowed time anyway. Because she would want more. She would *deserve* more.

"I don't know how long we have," he said quietly. "I want—" To be with you, to hold your body against mine, hear your laugh, listen to your ideas, drown in your warmth. But he couldn't have that, not forever. "I want to touch you, but we can't..." Damn this was hard. "We can't let emotions get involved."

The words felt hollow. As if he'd made this speech often enough to know the shape of it, even if he couldn't remember making it. As if they were just words, nonetheless. Words he didn't quite believe, even if he should.

Ellie stood silently, watching him with clear eyes that saw too much, the sounds of birds and insects loud in the forest around them. He waited stiffly, identifying bird calls —there was a blackbird and a starling, a woodpecker drumming in the distance—forcing himself to patience.

Finally, she replied, "Okay. I—" She let go of his fingers and shoved her hands in her pockets as she took a slow breath. "Thank you for telling me the truth."

He knew why she did it. He understood. He'd told her they couldn't get emotionally involved, and she'd distanced herself. But it *burned*.

And he found himself doing exactly what he'd stopped himself doing earlier. He gently tugged her hands back out and took them in his, holding them loosely, letting her pull away if she wanted to, but wishing she wouldn't.

And she didn't. She stood there, surrounded by the dappled light, looked at him, searching his eyes for something. Something he couldn't identify. Whether she found it or not, he didn't know, but she didn't pull away again.

"Can we have this?" he asked. "Can we trust that this is real and spend this time together? Even knowing it can't last?"

She was silent for so long that he began to fear she might not answer, but eventually she sighed softly. "Yes. We can have this."

He didn't speak. There was nothing he could say. Instead, he dropped a kiss onto the knuckles of each of her hands. Then they turned and walked quietly together once more.

They reached the iron gate embedded in her hedge, and

she pulled it open, leading the way into her garden. Daisies, poppies, and marigolds grew in riots of informal color while leafy shrubs and tall oaks created a private space. It was relaxed and abundant, a haven of safe nesting for the robins and blackbirds that would love the dense foliage. And yet, somehow unsettling. Its beauty did nothing to ease the emotions churning through him.

Ellie had drawn him here. And now she'd accepted that he would never stay. It was the truth. It was what he wanted. But it was still wrong.

He wished he could have had his epiphany about his name an hour later. They would have stayed in the woods. He could have kept her in his arms, kept his mouth closed over hers, and let their bodies drown out everything else.

But it was too late now. The moment was lost. And in exchange, he had a name with no memories, and a smoldering, unfulfilled need to hold her.

Ellie led him over the large wooden deck he'd stood on earlier, past a set of comfortable-looking rattan furniture with bright turquoise cushions clustered around a raised firepit. At the far side of the deck, a covered hot tub was surrounded by a privacy wall teeming with baskets of flowering geraniums and decorated with looping fairy lights. Two cushioned loungers stood nearby, and a storage closet was set off to the side.

He hadn't really looked at it properly earlier. But now he wondered. Did she come out here alone? Leave her clothes in the house and walk through the sunshine naked? Or perhaps she preferred the night. She would slip into the steaming water and lie with her head tilted back, looking up at the stars as her vibrant imagination created new adventures on fantastical worlds.

He would slide in beside her, listen to her stories. And

then, when she was languid and soft and the steam surrounded them, then he would touch her. He would finally have her close enough that he could drown in the heat of her body. He would bring her onto his lap, his hands stroking over her skin.

She must have seen the direction of his gaze and realized what he was thinking, because a tendril of color rose in her cheeks. Or perhaps she also imagined the exhilaration of gliding naked into hot water, the soft glow of the lights, and the velvet touch of wet skin against wet skin.

"Josh?" Her voice broke into the fantasy, and he blinked at her as the tantalizing image faded.

"Have you remembered anything else?" she asked as she opened the large glass bifold door that led from the deck to the living room.

And just like that, his body cooled. The wisps of the fantasy disintegrated in the dry glare of reality. "I haven't," he admitted. "I wish I could tell you that I did."

She led him inside and through to the kitchen, and he followed her silently, waiting for her to speak. Knowing there was more.

She grabbed them each a glass of water, put his on the table, and then leaned against the counter, looking out the window. Looking away from him.

The glass taunted him. His lips were so dry they'd cracked. But he wasn't sure he even wanted to try to drink something. He reached out a tentative finger to touch the glass. At first it seemed to slip. To slide away under his touch like melting ice, and he flinched back, away from the cold.

He straightened his shoulders and forced himself to concentrate. To focus on the glass. How it would feel to hold in his hand—cool and smooth and beading with water.

He tried again, and this time he was able to hold it, lift it carefully, and take a small sip.

It was icy and refreshing, exactly what he wanted. But he could only manage a tiny sip at a time.

Ellie turned away from the view and faced him. Thank fuck she hadn't seen his struggle with the glass, because her expression was back to being somber and a little dejected. She looked stoic in a way that he didn't like—as if she was preparing herself to be strong.

"Are you married?" she asked eventually.

He choked on his water, spluttering and coughing before finally being able to take a decent breath. "No!"

"Were you, though," she persisted, "before... this?"

Josh put his glass on the table and folded his arms over his chest. "No," he answered firmly, glad when his voice came out even.

Fuck. He wanted to be insulted. Honestly, he *was* insulted. But... it was a fair question.

She turned to face him more directly. "How can you know that?"

He grunted. "I just do." And he did. Somehow, without knowing the details or the events, he knew that he had never trusted anyone enough to want to be that close to them.

"And I have to take it on faith?"

It was unreasonable to expect. He knew it. In her place, he would ask the same question. He *liked* that she had asked it. But he needed her to believe in him.

"I know it. Like I know I love nduja sausage on my pizza, and lager but not ale. I know that ketchup should be dipped into and never poured. Socks should never be worn with sandals—ever! Toilet paper should hang over the roll, not under, and the jam goes onto the scone first. I know it like I know that I love being outdoors with the wind in my face.... Like I know that my name is Josh."

He stalked across the kitchen and pulled her close, close enough that he could lower his forehead to hers and look into her eyes as he spoke. "I know it's not rational. And I can't explain it. But I know that I wouldn't be here unless I was meant to be."

Her eyes flicked between his, looking at him. Seeing him. And she slowly softened. "I believe you."

Her belief filled him, sent warmth curling through his chest and over his body, and he couldn't resist turning his head and taking her mouth in his.

He could get lost in her kiss. Drown in it. She was so soft and warm and perfect.

Just for a moment. He could have this, but only for a moment.

# Chapter Ten

He was still with her. Sitting across from her. Watching her work.

Watching her *try* to work. Or, more accurately, *pretend* to work. But how was she supposed to work when her whole body was still tingling from that kiss?

Ellie ran her fingertips over her lips. They still felt swollen. Oversensitive. And so did the rest of her body. The way he'd held her. That soft grunt he made as he hauled her even closer, consuming her. It was the best kiss of her life.

But since then, he'd withdrawn. He'd been increasingly silent as she pulled out her laptop and tried to make some kind of progress against her ever-growing e-mail backlog. Now he was rocking back in his chair with his arms crossed over his chest, biceps straining against his T-shirt. Brooding.

He probably thought he had his emotions locked down. But he was wrong.

She focused on the screen, trying to forget how he'd growled her name, his breath hot on her neck. How he'd fit between her thighs. How she'd wanted him so much closer.

How easy it would be to walk over and straddle those big thighs. To unzip his jeans and free them both.

"Ellie?" His voice intruded on the fantasy.

"Mm-hmm?"

"Are you alright?"

"Of course," she muttered, not looking up. She was working. Anyone could see. She tapped a few keys to prove the point.

"You've gone pink."

She lifted her head at that only to see his knowing look, one eyebrow raised. And damn him. Damn him for breaking into her world and upending her life, and then disappearing. Damn him for making her feel so flustered. For stripping her control when she needed it most. For leaving her so obsessed. For kissing her in a way that made her come alive. For kisses that were probably only perfect because they came directly from her own subconscious.

She glared at him. "You know, for a hallucination, you can be pretty smug."

He rocked the chair forward, landing the two front legs with a sharp thud before standing up and walking to the window. The stiffness was back in his shoulders, his brooding turned more bitter.

Guilt prickled down her spine. He wanted her to believe, and she'd promised she would. At the very least, she could try.

She closed her laptop with a soft click and rose to join him, standing just behind his shoulder. He must have known she was there, but he didn't turn.

"I don't have to work all afternoon," she offered. "Why don't we do something together?"

"I thought you were on a deadline." He didn't sound annoyed, just resigned.

And he was right, she was. Usually, nothing would have dragged her away. But she was always on a deadline. And maybe that had been a mistake. "It's under control." The storylines were back on track. The game mechanics were looking good. The e-mails piling up... not so much, but this was more important. And for the first time in her life, she was ready to prioritize *living*. "What do you feel like doing?"

He shrugged, turning to look at her over his shoulder, frustration etched into his face. "We could go see my place... oh, wait." The words were sharp, but the pain beneath them was real.

She settled her hand on Josh's back. Josh. The name fit him, and she liked knowing it. His muscles were even tighter than they'd looked. And a wave of tenderness rose through her. She wanted to take away that tension. To protect him somehow.

"We could..." She cast around for ideas and realized he still hadn't eaten anything. "We could cook. How do you feel about shepherd's pie?" she offered. He turned to face her, and she let her hands rest on his chest.

"I love shepherd's pie... but I'm just—" He shrugged one shoulder. "I don't feel like eating. At all."

She wrinkled her nose at him, thinking. "We could play a game. It doesn't have to be mine; it could be anything. How about *The Last of Us*?"

His stress seemed to ease as he looked down at her, his rigid neck muscles releasing some small measure of their tension. He lifted a strand of hair from her shoulder and ran it slowly between his fingers before tucking it behind her ear. The rough pads of his fingers brushed over her skin with a soft sweep. "Could we go for a drive instead?" he asked.

She stiffened—all the tension he had lost transferring over to her. How did he manage to choose the one thing she really didn't want to do?

Josh frowned. "I thought maybe if we drove around, I might see something I recognize," he said, watching her. "I might remember something."

Ellie nodded slowly. She'd wanted him to look for answers, and now he was offering to try. And she had to do it sometime, right? She had to get behind the wheel and actually drive somewhere eventually.

More than that. She *wanted* to. She didn't want to be stuck in her house for the rest of her life. Maybe this was the right time? Josh wanted to find himself—and she wanted to help.

"Let's—" Her mouth was so dry she had to swallow and try again. "Let's go now."

He blinked. "Right now?"

"Absolutely." Because if she didn't go immediately, it was going to build up bigger and bigger in her head. She'd committed. She had momentum. She wanted to go *now*.

She turned away, ready to close up the house and grab her keys, but Josh stopped her with his hand on her arm. "Ellie?"

She tried to tug him forward, but he turned her instead, pulling her closer until she was flush against him. "What's going on?" he asked carefully.

Her hands tingled, and her breathing sounded too sharp, even to her. But Josh was so big, his arm that came up to wrap around her shoulder so reassuring, that she found herself nestling into him, tucking her head under his chin, her heart rate slowly settling. "It's fine. I'm fine. We can go now, if you want."

He rested his hand on her cheek and lifted her chin,

tilting her to look at him. Straight into his eyes. And a sudden vision of intense blue eyes meeting hers across asphalt assaulted her: Josh, lying in a spreading pool of blood, his hand reaching for hers....

Her heart rate shot straight back up, and she shivered helplessly. What if he was hurt? What if they went for a drive and had an accident? What if—

No. She forced that line of thought away, popping each new what-if like a bubble in her mind. She closed her eyes and leaned her forehead against his chest, reminding herself that he was with her. He was safe. And so was she.

"Speak to me, Ellie," Josh's voice was low and concerned.

She concentrated on slowing her breathing, sinking into the reassurance of his big body against hers. He'd wrapped himself around her, encompassing her in safety. She couldn't remember another time in her life when she'd felt so securely held. And she found herself talking. Telling him the truth. "I started having panic attacks when I was in senior school." She let out a self-deprecating chuckle. "I was a little obsessed with getting everything right, and when things didn't... When I failed... It was terrifying. My father thought I should try harder to control myself. You know? Like if I wanted to, I could stop panicking. And I really tried." She blinked against the prickle in her eyes as she remembered. "But it just made it worse."

His arm tightened, holding her even closer. "He seems... I mean—"

Ellie sighed softly. "Yeah. He grew up with nothing. His father was a coal miner who lost his job during the pit closures. I think he never forgot what it was to be cold and hungry. Things got better and he was happy for a time. But then when my mother died, he just retreated back into his shell. He remembered to hate weakness in anyone—including himself—but especially in me." She shrugged sadly. "I understand why money and success are so important to him, I do."

And Ellie understood all about throwing herself into work, trying to live in the one place that she could control. But she was starting to realize how cold and lonely that place could be. She was determined not to follow that path. Not anymore. "I just.... I wish he could try to understand the things that are important to me."

Josh grunted. "*You* should be important to him."

He sounded so outraged on her behalf. So protective. And he was giving voice to the thoughts she'd held locked away for so long. As if he truly understood. It helped her continue. "When I left home, I found a therapist who helped me get my panic attacks under control. I didn't have one for years. Although—" She gave a small smile. "I still have a bit of a perfectionist streak." She rested her hand over his heart, letting the steady beat soothe her. "For the last few weeks, I've been having panic attacks whenever I try to drive somewhere."

His frown grew deeper, but he didn't let her go. "What happened a few weeks ago?"

She loved his complete lack of judgment. He didn't tell her to try harder. Or that she was too sensitive. Or that she should know she was really safe. His tone held only empathy and an honest desire to understand.

"I was in an accident." The words came out quieter than she'd intended, and she tried again, firming her voice. "I was cycling... and I was hit by a car."

She'd been flying down the steep, narrow forest roads not far from her house. The air had streamed past her, the ground disappearing beneath her wheels. It was the closest a human could come to flying—no pressure, no demands, no one who needed anything—just her and the bike and the road. But then something started to feel off.

She was in the lead, the first of a large group, and she didn't quite know how she'd come to be there. She looked back to see a dark blue SUV overtaking the other cyclists. It was moving far too fast. And right down the middle of the road.

She leaned into the curve. The ground shot past, the trees a blur at her side. She glanced back again. But now, somehow, the SUV was right up behind her. The road straightened; it was clear. There was plenty of space for the driver to go around her.

She slowed. Made space. The side of the road was rutted, carved into channels from rain run-off and littered with potholes. She stood on her pedals, using her legs as shock absorbers, pushing herself as close to the sandy curb as she dared. But the SUV kept coming closer.

The wind buffeted her. The smell of hot rubber surrounded her. She looked back, another anxious glance. The SUV was close enough that she could make out the driver through the darkened windshield. It was a man wearing dark glasses and a cap pulled low. And his face was turned toward her. Was he looking at her? He seemed to be.

And then he turned the wheel. Deliberately. Right into her.

She swallowed. "It was a hit-and-run. I went down. Hard. And then the cyclists behind me couldn't stop. They all hit me. They all went down."

God. What an understatement. The jarring wrench as the SUV hit her back wheel. Flying through the air, so fast, so helpless, and then crashing into the tarmac, sliding, ripping up the thin fabric of her cycle kit. Down to skin, down to blood and muscle.

She had opened her eyes to agony. The knowledge that something was broken inside her. Stabbing pain through her chest, radiating down her shoulder, the struggle to breathe. Her body feeling as if it had been through a shredder, her blood slowly seeping out onto the road from her torn-up hands and legs.

The nearest cyclist lay face down. His helmet had broken free, revealing dark hair matted with blood. She didn't know his name. They'd all been introduced too quickly. Those happy, carefree greetings were a hazy blur, a lifetime ago now. She'd tried to reach for him, she called for him, he—

Josh's fingers swept up her cheek and down again, over her shoulders and back up again as if he was checking for injuries, and the movement dragged her back to herself.

"And you? Fuck. Were you okay? *Are* you okay?" His words were low and tense, as if he was caught somewhere between reassuring her and reassuring himself.

"I am." She pressed a gentle kiss over his heart. "I'm fine now."

"What about then?" he asked roughly.

"Broken ribs, one pierced a lung, a really bad graze with a couple of deeper cuts that needed stitches, but those came out after about a week." She tried to sound nonchalant, but his look of horror told her he wasn't buying it.

"It took a while," she admitted. "My ribs still ache a bit. There are some scars at the top of my thigh. But I got good care, and I had a great physio. They helped me get back on my feet."

He tucked her closer into his arms. "And the other cyclists?"

"All okay. Only one was seriously hurt; he hit his head. I felt—" She shook away the strange shiver that rose in her. The whole thing had been so quick. And then so hazy. Too much pain, too much confusion. "I wanted to check on him. I tried to find out his name, but the police wouldn't release any information. Privacy laws, you know. Later, when I got home from the hospital, I called the cycling club, and they let me know everyone who had signed in was fine and back home."

"And did they find the person who hit you?" Josh asked.

"They found the car. It had been stolen from a nearby village. Do you know Duncton?" She snorted roughly, embarrassed. "Sorry, that's a stupid question."

Josh grunted, but he didn't seem offended.

"Anyway, it was abandoned in a field afterward, and set on fire. It could have been taken by anyone."

"They never found the driver?" Josh asked, blue eyes intent.

"No. The police think it was someone joyriding. Teenagers."

"And you?"

A man. Dark hair. Dark glasses. Collar high. Cap low. No defining features. "Not teenagers. It was a man, but I didn't see enough... I couldn't be certain."

"And now, driving is...?" He let the sentence hang. A question.

"Difficult."

He nodded slowly, his gaze locked on hers. "Okay."

And somehow, it was. More than that, for the first time, difficult didn't feel impossible. She'd climbed behind the wheel every day and gone a little farther every time. And she could go farther today. For him—and for herself.

He pressed a soft kiss to her forehead. "I believe in you, Ellie."

God. How could such simple words mean so much?

"Thank you." She cleared her throat, forced her spine straight. "Shall we go then?"

He stroked her hair slowly, never looking away. "It's up to you. We can go now, if that's what you want. Or another day, if you prefer. Either way, I'd like to spend the afternoon outside. With you."

# Chapter Eleven

THEY SPENT the rest of the day working in her vegetable garden. He'd asked her what she wanted, and this was what she wanted.

If he was going to disappear, she wanted some time with him first. Time when they could both relax. And she wanted to share this special place—a place she'd never shared with anyone before. Most of the men she'd dated had been firmly rooted in the city; even Vic had barely taken a glance—but it was one of her favorite places in the world.

A small courtyard of stone walls formed the perfect suntrap. Tomatoes, peas, and zucchini were planted in neat rows. Runner beans climbed frames alongside a wall of lettuce growing in vertical hanging planters. Strawberries were just starting to show fruit in the baskets she had placed in every free corner.

When she was stuck, when she needed to think, this was where she went. Something about working with her hands outside in the fresh air gave her the mental space she needed. And it didn't hurt that she could eat the results later.

Josh clearly loved being outdoors. There were a few slightly strained moments at first when she passed him tools or he started working on something new, when he seemed to falter. His expression got a little more closed, and he'd rub the back of his neck or scratch his thumb through his beard, looking like he'd never seen a garden tool before. But after a few seconds, he would take whatever she'd handed him, test the grip a few times, and carry on. And over time, it seemed to come easier, until the lines of tension around his mouth softened and the shadows in his eyes seemed to lighten.

After an hour of companionable side-by-side digging and planting, Nissy came out to join them. She padded over, getting under Ellie where she kneeled beside a bed of beetroot, bumping Ellie's chin with the top of her head and purring softly.

Ellie pulled her glove off and stroked her soft fur, crooning quietly. "Hey, pretty girl. My beautiful Nissy." Nissy stepped delicately back and forth, rubbing herself on Ellie's arms, her tail high and swaying as she walked.

Josh looked up from the hole he was digging. His shoulders were relaxed, his lips turning up into a smile. "Missy? Is that her name?"

Ellie chuckled. "No, her name is Niss, but I call her Nissy."

Josh blinked at her a few times and then he threw back his head and laughed. "You called her Cat-Niss."

It was glorious. Magical. He'd been so stoic and so shuttered that she hadn't imagined it was even possible for him to laugh like that. "Yes," she admitted. "Yes, I did." And her own lips twitched into a huge grin, until she was also laughing, laughing just from the joy of seeing him so free.

By the time they settled, Ellie's cheeks ached from

smiling, and she returned to her work feeling somehow lighter than ever before.

As the shadows lengthened and evening approached, Josh leaned back on his heels, eyes closed. A bird sang nearby, trilling and warbling, whistling and gurgling, and Ellie stopped to listen. "It's so lovely," she murmured. "I wish I knew what bird it was."

"He's a nightingale," Josh replied.

Ellie stretched out her legs as she began packing up. "Don't they sing at night?"

"Not always. The male is looking for a mate and marking his territory. He'll sing during the day sometimes while he's focused on that." Josh dusted his hands on his jeans and stood. "They'll be together for a handful of months, and then they'll move on. He'll go back to singing in the night by the end of summer."

A shaft of something—not pain, not envy, but *something*—struck her. Josh had been clear that he wasn't looking for anything permanent from her either. Maybe he would stay for a while, but then he would be gone. Whatever happened—whether he was real, a fantasy, or some kind of spirit—he had no plans to stay. By the end of summer, she'd be alone once more too.

Would it be enough? No. Almost certainly not. There would be a price to pay for afternoons like the one they'd shared.

She rested back on her heels and watched him. His face was turned up toward the clear, pale blue of the late afternoon sky. Perhaps watching for the nightingale. Perhaps enjoying the wisps of cloud lit up in peach and orange from the sinking sun. His lips settled into an almost smile, and it held her captivated. For the first time since she'd met him, he seemed at peace.

And she knew she would pay the price in the end, if that's what it took.

She pushed herself up to stand beside him. "Thanks for helping. I couldn't have done this on my own." It was true. Together, they'd done all the clearing and planting she'd put off for weeks.

"You're welcome. I needed that more than I realized." He wiped a bead of sweat away with the back of his forearm, and his T-shirt rode up, revealing a muscular abdomen with a smattering of dark hair that she longed to run her fingers down.

"How are you holding up?" she asked instead.

He dropped his hand and looked at her with a serious—yet slightly bemused—expression. As if he wasn't used to being asked how he was. Perhaps the people in his life were used to his brooding or the innate competence he exuded and didn't think to check if he needed help.

"I wish I remembered more," he admitted. "I don't like feeling out of control."

She stepped closer and rested her hand on his forearm. "I feel the same about being out of control. I think that's part of what made recovering from my accident so difficult." She squeezed his arm gently. "I can't even imagine how much worse it is for you."

He didn't reply. Didn't admit to the depth of how terrible it must be for him—or deny it. But he didn't move either, and they stood together in the cooling air for long moments before Ellie led the way back inside. Josh cleaned up while she packed away the gardening tools, and then she took a quick shower and threw on yoga pants and a soft cotton T-shirt while he warmed up some lasagna from a batch she'd frozen.

He complimented her on the aroma—which she could

admit was delicious, thick with tomato and herbs and rich with cheese—but he still seemed vaguely disturbed by the idea of eating. Instead, he drank some ice water while she ate, and they chatted about books they'd read and movies they'd seen.

And all the while, their hands brushed and their gazes met. She was aware of him. Of his presence.

They moved to the living room to sit on the sofa, and her legs pressed against his. His warmth spread through her thin leggings, and when she moved, he grunted. A sound that traveled right through to her most primal senses.

They decided to watch a film, and when she stretched over him to reach for the television remote, his hand settled on her waist, so hot and compelling that she couldn't help but turn to look at him. She was almost straddling him, her face close enough to his to feel his breath.

She held herself over him, drinking in the way his pupils flared and his fingers tightened on her waist. And then, when the torture of being so close and not quite touching grew too much, she dipped her face to his and kissed him.

His mouth sealed over hers, and his hands dragged her closer, pulling her down to meet the heavy bulge in his jeans, hard and straining and impossible to miss.

He lifted the hem of her shirt, his fingers gliding around her waist to settle on her back while his other hand cupped the back of her head, bringing her closer, angling her to taste her again and again.

He kissed her like she was a siren who had called to him for hours and he had battled through the oceans to reach. And she felt like perhaps she could be. As if she was beautiful and wanted and worthy of risking the sharp danger of the surrounding rocks. And even when they broke apart, both breathing hard, both flushed and slightly dazed, the feeling stayed.

She leaned back, turning on the movie they'd chosen, but he kept her legs across his thighs, rubbing her feet while they watched whatever was on—she was too focused on him to notice—and then he leaned over and kissed her again until they forgot the film entirely.

They made out like teenagers, until their lips were swollen and their hair disheveled and she had beard burn down the side of her neck.

And neither of them brought up anything about the future, or Josh's past.

She didn't even realize that she'd eventually nodded off until she woke up in his arms halfway up the stairs. He lowered her gently onto her bed and helped her strip down to her T-shirt, then after her mumbled insistence, climbed up beside her and pulled a blanket over the top of them both.

She woke up during the night wrapped in his arms. His jeans were rough on the back of her legs, his hand warm where it rested against her breasts. His breathing was slow and deep, and she closed her eyes, settling into sleep once more.

But when she woke in the morning, he was gone.

# Chapter Twelve

"How to tell if you're being haunted." Ellie's finger hovered over the Return key for a long moment. And then she slid it higher and hit Backspace instead, deleting the search.

She wasn't being haunted. It didn't feel that way at all. If anything, she felt more alive, more present in the real world than she had for... maybe ever.

She was beginning to make peace with the idea that he was real. That whatever they were sharing was real. She didn't want to know whether she was being haunted. She wanted to know how to help Josh to *stay*.

She wrote a new search instead: "How to help a ghost return to its body." Then read the results for five minutes before dropping her head onto her hands with a tired groan. Honestly, she should've known what she would get. A lot of ideas more relevant to one of her games than the real situation she was in. Sacred rituals. Quests. Buying spells. Seeking out a blessing.... None of them helped. Offering a sacrifice was more doable; perhaps she could offer Josh her body? She snorted to herself as she closed her laptop. Yeah, she wouldn't mind offering him her body.

It had been a long, crappy day. After finding Josh's side of the bed cold and empty, she'd wandered through the house already knowing he wasn't there. She'd burned her toast at breakfast, dropped a glass, which shattered into a million pieces, and picked up a text from her father wanting to catch up about selling the *Shadow-rift-binding Chronicles*, which she'd read and then left without replying —not even to point out he'd got the name wrong again—but hadn't been able to forget. Then her Wi-Fi had gone down. Living so far off the beaten path meant a low-priority network grid, and she hadn't been able to get online until midafternoon.

Then, when she finally did get online, it had been to wade into the very swamp she least wanted to spend time in. She'd spent hours doing the due diligence she'd promised Vic. Running numbers, analyzing the opportunities and threats associated with the offer, evaluating long term trajectories. And every way she looked at it told her she'd been right all along. She didn't need to sell her game. And she didn't want to.

The problem now was figuring out the best way to let her Dad and Vic know that she had made her decision— and she wasn't going to change her mind. They were the only family she had left. And they would both be disappointed. And Vic... hell. If she was back with Warren, that made everything a thousand times more complicated.

Of course, those weren't the only thoughts plaguing her. Memories of Josh had tortured her all day. Josh in her kitchen, watching her with that intent focus. Kneeling in her garden, head tilted up to the sky. In her bed, wrapped around her. Josh pressing her against the tree, his big hands gripping her waist.

Gah. She stood and walked away from the laptop. Stalked back to it because there was still work to do. Her inbox was just as full as it had been—probably even more full—but her mind was agitated and distracted. She hesitated, and then strode away again.

Her kitchen garden had never been so orderly; there were no chores for her to do outside. And the new mafia romance she downloaded—by an author she usually loved—couldn't hold her attention. It didn't help that the hero on the front cover, with his piercing blue eyes and brooding stare, could easily have been replaced with Josh.

Maybe he *was* haunting her. Damn it.

She did another lap of the house—Josh still wasn't there—and finally found herself standing in front of the mirror in the hall. Remembering the first time she'd seen him.

She reached out and touched the cool surface of the mirror. Since her accident, she'd kept asking herself what the point of anything was. Why bother, when it could all be lost so easily?

But maybe *this* was the point. She was still standing. She existed. She could see herself, staring back.

*"What does real feel like?"*

Real felt like life. Like second chances. Like taking action, even when it was terrifying.

Ellie strode into the dining room and dropped a kiss to Nissy's forehead, then jogged back to the hall, snatched up her keys, and stepped through the doorway, hardly even stopping to think. She wanted Josh, and she had no way to bring him back, but he'd given her a gift, nonetheless.

*I believe in you, Ellie.*

His faith in her was a precious thing: it reminded her

that she had faith in herself. She'd followed her dreams and her gut all her life. She believed in love. She believed in hope. And it was time to find that strength once more.

She stepped outside, paused for a moment to rest her hand on the smooth, solid wood of the front door, and then made her way across the driveway and into the driver seat.

She checked her position. Turned on the cold air and then turned it off again. She'd been too hot in the house, but now she felt chilled. She took a moment to fix the rearview mirror. Her hands were shaking, but she ignored them, just as she ignored the temptation to get out and check the tires. They were fine. She was fine. Wherever he was, Josh was fine—she hoped. Dear God, please let him be fine.

No. She couldn't think about that now. Later, she would find a way to help him. First, she wanted to do this.

She closed her eyes and concentrated on slowing her breathing. On her safe place. And then on relaxing the muscles in her face and shoulders, one by one. The panic receded, and she opened her eyes.

The air was clear, the sky a hazy blue, clouds building in the south. She opened her window and listened to the birds calling, wishing she could make out the nightingale, but he wasn't singing or wasn't nearby. She moved her foot to the accelerator and rolled forward. Through her gate, down the single track, all the way to the main road.

This time, there were no cyclists, no dark SUVs, just the open road. She inched forward. Checked, and checked again, and then moved out.

Her breath came sharp and uncomfortably, too high in her chest. Too tight.

She wished Josh was there. But she didn't stop. She needed to do this. She *could* do this. And maybe, one day, she would show him the places she loved. The nearby sandy beach. The ancient forests.

She released a rough breath, holding on to that thought. And, for the first time in weeks, she drove.

She made her way down the main road at exactly the speed limit, getting used to the feel of the wheel in her hands, the sound of her tires humming over the tarmac.

She kept breathing. Kept moving. And with every mile, her anxiety slowly eased. Driving became more natural.

She had done it.

Slow tears rolled down her face, and she wiped them away with the back of her hand and smiled—even if it was a little shaky—letting all her built-up emotions release; relief and gratitude warm within her.

She turned the radio to classic rock and left the sound low as she moved to the back roads for the journey home, driving past houses and through villages. And at the last minute, she drove past her turnoff and down to the beach instead.

The car park was long and narrow, running along the promenade, and still full even so late in the day. She found a spot right at the back and pulled in.

She wound down her windows, and the sea air filled the car, it was starting to cool and full of salt, teasing against her skin. Children played and shouted in the distance, teenagers listened to music a little way down the beach, and the sound of the waves formed a lulling backdrop to it all. It sounded like joy.

Had she ever felt so alive?

Next time, she would take him with her. Next time—if there was a next time—she wouldn't hold back.

# Chapter Thirteen

THERE WAS DARKNESS. There was a woman—Ellie. And now there were also memories. Memories of soft skin smelling of vanilla and jasmine, a quiet laugh, a quick wit, and a vibrant imagination. Memories of her body so close to his. Her hand on his chest, just above his heart. Memories of the all-consuming need to touch her. To hold her. To keep her. And twining though those memories, the sharper, colder, instinctive knowledge that she was not his to keep. That he shouldn't get too close. That he needed to control his feelings.

He remembered a man, older than him, someone important, ruffling his hair. "Be good, Joshy. You're a big lad now. Your mum needs you."

*No,* he wanted to scream. She needs *you*! *I* need you! But he didn't open his mouth. Why not? He kept silent. And the man walked away.

And there was also the memory of a dark SUV and a steep road. He hated that memory. And the fear that came with it. What if he remembered it because he was there? What if he'd been involved?

He forced away the thought. Allowed himself to sink deeper into the darkness. Away from all the things he didn't know and didn't want to know.

He floated for a long time, in that dim, silent place. Until the sound of beeping drove him to the surface.

Where was he? He forced his gritty eyes open. Tried to understand. He didn't know this place. It was cold and bright. His lips were cracked, his mouth dry. It wasn't Ellie's house. She wasn't there. There was no sunlight, no warmth, no lilting voice. And his body didn't move. It was locked in place.

He would have howled, if he could.

"His eyes are open." A voice spoke loudly beside him. A voice he knew. His... brother's? He tried to turn his head. Couldn't.

"Why are his eyes open?" There was a flurry of activity. Someone new. A light shone in his eyes, but it hurt so he closed them again.

He didn't want to be here. He wanted to be back with Ellie. And he'd promised. Somehow he knew—he'd promised.

He let himself drift back into the darkness.

# Chapter Fourteen

Ellie leaned back in her ergonomic gaming chair, the glow of her three screens casting a shifting blue light over her skin.

She was sitting in her home office—and gaming room— which had always been her happy place. The place where she could live in worlds that were fast and bright and full of adventure, with a set of online friends she enjoyed supporting, competing, and joking with.

When she'd first come home after her accident, her whole body battered and aching, this was where she'd come. And she'd been immediately welcomed back with a flood of messages pouring through her open chats. But even the people she'd played with for years didn't really know her. And she hadn't wanted to bring her problems into a gaming chat any more than she wanted to take them in to work, so she'd kept the details to herself.

Since she'd woken up in hospital, the only time she'd felt truly, authentically connected was with Josh. And he was gone. It had been two days, and he still hadn't come back.

She turned her focus back to *Balrog's Bridge*, a next generation RPG set in a far darker Middle Earth than even Tolkien had imagined. Despite it being a Saturday, she'd spent several hours working, and then moved onto her current favorite game. It was what she needed; something twisty and creative, with an array of challenging side quests to keep her busy. To keep her mind occupied.

By the time she'd finished freeing an Uruk-hai rebel from the Witch King's hold, it was midnight. She was exhausted but wired. High on the adventure and buzzing from too much adrenaline with no outlet.

And the quest she'd completed had teased her with the potential of an orc romance and then left her unfulfilled.

What if the rebel had been her character's soul mate?

Yes. That would work. The orc would be grim and huge, the leader of the rebellion against the Witch King's cruelty and avarice. Her female character would be a witch, her magic wild and dangerous, and utterly forbidden—only human men would be allowed magic. Not women. And not orcs. The witch and the orc, thrown into the dungeons to die, would meet by chance. And their first contact would be *primal*, their mating tattoos flaring to life as soon as their skin brushed.

Ellie grabbed a pen and started to write. The witch and the orc would hate and mistrust each other. But what if they had to flee the castle dungeons together? What if they had to travel, side by side, through dusty ravines crawling with the king's neophytes and witchlings? Dangerous winged beasts would fill the air above. They would fight back-to-back. Sleep in caves. The orc would be powerful, dangerous, and sexy as all hell. The witch would be smart and sarcastic and just as lethal. Together, they would be explosive.

Damn. It was a pity there was no way to write this story into the game they were working on. But... maybe it was worth a whole new world. A new game. A world full of betrayal and lies and sexy orcs.

She chuckled to herself as she scrawled ideas onto the pad she kept on her desk. Just one cave. Just one bedroll. Sniping and banter as sharp as the swords and spells. And passion. So much passion.

*Strong-Hold.* That would be the name. Damn. She loved it already.

But it was late, and she should have gone to bed already, so she packed away her pen and stuck her notes to her whiteboard. Nissy had been asleep in her cave for some time already, and she didn't stir as Ellie turned off the lights.

She made her way upstairs to her bedroom with her mind spinning. Glittering pictures and enticing storylines wove together to form the beginnings of a new world.

It was like coming back to life. Or the sun coming up after a long night. She'd driven beyond her road. She'd taken herself to the sea and walked on the sand. She'd felt the cold, salty water lapping against her toes. And now she was imagining again. Creating again. Seeing possibility in the world again. Seeing something more than work and survival.

Heat danced over her skin with the flush of excitement, and she longed to feel more of the cool night air drifting in through her open window. She dragged her T-shirt over her head, then slid her leggings off, dropping everything to the floor.

There was something empowering about standing naked and unashamed. Ellie moved to the massive mirror that leaned against the back wall. She'd rested it there, loving the idea of lying in bed, able to see the sky whichever way she turned—whether through the window or in the mirror's wide reflection—and maybe she'd imagined sexier uses too. Uses for times like this, when she was wide awake and burning with ideas and stories.

She stood in front of her mirror, watching as her nipples pebbled in the teasing breeze, and she lifted her hands to cup her breasts, thumbs slowly circling the aching tips. *She* was the witch, magical and fierce.

Her orc rebel would stand behind her, his scarred hands drifting up her sides, over the curve of her hips, skimming her ribs. The tips of his claws would pinch her nipples, tugging them. His fangs would be sharp and lethal at her throat, scraping gently.

Her heated flush spread and deepened as her fingers followed the path of the orc's big hands, down her abdomen, over the bones of her pelvis. She let the fantasy fill her. Rough hands on her skin, teeth on her shoulder, eyes meeting hers in the mirror, blue and intense.

Only now the orc had faded, and the eyes belonged to Josh. *His* hands petted her skin. *His* tongue laved her neck.

She slid her fingers over the soft curve of her stomach, letting one hand drift down, slide through the tight curls, farther. Her breathing grew shallow as she found the heated flesh and pressed a finger against the swelling nub of her clitoris before dipping lower, stroking deeper, gathering wetness.

She closed her eyes and let her head fall back, remembering Josh's kisses. The glide of his tongue. The way he growled. His hard cock pressing against her, heavy and thick and not nearly close enough.

Her pulse thudded in her ears, her body tingling and aching. But she needed more. She reached for the vibrator in her drawer and dropped it on the bed with a bottle of lube.

And then the air changed.

Pressure grew. A tang of ozone and electricity raised the hairs along her arms, and she knew he was back. He was in her house.

"Josh?" Her voice was husky and full of need.

"I'm here," he rumbled from the corridor just outside her bedroom.

She had a second to decide what to do. Whether to fling on a gown or throw herself under her covers. And maybe she should. Maybe she should protect herself from so much uncertainty. From a situation she had no control over, but which she was so thoroughly invested in. From the knowledge that she thought about him—wanted him, needed him—constantly. While he clearly wanted none of that.

But she did neither. She knew he would walk away if she told him to. And she knew she wasn't going to.

She was coming back to life and taking charge of her own pleasure. She turned to face the doorway, straightened her spine, lifted her chin, and waited for him.

He came around the corner and stilled. His eyes tracked slowly over her curves, taking in her peaked nipples and flushed skin.

"Ellie?" His voice was gruff.

Her eyes flicked to the toy abandoned on the covers before returning to his, and she saw the moment he recognized what she'd planned. Recognized it, and was ensnared.

He stepped through her doorway, making his way across the floor, each step intentional. Confident. Drawing closer and closer as the air between them thickened.

His eyes stayed locked on hers, intense and focused as she'd known they would be. "Is there room for me?" he asked, hands lifted, ready but not yet touching.

"Yes," she admitted. She kept her gaze steady on his. "I was thinking of you."

"Were you?" He stood over her, tall and imposing, as one big hand brushed deliberately down her side before settling on her hip.

"Yes." She licked her lips, one side of her mouth tugging up into a half-smile. "I was imagining you as an orc."

He dipped his face into her neck, running his nose along her skin as if he was memorizing her scent, and she felt the huff of breath as he chuckled. "And what would an orc do, once he'd caught the...?"

"Warrior witch."

He grunted, tugging her even closer. "Yes. His witchy warrior queen. What would he do with her?"

She slipped her fingers under the hem of his T-shirt to touch him, needing his skin. It was cool and firm. The muscles of his abdomen clenched and rippled as she skimmed her fingertips over the rough smattering of hairs leading to his chest and then dragged her nails lightly back down. She tilted her head further, offering more of her neck. "He would bite her."

Josh's teeth sank into her shoulder before she'd finished the sentence. Not too hard, but hard enough to hold her still as his tongue laved the flesh he'd captured. Hard enough to electrify her nerves all the way down to her core. She shuddered, her entire body inflamed as he released her shoulder to scrape his teeth along the tendon of her neck, up to capture her earlobe.

She pushed at his shirt, needing it gone, and he released her just long enough to tug it over his head, revealing his tanned chest lightly sprinkled with dark hair, and the heavy lines of ink covering his right bicep and over his shoulder. Then he immediately leaned closer, all the way into her space. Crowding her. Surrounding her. He cupped her face with his hands and took her mouth.

There was no teasing this time. No gentle introduction. They met each other with all the desire and need that had been growing between them. And then ramped it even higher in a wild dance of lips and tongues and give and take.

His chest hair rasped over her nipples with every movement, and she squirmed against him, pushing herself closer. He sucked her lower lip into his mouth as his fingers threaded into her hair, tugging lightly, positioning her perfectly for him to consume her.

She slid her hands to his zipper and tugged it down, opening his jeans, giving herself space to slip her thumbs into the top of his underwear, reveling in the smooth firmness of his skin and the fire growing between them. The way his cock swelled and hardened even further. God. She had never wanted someone with such ferocity before.

Josh released her mouth, whispering against her skin as he pressed open-mouth kisses down her chest. "I don't think an orc would leave it there, would he? I think he'd need more to bite. More to claim."

Her brain scrambled as he scraped his beard over her breast, a torturous brush over her skin, before sucking the tip into his mouth and tugging with his teeth. It was a live-wire connection straight to her pussy, and she moaned, arching her back. "Yes." It came out on a moan. "He would take more."

And Josh took it without hesitation.

He dropped one hand to her hip, holding her still as he

licked a line between her breasts, his other hand reaching to tug and twist her dampened nipple.

She slid her fingers down to wrap around his solid length, squeezing with the rhythm of his scorching mouth, loving how he shuddered and groaned, his hips thrusting forward into her grip, demanding more.

His mouth closed over the other breast, lashing it with his tongue and teeth. Again and again. Building an inferno inside her and fanning the flames. God. She *needed*. She writhed against him, panting. "An orc would take it all."

He left her breasts with one last teasing nip and straightened, her hand still locked around his length, his eyes almost black with desire. "You're gorgeous, my warrior witch." His voice was rough and strained. "I want to taste your skin. I want to suck your pussy into my mouth and torture you with my tongue." His hand slid from her hip, gliding between them until his middle finger found her clit and slowly, softly, began to rub, creating a sparkling, tingling point of contact that drew all her awareness, all her desires. "Can I do that, Ellie?" He swallowed. "Even knowing—" He hesitated for a fraction of a second before continuing. "—how little I can promise?"

His words stung, but she'd known them going in. They didn't change how much she needed him. Needed to feel him. She'd chosen this for herself.

Maybe, just maybe, there was a chance for them. Maybe, if she looked hard enough, she could find it. And for now... she would take everything he could offer. She would *live.*

"Yes." Her voice was husky. "Yes, to all of it."

She leaned into him, letting him hold her up even as his fingers dipped lower, finding her wet core and spreading the cream he found, gliding it over her swollen, desperate flesh.

"Fuck, Ellie." He rubbed slowly, watching her with glittering eyes as she heaved in a shaking breath. "I don't deserve you. But I want you too fucking badly. I have to take you." He slipped his hand away, and she groaned at the loss. But then he lifted her, carried her to the bed and laid her down. He dragged a pillow under her hips before coming to kneel between her legs.

He nuzzled into her, breathing deep, and her hands came down to his head, tangling in his hair. And then he licked her, just as he'd promised. A long, slow lick, through her slit, coming to rest briefly on her clit before moving away. He focused on kissing all the desperate parts of her before returning to circle that desperate nub. Moved away and came back.

His eyes lifted to watch her face, noting when she gasped, when she held her breath, when her fingers tightened in his hair, finding the rhythm that pulsed and spiraled through her. And then he did it again, over and over, pushing her higher.

Her legs were bent, her body open and offered to him, the pleasure rising through her until she was so close she could cry. And then he slipped two fingers inside her, unerringly finding her swollen front wall, and she exploded.

He held her close, whispering how gorgeous she was as she slowly came down. Then he met her eyes and grinned. "Let's do that again."

"You don't have—"

He growled and nipped her inner thigh, and she swallowed the rest, gladly. His lips found her clit once more, his tongue teasing, slowly stroking, building her pleasure. Using everything he'd learned until she could barely breathe.

Her hands fell back from his hair, and she gripped the

sheets, drowning in sensation. And then she heard the buzzing of her vibrator, set to its lowest, rumbliest setting.

He pulled away for a moment, spreading lube over the vibrator before turning back to her.

"Oh God. Josh. I..." She forgot what she wanted to say as he guided the vibrator inside her, just to her entrance, and licked her clit once more.

His free hand came up to pluck her nipple, and she gasped. He was everywhere. His lips and tongue teased and circled, his fingers tugged and tortured, and the deep, powerful vibrations spread through her in heated waves.

"Are you ready, Ellie?" His mouth moved over her clit. "Can you take more?"

She lifted her hips, pushing closer, and he chuckled, sliding the vibrator deeper even as he returned his attention to her clit, tonguing her in tight circles. She was sweating now, the pleasure shuddering through her. All the blood in her body pooled in the places where he was touching her. Her hips pushed forward, taking more, every part of her rushing toward him, toward the paradise he offered. She whimpered, reaching for it.

"Ellie. God. That whimper. I've been dreaming of it. I've been needing it." His lips closed around her clit, and he sucked. She shattered once more, keening as her body shuddered through the most intense orgasm she'd ever had.

Josh crawled forward to hold himself on his elbows over her. His bare chest pressed against hers, a comforting weight, and his skin smelled of heat and salt. "More?" he asked.

She lifted her head to kiss him, tasting herself, musky and sweet, before agreeing. "More. I want you inside me now." She pointed to her bedside table. "Condoms are in there."

He rolled off her to strip out of his jeans and then pulled out the sealed box, ripping off the plastic and pulling out a condom. He tore open the wrapper and rolled it on before crawling over her again. His heavy cock settled between her thighs, nudging at her entrance. "How are your ribs?" he asked, voice rough.

The ache had faded far into the background. "Fine." She cupped his face with her hand, wrapped her legs around his hips, and dragged him closer. "Thank you."

"Good." He bit his lip, brow furrowed as he concentrated. And slid into her so steadily, so smoothly, that she could feel every inch of him joining her in one long, lush penetration. Their breaths heaved together, bodies slowly merging until eventually he was fully seated inside her. And even then he held himself tightly controlled, letting her get used to his length. Letting the need to move build.

Ellie was still tingling with the power of the orgasms she'd had, her body floating and languid, but the strength of his body over hers, the way he filled her, brought her back. She raised her head to lick his tortured lip. To tease and soothe it. The movement settled her body even closer to his, and she reveled in the connection.

Josh began to move, a sensuous retreat followed by an intoxicating return. She was soft and flushed and molten, awash in a sea of pleasure. He lifted his head to watch her, his eyes on hers, and she couldn't look away, couldn't break that primal connection. He saw her. And she saw him.

And then he pressed his pubic bone against her clit, and her pleasure started to spiral upward once more. Her body tightened, clasping around his, and she moaned, lifting her hips, trying to drive him even deeper.

"You're so beautiful when you come, Ellie. I want to see

it again." Josh's voice was hoarse, the skin on his back hot and sweat-slick as she smoothed her hands over him, needing to hold him. "You look like a forbidden feast. For me to lick and taste and devour." He dipped his face into her neck and thrust harder, deeper, grinding against her clit with every motion, somehow finding that swollen, aching place inside her.

Her hands slid into his hair, holding him against her neck as she arched her back, hunger building once more. He circled his hips, sparking new currents through her feverish nerves. "And you sound... God. You sound like an erotic fantasy. You sound like I dreamed you."

His pace picked up, and she met him thrust for thrust. His teeth were on her throat, his body locked with hers. He dragged his free hand along her arm to find her hand and thread his fingers through hers, and she gripped it tightly, clinging to him as he drove into her, as he took her all the way to the top.

"Are you going to come for me, Ellie? One more time? Are you going to take us over the edge?"

"Yes." She panted the word. "I am." She tightened her inner muscles, holding him deep inside her. He ground against her clit as she arched into him, his breath hot on her neck as he whispered her name, and she flew.

Incandescent pleasure flowed over her in wave after wave as she clung to him. He lost his steady rhythm to desperate thrusts, finding his own peak and exploding through it.

And then he collapsed over her as they both shuddered, holding each other through the aftershocks as they slowly found their breath and returned to earth once more.

He shifted to her side, pulling her with him, pressing soft kisses to her cheek and hair. And she held him long after, turning to rest her head against his chest where she could hear his heart beating. Taking her chance to trace the lines of ink up his arm, following the story they told. They were trees, she could see them now. A dense, impenetrable forest.

Perhaps it would be wiser to let him go. To stay clear of the forbidden woods and the dangers they held. To keep emotions out, as she'd promised.

But she didn't. She *couldn't*. Whatever hurt came later as a consequence, she'd take it.

# Chapter Fifteen

Josh tightened his arm over Ellie's shoulder where she lay cuddled up against his side. Their bodies were naked under the covers, heated skin pressed against heated skin.

She unlocked him. Her kiss had given him back his name. Sinking into her body... God. It had given him so much more.

His memories—his life—were closer than ever. He could feel the shape of them, almost in reach. He could recall individual moments. Raising a pint glass to his lips in a familiar pub. A heron taking flight over a canal as he hurried to class. Serving breakfast for a younger boy, helping him with his homework. He remembered the moment he'd cut his lip: flicking a skateboard up through the air, intending to catch it and impress a girl he liked. But he'd misjudged and slammed it into his face instead. His teenage friends thought it was hilarious. And the girl... He reached for the memory and found only fog.

He didn't know what she'd thought. Or who she was. Or if he'd ever even seen her again. He didn't know who the boy was, only that he was important. Or where his home was. He had images and flashes, but the complete picture was still missing.

Outside Ellie's house, a pair of tawny owls called to each other, their soft hooting a haunting melody drifting in through the open window. Goose bumps rose along his arms; his body heat was slowly fading. He pulled Ellie in a little closer, sharing her warmth, the comfort she offered so freely.

She turned her head up to look at him, one brow raised in question.

"I heard the owls," he explained, as if that was an answer. He lifted a lock of hair and caressed it between finger and thumb. "They're calling to each other. Claiming their territory—and each other."

"Owls?"

"A pair."

Not only was Ellie haunting him, now even the owls were taunting him with their duet. Calling back and forth. Choosing to share their lives.

"I didn't realize that hooting was more than one owl," Ellie said, only half awake.

"Tawny owls," he replied, tucking the soft strands behind her ear. "They mate for life."

"That's beautiful. Better than the nightingale." She lowered her head back to his chest and closed her eyes sleepily. And then shot back up, eyes wide. "I didn't know that," she whispered.

"About the owls?" He let out a self-deprecating huff. "I don't know where I live, but I can tell you all about the local bird life."

"No." She cupped his cheek with her hand, turning his face to look her right in the eye. "I didn't know that tawny owls mate for life. The same as I didn't identify the nightingale." Her expression was completely serious. "Josh, I couldn't have hallucinated something I didn't know."

He stilled. "Did you still believe I was a hallucination?"

"No." She shook her head roughly. "I mean... I didn't think so. I wanted..." She let out a long breath. "I wanted you to be here, with me."

"I *am* here."

Doubt and fear and hope tangled together in her expression, and he wanted to give her something. Give her some of what she gave him. He lifted her hand from where it rested on his chest, brought it to his lips, and pressed a soft kiss to her knuckles. And then another. "I was just thinking that you—touching you—makes me remember myself."

She settled onto her side, resting on one elbow. "What do you mean?"

"When you touch me, I feel as if I'm coming back. I start to remember pieces of my life. It's like..." He paused, not quite finding the words he wanted. He let go of her hand, and she settled it back on his chest, a warm weight right over his heart. "It's like you're a candle, casting light, showing me where I am. Showing me *who* I am."

She leaned down and pressed a gentle kiss to his forehead. And if he was another man, a man who could really allow himself to feel, he might have wept for how tender and gentle it was.

She stroked her thumb along his jaw, rasping through the bristles. "And do you? Remember who you are?"

She sounded so encouraging, and her eyes held so much empathy, that he almost didn't want to tell her no. But lying was not in his nature—and Ellie deserved the full truth. "I know my name is Josh. I know I cut my lip with a skateboard when I was trying to prove how cool I was. And

I know that, right now, there's nowhere in the world I'd rather be than here, holding you."

She stayed there, looking down at him for a beat, and then dipped to press a soft kiss to his lips. He slid his hand up her back, savoring her smooth skin, letting the kiss take them both away. But not for long enough. She had more questions.

Ellie raised her head, her eyes flicking between his as she met his gaze. "And do you remember the other place? The place you go when... when you're not here."

An image of a large navy blue SUV flickered in his memory, but he blinked it away. "I'm only aware of three places: here with you, the darkness, and somewhere cold and bright and painful." He threaded his fingers through her hair and kissed her again, needing her lips on his.

She drew away and settled herself back down, nestling her head under his chin and wrapping her arm around his chest. Perhaps to get closer. Perhaps for reassurance. Perhaps so that she could look away as she asked in a low voice, "Why here, Josh? Why do you come?"

There was an answer, somewhere lost in the mist of his memories. Like a word he couldn't remember, sitting at the tip of his tongue, scratching at the back of his mind. But he couldn't reach it.

But there was one thing he knew, one certainty he could offer unreservedly. "Because *you're* here."

# Chapter Sixteen

"Are you sure you want to do this?" Josh asked as Ellie stepped outside and locked the front door behind them. Going for a Sunday afternoon drive was her idea, but she'd been looking a little pale since she suggested it, and the idea of watching her suffer made him feel... something. Something he didn't like.

"Yes. I want to take you out for a while. I want to show you some of the places I love." She flashed him a small, determined grin. "Maybe you'll even recognize them."

He forced himself not to take a step back. Hell. That was even worse. "Don't do this for me, Ellie. Please."

She tilted her head to the side watching him. "Don't you want to go?"

What was the right answer? Leaving the cottage meant accepting that there was a life outside their bubble. It was a reminder that all bubbles popped, eventually. But even more than that, the idea of Ellie making herself do something she was afraid of for him made him uneasy. It was too thoughtful, too compassionate. They were supposed to be having fun and living in the moment. This was something else.

And yet... how could he say no? She had taken this massive step on her own already; she had faced this demon without him. How could he not support her now?

And deep inside him, somewhere buried, he'd dreamed of someone to care for him like this. Someone who he could stand beside and trust that they would face the monsters hiding in the darkness together.

He swallowed his concerns and reached out to tuck a lock of wind-blown blonde hair behind her ear, letting that small contact fill him with warmth. "I'd like to go wherever you'd like to take me."

"Okay. Good." Ellie glanced back at the house—Nissy was washing her paw daintily in the window—and then gave him one last quick smile before climbing into the car.

Opening the passenger door was harder than he expected. He'd become used to holding Ellie. Interacting with her. And when he was touching her, everything else was easier. But the door was heavy, metallic, and cold. His fingers slid through the surface as if it had been formed from freezing mist, and he had to concentrate to get a good grip. It was a relief to finally climb inside and settle onto the soft leather seat—even if her mini was small enough that he had to fold his legs up to fit.

Ellie was quiet as she drove them out to the open road. She checked and re-checked her mirrors and her speed, her hands clenched tight around the wheel. It clearly cost her, this idea, but she didn't suggest they go back. And mile by mile, she seemed to find her rhythm.

Josh leaned back in his seat, watching her as she settled into the drive and slowly began to relax. Her breathing deepened, color came back into her cheeks, and he couldn't help remembering the way her skin had flushed and warmed under his hands the night before. The way she'd stood, naked and proud and magnificent. He cleared his throat, trying not to shift in his seat. "So, tell me more about your orc."

She huffed out a strained laugh. "What do you want to know?"

"Anything... everything. Where did you get the idea?"

"I was playing Balrog's Bridge and there were Uruk-hai"—she glanced sideways at him, eyes twinkling—"and I started thinking about all the awesome orc romances I've read...."

The more Ellie spoke, the more comfortable she seemed, and the more the world around them seemed to lighten. She told him about her favorite novels and promised to lend him some books that would make him see the world of orcs in a whole new way. And then she began to explain and build on her ideas for a new game, and as she did, as her passion and excitement filled the air, she seemed to grow even brighter. As if he could almost reach out and touch that spark of joy that she shared so generously. The warmth that he would take back with him, wherever he went.

The thought pierced through him: one day, maybe soon, he would be gone. He rubbed his chest, trying to ease the ache, and Ellie glanced over at him with a raised brow.

He didn't want to break into their moment, so he simply gestured to the small space and his bent legs.

She chuckled, and for the first time her grin seemed genuine. And after that, they settled into a companionable conversation about books they'd loved and occasional easy silences. The radio was set to indie rock and the air filtering in through the open windows was warm and pleasant.

Ellie drove them down to the beach and they parked for a while, soaking up the sea air and the sounds of families. It seemed like the kind of place he would have loved to visit, but it didn't spark any memories for him.

They turned inland and drove through the nearby town with its narrow streets, towering medieval cathedral and Georgian architecture. It was charming, but he still didn't see anything that he recognized. In a way, it was a relief. They still had their bubble; they'd just taken it with them.

After a while, Ellie drove them out of the town center and back onto the ring road. But instead of turning south toward her home, she turned north. "I thought we could loop around closer to London," she explained. "It's busier. There are more villages. Maybe something will come back to you."

The traffic got heavier. Ellie's attention focused more closely on the road, and their relaxed drive slowly grew more tense.

And then something worse happened. He started to get cold. The kind of bone-deep, soul-deep cold that he couldn't shake. Closing the windows and turning up the heating didn't help. Ellie's glances full of quiet concern didn't help. He could feel the darkness, pulling at him.

"Ellie." His voice scraped at his aching throat, and he swallowed heavily. It was as if he could feel something lodged there. His hands tingled with pins and needles, and he flexed his fingers trying to get feeling back before tugging at his shirt, desperate to make space to breathe. But his fingers slipped through the fabric as if it didn't exist. God.

Pain began to filter through the cold. Pressure through his temples became a sharp, stabbing ache. The radio was too loud, but when he tried to turn it down, his fingers slid through the dial.

He hunched over, closing his eyes against the undulating shimmer of the world and the pain stabbing through his skull, wishing he could block out the acrid scent that filled his nostrils: something harsh and pungent, like bleach or chemical cleaners.

Ellie's words came from far away. "Josh? What's wrong?"

He shook his head. He couldn't answer. And he knew that if he lost concentration he was going to fade completely.

"I'm turning around." Ellie's voice was comforting and safe, precious to him, and he clung to it, as he had so many times before.

He nodded carefully, keeping his eyes closed. And then her hand settled on his thigh. Warm and gentle and holding him like an anchor. She spoke to him, telling him about how close they were to her home, and how pleased Nissy would be to see them both.

And slowly, slowly, he came back to himself.

"I'm—" He cleared his throat roughly. "I'm feeling a bit better."

"What happened?" Ellie's voice was full of worry.

"I don't know. I think we got too far away."

"From what?"

He couldn't be sure. Too far from Ellie's home perhaps —the only place he ever woke. Too far from where she felt herself safe and grounded? Or from his own body, wherever that was. "I'm not sure. Maybe from myself."

"Okay." Her fingers gripped his thigh a little tighter. "I've got you."

With every mile they drove, the darkness receded, and

the harsh smells eased. His body began to feel more solid, and the pain eased until it was only a vague echo in his head. And through it all, Ellie didn't falter. She did have him.

She faced the darkness at his side.

# Chapter Seventeen

Ellie took a sip of her coffee, forcing herself not to look at Josh. Or, if she were being honest with herself, look at Josh *again*. Damn, the man was distracting. A low thrum of awareness pulsed through her whenever he moved, whenever she caught sight of his big, competent hands, or the way the muscles moved in his tanned arms.

She'd set him up on her spare laptop so they could work side by side in her office. She usually worked at home on a Monday anyway, and after the stress of almost watching him fade during their drive yesterday, it was a relief to stay at home where she knew he was safe.

Josh was browsing; looking for anything that might be familiar. Places. People. Jobs. Somewhere to start. While she was finally going to crack the mayhem in her e-mail inbox. Which would probably be moving a lot faster if she didn't take a break every ten seconds to watch him.

Her body was still responding after the night—and the morning— they'd shared. Nearly losing him yesterday had created an urgency in them both. A constant need to touch and be touched. And of course, the touching led to more touching, until they were both naked.

Waking up and finding him still in her bed was magical. An unexpected, thrilling gift that she hadn't dared to hope for. He'd been watching her, those clear blue eyes locked on her. On her hair, spread out over her pillow. On her breast, half peeking out from under the fallen sheet. And then his calloused hand had stroked over her body to take hold of the sheet and slowly drag it away, his gaze never leaving hers.

He'd leaned down and whispered, "Are you awake, Ellie?" and she'd gone from half asleep to wide awake and tingling with arousal as his hot breath whispered against her ear, the cool air flowing over her tightening nipples.

She'd reached for him, pulling him over her... and it had taken another hour before they finally managed to leave the bed. And yet another hour after that when he joined her in the shower.

The temptation to suggest they take the day off and go back to bed was almost irresistible. But her inbox had become totally insane, and she had to get it in order first.

She dragged her eyes off him, took another fortifying sip of her now cooling coffee, and dived in. And almost immediately lost the will to live. So much of it was junk. Even when it wasn't outright spam, there were multiple copies of meeting minutes she didn't need to see, bills that accounts should deal with, a few blatant covers—copying her to prove a point—and...

That was weird.

She opened the e-mail from ProClimate Air. It was a cost estimate for an annual service plan for a precision cooling system designed for a server room. For a very specific dedicated server room. A server room for

Dangerous Business Games. Her company. The only thing was, they didn't have a server room.

"Huh." She leaned back in her chair and opened the attachment, trying to make sense of what she was seeing.

"What's wrong?" Josh watched her, his brow creased.

"I don't really know," she replied slowly, reading further. It was the fifth e-mail in the chain, but the first time she was copied. Someone had added her, perhaps accidentally, because she certainly hadn't been copied before. Not on any of it. "Something isn't right. I have to—"

She let the sentence fade, already picking up her phone, dialing, waiting with increasing... worry? Anger? Some combination of them both.

"Hi, Ellie," Victoria answered eventually. "How are you feeling?"

"Right now, I'm feeling a whole lot of things." She forced her voice to calm. "Vic, why am I looking at a quote for air-conditioning for a server room we don't have?"

There was a long silence, and then footsteps, followed by the sound of a door closing. Presumably Vic's office door.

When Victoria spoke again, it was with the measured calmness someone might use to talk to an overtired child. "We do have a server room, Ellie."

"No." She had to fight to keep her voice steady, to not give into the rising fury. "That's not possible. Because I distinctly remember deciding that the costs of setting up and maintaining a server room were prohibitive—and it wouldn't add any kind of value anyway. Because our games have always been intended to be played either as a single player or locally hosted for couples and small groups. The *Shadowbound Rift* is meant to be experienced as a *story*. It's not designed to be a massive multiplayer game. That's the whole point."

Vic huffed. "Part one, maybe, but when the new game comes out—"

"Not *maybe*. God, Vic. You know this. *The Binding* continues the story with the same characters and the same style of play."

Vic continued as if Ellie hadn't even spoken, and for the first time her tone contained a hint of something less patient and a lot less friendly. "What I know is that you weren't here, and somebody had to decide what direction to take. I made the choices that were best for everyone."

Ellie pushed back her chair and stood, pacing around her office as she spoke. "I was in hospital. And then in daily physical rehab, and then working from home. I wasn't even gone that long." It was as if Victoria had leaped at the chance, taking sweeping actions she must have known would never be approved otherwise. Ellie rubbed at her chest, trying to soothe the rising ache. "I left you in charge. I trusted you."

Vic laughed, a brittle, high sound. "You don't trust me, Ellie. You don't even listen to me. I asked you to sell. I asked you to let the storylines evolve. You haven't—"

"Oh, my God." Ellie cut her off as cold understanding flooded through her. "That's why you installed the servers! Not for the game. Not for our staff. You did it to sweeten the sale. To offer a European data center for Silver Wolff to use."

For the first time, Victoria was silent.

Nissy stalked out of her bed, fur rumpled and amber eyes narrowed, irritated at being disturbed. Josh rose from his seat and came to stand at her side, his hand resting on her shoulder, tethering Ellie to the earth.

"I told you how I feel about this, Vic." She'd built her company from nothing. It was *hers*. Victoria was her sister in everything but blood—but she had pushed too far. It was time to go back and see her face to face. "Fine. I'm coming there. I'll be in London by this afternoon. We'll talk about this more when I get there."

She put down the phone feeling a hundred years older and infinitely betrayed. Damn, she hated conflict. And Vic knew how tension and confrontations made her anxious. How she'd spent her entire childhood trying to be perfect enough to avoid being the focus of hostility. But Vic also knew Ellie'd never wanted to host a massive multiplayer RPG. She didn't want to create a platform where strangers could spend their days shooting each other. She'd wanted an intimate story to share between friends. One with a happily ever after. Because God knew, life didn't hand out HEAs.

Josh was still standing beside her, his gaze troubled, and that made everything even worse. She didn't want to leave him, but she didn't see how he could come with her. She didn't want to think about whether he would be there when she got back. Or how she would ever find him again if he wasn't.

*She didn't want this to be their end.*

It was a terrible choice, and she hesitated. But Josh didn't. He turned her to look at him, his hands warm and reassuring on her arms. "You have to go, Ellie."

"But—"

He pressed kisses to her cheeks, her eyes, even her nose. "You need to do this. We both know you do." He kissed her again and then stepped back, giving her space, waiting patiently while she came to the same conclusion, the conclusion she'd already reached while speaking to Victoria: she had to go.

Damn Vic for putting her in this position. But now that

she was in it, there really was only one choice. She rolled back her shoulders and lifted her chin. It was time to set this straight.

Ellie ripped through her house shoving her laptop into its case, grabbing an overnight bag, and throwing in toiletries. In the past, she'd always stayed with Vic. This time, she would need to book a hotel.

She double checked Nissy's cat flap, water, and food dispenser and cleared out her litter tray. She would be fine for one night and if Ellie had to stay longer, she could call her usual cat sitter from the village.

And through it all, Josh was a reassuring presence. He passed her things, reached onto high shelves, promised to keep an eye on Nissy. And then finally, after she'd buckled her bags, he wrapped her in his arms and kissed her again.

She leaned her head against his chest—so much warmer now than when he first appeared in her life—listening to the steady thump of his heart. And spoke into his neck. "I wish you could come with me."

His arms were big and strong and safe. And his voice rumbled against her ear as he spoke. "I can stay here and wait for you. I'll keep up the garden for you." He chuckled. "I'll keep your bed warm."

She held him tighter, pressing herself even closer. "Will you be here? When I get back?"

"I hope so."

She did too. He'd already become a part of her home. Of her life. And she wanted to share more. She wanted the house filled with their laughter, she wanted barbecues on the deck, long walks to the sea, and lazy Sunday mornings wearing nothing but skin. And she wanted them with him.

But that was all a dream, and even this brief interlude was already over.

She forced herself to step back, hoping she looked more confident than she felt. "When you get tired of scrolling through random websites, why not play *Shadowbound Rift?* There's a link on the laptop."

"I'd like that." He grabbed her bag and slung it over his shoulder to carry out to the car.

They both hesitated on the drive.

"Will you be okay, Ellie?"

She swallowed. He wasn't only asking about the long drive, but about Vic. And a part of her wanted to say no and run back inside with Josh beside her. A part of her wanted to avoid the confrontation that was coming and stay with him in the strange and inexplicable dream they'd been living in. But she didn't run or hide. This is what she did: she kept working, kept trying, until she got things right. Vic had pushed her too far this time. Ellie had created something special, and now she would take on the battle to keep it safe. "Yes, thank you." She took her bag from Josh and swung it onto the back seat. "I'll be fine."

"I'll see you when you come back," he promised. Although they both knew he couldn't make that vow.

But he sounded like he meant it. As if, for all his talk of no emotions and having nothing to offer, he would be waiting for her if he could. And that was the hardest part.

She climbed into the front seat, slid on her sunglasses, and prepared to do what she always did: smile to hide how much her heart was aching as she waved and drove away.

But then she saw Nissy, sitting regally in her window, watching the world with big eyes. Josh stood just in front of her window, his hands in his pockets, his expression back to stoic and withdrawn.

A bird sang somewhere in the distance, and she didn't know what kind of bird it was, but he would. Their eyes met, and she didn't hesitate or stop to think, or try to do what was right or expected. She ripped open the door, flung her glasses on the seat beside her, and ran to him.

He caught her out of the air and lifted her high into his arms and laughed. God. He *laughed*. Genuine and free and full of delight. She cradled his face in her hands and bowed her head to kiss him. There in the sunlight, surrounded by the scent of sunshine on green leaves. And he kissed her back like she was rain on a summer's day, and he was dying of thirst.

And when he finally set her down, he held her a moment longer. He pressed his cheek against her hair and whispered so softly she didn't think she was meant to hear him. "I'll miss you, Ellie. More than you could know."

# Chapter Eighteen

Ellie's London offices were in an airy old warehouse with big windows and high ceilings. She'd worked closely with an amazing designer to create a techy-steampunk hybrid full of rich jewel-toned fabrics, exposed copper piping, old leather-bound books on cluttered shelves, and antique maps of London on the brick walls.

There was a battered brown leather sofa at reception, every available space was filled with a jungle of leafy plants, and a massive wrought iron clock oversaw it all. But if a visitor looked closely, they would soon see that it was threaded through with elegantly designed technology. And it was all cutting-edge; from the biometric entry to the voice-activated, customizable drinks machine, to the solar panels providing nearly all the energy.

Usually, Ellie stepped inside with a spark of pride and awe, a deep-seated gratitude for this magical place. Usually, it reminded her that she was part of something special. But not this time. This time, she was frazzled from the stressful drive, anxious about seeing Vic, and Josh's last whispered words played on repeat in her head.

Within seconds of opening the door, Sally looked up from the reception desk and saw her. Then the madness really began. Everyone poured out of offices and meeting rooms to greet her, hug her, and see how she was recovering. There were only twenty of them all together, so everyone knew everyone, and over time, they'd become a kind of family. People joined and stayed.

For the first time since seeing that e-mail, Ellie felt her shoulders soften. She should have come back earlier. She had needed this. This feeling of belonging. The excitement of working with talented people to create something wonderful.

But then she saw Vic. Standing apart. Always the most elegant person in the room. Victoria's hair was styled into a perfect spiky bun, and her designer skirt landed just above her knees to reveal her long legs. She had folded her arms over her chest, watching the excitement with a frown. And Ellie's sense of belonging slowly dissolved.

Vic was her best friend... but she was also the only person who looked like she'd rather Ellie was somewhere else. Somewhere far away.

Ellie finished chatting and finally faced Victoria as the last of the designers took their leave. Neither of them spoke as they strode toward Ellie's office and settled at the glass table beneath the window. She considered sitting at her desk and letting Vic sit across from her, giving herself space and authority—armor to protect the vulnerable softness she was struggling to hide—but it felt petty. This conversation was going to be hard enough.

Ellie looked at her friend for a long moment, noting the dark rings under her eyes, the fine lines bracketing her mouth. She looked like she'd been eating badly. As if things had been tough for her. And for the first time since learning about the new server room, Ellie felt concern threading through her anger. She reached out to settle her hand on Victoria's arm. "What happened, Vic? Talk to me."

Vic leaned back, away from her touch. "Nothing happened. I made a decision for the business."

Ellie pulled her hand back and straightened. "You made a decision you knew I wouldn't like."

Victoria's eyes narrowed, her face setting into the expression Ellie had seen multiple times over the years—stubborn pride and defensiveness. "You left me in charge."

Ellie dragged in a breath. She hadn't *left*. She'd been catapulted into a nightmare. She raised an eyebrow, and Vic had the grace to look guilty.

"You know what I mean," Vic muttered.

Did she? Ellie wasn't sure. Still, it didn't really matter why she hadn't been there. "That isn't the point. I couldn't be here, and I trusted you to represent me while I was gone."

Vic winced, the expression fleeting and almost unnoticeable unless you knew Vic well. Which Ellie did. But Vic still didn't back down. "You expected me to do what was best. And I did."

"I expected you to do what was best for the company." Ellie's voice started to rise, and she forced it back to calmness. She leaned forward against the table, ignoring the headache creeping up to hammer at her temples. "Selling is not best for the game, for the people who work here, or even for our players. It's not good for me—and you know, better than anyone, my opinion on this. It's only good for a lot of immediate cash."

Victoria shook her head. "You don't really think that, or you would have refused the offer straight away. I have no idea why you're dragging this out, but it's painful for everyone."

Ellie flinched. God. She'd been trying so hard to find a compromise when there really wasn't one. She'd delayed because she didn't want to hurt her friend or alienate her father. But clearly that was a mistake. "You're right; I should have made this decision weeks ago."

Vic leaned forward, her elbows coming to rest on the table. "Think of what you can do with that cash, Ellie. You could create a whole new game. You could create a whole new life. You wanted to travel.... Do it. You wanted to work less.... Do it. You wanted to find someone; now you can."

Ellie watched her friend, noting the relief glimmering in her eyes. Vic thought she'd won. And it *was* a good list, all things Vic knew Ellie wanted. Things she'd put off for so long that if she'd died on that road, she would have missed them entirely. And perhaps if Vic had come to her in the difficult days when she first came home from hospital, Ellie would have been swayed. But she hadn't. Ellie had faced those days alone and kept trying. She'd kept getting out of bed, even when it was hard. She'd begun to find herself again. And she'd given the sale all the thought it required. She had done her due diligence, and she was confident in her decision.

In the past, Victoria would have been her biggest cheerleader. But not this time. Why not? That was the real question. Why was Victoria pushing this so hard? "And what would you do with *your* cash, Vic?"

"We—" Vic swallowed the word immediately. But it was too late.

Ellie straightened. "Who's we?"

"I meant to say I—" Vic started, but Ellie cut her off.

"It's Warren, isn't it?"

Vic shook her head, looking away, but she didn't deny it.

"I knew you were back with him. God." The words spilled out. Too judgmental. Too harsh. But it was too late to take them back.

Vic swung her arctic gaze back to Ellie. "*You* might be happy in your imaginary world where you live with your book boyfriends and fantasy men. *I'm* trying to make a real relationship work."

That hurt. Ellie knew she was a perfectionist. She knew she sometimes hid in her fantasy worlds rather than face the messy, unpredictable dangers of the real world. And Josh... was that what she had done? Invented him?

No. Vic didn't even know about Josh. Ellie pushed those worries away. "How can you say that, Vic? We've been friends for years. You know the truth."

"Do I?" Vic scraped her hands over her face, smudging her mascara.

It was jarring. In all their years of friendship, had she ever seen her friend less than perfectly put together? A horrible suspicion began to form. "Did you tell Warren about the sale? Is this all his idea? Damn it, Vic."

Victoria glared at her, high red streaks marking her cheeks. "You don't get to police my relationships, Eleanor. You don't tell me what I can share and what I can't."

"I'm not policing your relationship, Vic! See who you want. Sleep with who you want. But I wish you could see that you're worth so much more than that arsehole who has never made you happy, who has never prioritized you in any way." Ellie gave herself a second before voicing the rest, Vic was not going to take it well, but it had to be said. "But actually, I *can* tell you what you may and may not share. You're an employee here and—"

Vic's face pinched. "Fuck you, Ellie."

"We're friends, Vic. We've been friends for a long time. So I'm going to forget you said that." Ellie gripped her hands together to stop them shaking. "I'm worried about you. I don't think he's good for you. And now he knows things about my company that—"

"Why should it be yours?" Vic demanded. "I work just as hard as you do! That's my blood and sweat and tears out there too!"

Ellie held her gaze. "It's mine because I created it and nurtured it and loved it for all these years! It's mine because it means more to me than a number on a bank transfer. It's mine because *I* am your boss." Ellie took a breath, working hard to hold her outrage from spilling out any further. This wasn't her friend speaking. Vic's words were straight out of Warren's mouth. And before she decided how to handle Vic's actions, she needed to know exactly what she was dealing with.

She clasped her hands together even tighter as she found her control and held it. "What did he promise, Vic?"

"This has nothing—"

Ellie leaned forward and locked eyes with her best friend. "What. Did. He. Promise?"

Vic stared out the window in silence for long minutes. Long enough that Ellie assumed she wouldn't reply. But eventually she answered quietly, "We'll get married. He doesn't want to start our life together in debt."

And there it was. "How much debt is he in?"

"He got scammed. You know how hard he's worked to set up himself up as a trader."

Ellie didn't know that at all. She knew Warren liked to stay at home in sweatpants doing things on his computer no one else was supposedly clever enough to understand. But she couldn't say that. Not now.

"He knew someone who could get him in on an IPO on this mining company that had developed a new way to extract rhodium," Vic continued. "Do you know how much rhodium is trading at right now? Twenty-five thousand dollars per ounce. It was going to be huge."

Hell. Ellie was gripping her hands together so tightly that they hurt, and she forced them apart as she waited. There was only one possible way that could end.

"It was a scam." Vic swallowed thickly. "But he'd already put everything up as collateral."

Ellie's heart broke for her friend. And she had a horrible feeling this story was about to get worse. "How much debt is he in?"

Vic's shoulders slumped. "Over a million pounds. Not including his mother's house—" She took a ragged breath. "—and mine."

"He lost your house! How could he even... How does he...?" Ellie's stomach clenched. "How is that possible?"

"I gave him permission," Vic admitted. "I signed the forms and let him use the deeds as surety."

Ellie reached out and took Vic's hands, holding them tight, wishing she could surround her in support. And maybe it was a measure of her distress, because Vic didn't pull away. "Why did you do it?" Ellie asked.

"Because he was so excited. He was so sure he was going to make it big, and I wanted that for him. He loves me, and I could do this one thing. And I had to trust him, right? If we're going to have a life together, we have to trust each other." Vic's voice dropped to a whisper. "We were going to be happy."

"God." Ellie held in the rest of what she wanted to say. She held back the flood of how much she hated Warren for his snide comments and his constant gaslighting. For making her friend—her bright, capable, beautiful friend—doubt herself. For making her believe she had to do something so reckless to prove her love. And for working so hard to drive a wedge between them.

Vic's fingers closed around hers and for a moment, Ellie had hope. But then Victoria spoke. "We can still fix this." The harsh red had faded from Vic's cheeks, leaving her pale and tired-looking. "Sell the company, Ellie. Take the cash. Set us all free."

Hell. Just do this one thing for Vic. Like Vic had just done one thing for Warren. Prove her love to her best friend, just like Vic had proven hers....

Where did that end?

How many people could be hurt? Her staff. Her game. The community of players she'd nurtured and loved; that beautiful group of people creating character art and writing fanfic and bonding over plots on social media.

Ellie shook her head. There had to be another way. "I'd be happy to loan you—"

Vic tugged her hands back, her mouth turning down at the corners. "I don't want to borrow money from you. I want the money I've earned."

Ellie sucked in a breath. She hated everything about this. The conflict. The fear of losing her friend. Everything. But she was finding a new kind of strength. The strength to say *no*.

She reached across the table, holding her hand out palm up, and tried again. "Please don't ruin our friendship over this. We can work together. I'll help—"

Victoria stood up, pointedly ignoring Ellie's open hand, and stalked to the door. "All I want is my share of the company that I helped build." And then she left.

# Chapter Nineteen

Ellie opened her eyes at the discordant beep, blinking slowly as she tried to work out where she was. The lights were bright, almost glaring, contrasting with the darkness at the windows, and other than the sporadic beeping, her office was silent. A cup of cold coffee sat half drunk beside a stack of papers that she still hadn't read. She had fallen asleep with her head on her desk.

She pushed herself up, wiping the grit from her eyes. A quick glance at her laptop clock showed it was almost 2:00 a.m.

After Victoria left, she'd taken a minute to get herself together, and then gone to do the worst job of her entire career: speak to HR about how to handle Vic's breach of confidence and start an investigation. When she got back to her office, she'd planned to spend some time working out what to do about the trouble her friend was in... and how far she should go when Vic had been clear she didn't want help. But it had only been a minute before the first of her staff arrived and the floodgates opened.

Everyone needed her. Her accountant wanted her to go

through month-end spreadsheets, the designers had reams of concept art, the story team wanted to share the improvements they'd made, marketing had ideas for a teaser campaign.... On and on and on until she was spinning.

It was after eight by the time the last person had left her office. Ellie had ordered Chinese food and gone back to her desk, planning to catch up on some of her own work before heading over to a local hotel to get some sleep. But her exhaustion had caught up with her first.

Her mouth was dry, lips cracked, and her eyes still felt as if they were still half glued together. She took a sip of the ancient coffee and winced. It was bitter, and the milk had started to separate.

She pushed it away and dragged her hands through her hair, pulling it back into a ponytail out of her face. There was no point in sitting there for the rest of the night. She needed a shower and a bed.

A cold bed. A bed without Josh in it. She rubbed the ache in her temples and sighed. The desire to speak to him, to hear his voice, was visceral. But it wasn't as if he had a phone. Or an e-mail address. Assuming he was even still... there.

Ellie stood slowly, easing the kinks out of her back and shoulder, and began packing her things away. But then her laptop chimed again.

She glanced at the screen, and then looked again, properly. There was a string of security warnings.

She sank back into her seat, pulled her keyboard and mouse closer, and scrolled down. There were multiple alerts over the last twenty minutes. All coming from her firewall. Someone was making repeated attempts to get into her private system.

She was used to seeing hacking attempts on her IP

address. That was just standard. But this was different. This was a relentless, coordinated attack.

Her fingers flew over the keyboard as she followed the digital signature of whoever was trying to get onto her system. It was weirdly easy. Too easy. They were making no attempt to hide themselves at all. They were...

Her body filled with ice. They were *her*.

Someone was trying to hack her system using her login. And if they got past her firewall, they would have everything they needed to steal the game design document for the new game—concept, characters, gameplay, easter eggs, even her own personal notes—*everything*.

All new staff signed an NDA when they joined, and it was to protect the GDD. If a thief got hold of it, they could sell it to anyone. Everyone. Her launch would be over. Hell. Her business might be over.

She'd invested too much already. She'd invested too much before Vic had sunk tens of thousands of pounds into a server room they didn't need.

But where...? Her fingers flew over the keyboard. Searching. Tracing the person pretending to be her.

And... crap.

They were using her login from her own IP address. From her personal computer. She recoiled, heart thundering. They were *inside* her house.

And this was no ordinary robbery. This was someone who knew her name. Who knew her login. They were struggling to crack her twenty-character password—thank God for her insane levels of security—but they had everything else.

Where was Josh? Was he still in the house? Was he okay? God. What about Nissy?

She sucked in a ragged breath and pressed her fingers

into her cheeks, forcing herself to think. If only she had bought those security cameras when she first thought of them....

She dropped her hands, eyes flying back to her laptop. There *was* a camera.

She hunched over the keyboard, typing as fast as she could, taking control of her computer remotely. And then she turned on the webcams and told them to record.

A man was sitting in her office. At her desk! He wore a black ski mask completely covering his head and mouth; only his eyes were vaguely visible in the dim room.

He flinched and then tilted his head, facing directly toward the camera. Dammit. The light must have come on and alerted him. He looked at her for a tense moment, clearly aware of her. His eyes were wide, pupils dilated in the dim light.

Then he jerked to his feet and hurriedly sprayed all the surfaces from a bottle spray he'd brought with him. Alcohol or vinegar maybe. He was clearly rushing, but still meticulous.

She reached for her phone to call 999 at the same moment that he scanned the room, perhaps checking that he hadn't left anything, and then jogged away. But he didn't run. He never panicked.

Almost as if he knew he still had time. As if he knew she was too far away to stop him.

# Chapter Twenty

Josh felt the distance between them growing with every minute after Ellie drove away. And as the distance grew, his hold on himself—on his connection to the earth—diminished.

He tried lying on her bed, surrounded by her vanilla and jasmine scent. But it wasn't enough. He fell into a fitful, broken sleep, only to wake hours later, dazed and brain-fogged, with pins and needles in his hands and feet, and a cold tingle lapping along his spine.

Despite the exhaustion dragging at him, he made himself stand and close the curtains against the midnight dark and go downstairs to find Nissy. She roused herself from her bed in Ellie's office and chirped as she wound herself against his legs. He leaned down to scratch behind her ears before checking her feeder and water.

Had he ever had a pet? He felt certain that he never had. And yet... why not? Nissy was a joy. He could easily get used to her gentle companionship and charming certainty that she deserved to be treated like royalty at all times.

Josh rubbed his chest, reminding himself that it was a good thing he didn't have a pet. He didn't want there to be an animal left behind somewhere, wondering what had become of him.

He had a few sips of cold water and then walked through Ellie's house, touching the things she loved, looking at her art, trying to ground himself.

And trying to find himself. What did *his* house look like? What art decorated *his* walls? Where did *he* live?

He spent long minutes standing on her deck, looking out at the dark woods. Little night animals called and scurried, and their names rose and fell in his mind. He knew their diets and their habits. The dangers they faced.

A memory drifted into his awareness like a dream. A scene of people wearing scrubs, surgical masks, bright lights overhead. The memory sharpened, clarified, until it was the clearest one he'd had.

He was so close. So very close to knowing everything.

He stumbled across the deck to the far corner and sank onto a lounger next to the hot tub. The world was spinning, his ears ringing, and he leaned his head between his knees in the dark as the memories welled within him.

He could recall that procedure vividly. A rare white-tailed eagle had become tangled in a large hedgerow. Her wing was badly broken, and the surgery to repair it was brand-new and very challenging. He'd traveled north, to Scotland, to work with the conservationists there, and then stayed.

He remembered watching the majestic bird take to the skies once more. The visceral joy and relief, and the bittersweetness of whispering goodbye as he set her free.

How long ago was that? Did he live there? He wished

he knew. But at least he knew one thing: he was a veterinary surgeon. He worked with birds of prey. Thank fuck. He wasn't a criminal. He wasn't a murderer. Hopefully he was far away when Ellie had her accident.

He gripped the back of his neck with his hands. The relief uncurling through him was so powerful he wanted to laugh. He almost wanted to cry. He was starting to remember who he was.

He wanted to tell Ellie. To share this revelation with her He wanted to hear her voice. Even better, to see her face. She wore her emotions so honestly—so much more openly than him—and he couldn't wait to see her joy.

Josh stood, thinking. He could reach her through her computer. He could send her a message. If there was one thing he knew, it was that Ellie would have her laptop nearby.

But then he stilled, lingering in the shadows. Something didn't feel right. Had he heard something?

He crossed the deck and slipped into the house through the living room doors, pausing to listen. He *had* heard something. Someone was moving through the house.

He crept into the empty hallway. The front door was shut. No lights were on. The bowl on the hallway table where Ellie kept her keys was empty. It definitely wasn't her. Whoever was in the house must have come through the vegetable garden, hidden by the stone walls, and through the back door into the kitchen. But what the fuck were they doing there?

Josh walked through the house on silent feet, hunting for the intruder. Goose bumps rose over his arms and lifted the small hairs on the back of his neck. The pins and needles were back, but he fought them.

He couldn't fade away now. He couldn't bear it. Ellie needed him. And he'd *promised*.

How had he promised? What had he promised? He didn't know. But that didn't matter now. What mattered was Ellie. He'd told himself he wouldn't get involved. That he wouldn't care for her. But now... now, he couldn't bear to think about her being hurt.

His muscles tightened as he crept down the quiet corridor and drew closer to Ellie's gaming room. The door was ajar—whoever was there hadn't bothered to fully close it—and he could hear the sound of her chair being pulled out, someone settling into it with a quiet grunt.

Fuck. It wasn't just her gaming room. It was her office. It was where Nissy slept. Where was she? Ellie would be devastated if something happened to her cat. And honestly, so would he.

But the cold was all over him now. Waves of freezing mist enclosed him as the color slowly leached out of his surroundings, leaving everything gray and bleak.

He stepped forward, through the door, to see a man, hidden beneath a balaclava, his leather jacket hanging on Ellie's chair, gloved hands tapping at the keyboard.

Something about the man was familiar. The way he sat. The angle of his head. Something struck a chord. But what?

Josh opened his mouth to demand answers, but even as he did, he knew it was too late. No sound emerged. Everything was amorphous, turning to mist.

Ellie wasn't there to hold him to the earth, and he'd already clung on long past what he'd hoped might be possible. He stumbled forward and peered into the cat cave —desperate, knowing it was the last thing he could do—and thank God, it was empty. Nissy was somewhere else, hopefully safe.

But it wasn't enough. He was leaving them at the worst possible time. He was leaving them in danger.

Darkness flooded over his vision, and Ellie's world disappeared, leaving him to float, alone, in the icy shadows, howling out his fury and desperation.

# Chapter Twenty-One

It was early morning by the time Ellie got back to her forest road, the sky transforming from pink and gold to a clear, light blue glinting between the trees.

The emergency responder who answered her call had promised that a team would visit first thing in the morning and told her not to go back to her house in the meantime. There had been no point in them sending a quick response team when the intruder had almost certainly already left and Ellie was safely miles away.

But Josh and Nissy were there—Josh who she couldn't begin to explain, and Nissy who the responder was sympathetic about, but she wouldn't send an entire team for a cat—and Ellie couldn't reach them. She didn't have a landline to call Josh, he didn't have a phone, and she couldn't see Nissy through her webcam. She didn't know what had happened to them.

What if they needed her?

She forced herself to stand still and think. To not give into the panic as it twisted and churned. She would go to them as soon as she could—she was too far away to be of any immediate help, and she had to secure her business first.

She grabbed her phone and lifted her finger to hit the button to call Vic, the person she would always have turned to in the past... and then stopped. Vic wasn't the same, she'd been—

God. Vic couldn't have done this? Could she? No, Ellie couldn't bear to believe it. But she hesitated, nonetheless. And then she scrolled away and called her security company instead. She arranged extra protection for the office and then manually changed all the administrator passwords—including Vic's. Until this was resolved, nobody would be able to access anything sensitive without a double login and Ellie's personal approval.

Once that was done, she called Duane and left him a message explaining what had happened and asking him to call as soon as he woke up.

Finally, she rushed through the office, dropping Post-its on desks with last thoughts and notes of encouragement. And then she locked up and left in the darkness before dawn. She couldn't sit still miles away if Josh and Nissy were in danger.

The roads were empty, and she made the journey quickly, despite the worry slithering through her mind, presenting her with every dark possibility over and over. Finally, she pulled into her drive just as the world brightened from the misty darkness into daylight.

Her cottage seemed peaceful. Slumbering. And the first thing she saw, thank God, was Nissy. There was no sunbeam, but she sat in the window licking her paw, completely unconcerned about the riot of emotions pouring through Ellie.

She slumped in her seat, wiping tears of relief away

with her fingers. Tears that she'd held in all through the long night.

The only thing that would have made it better was for Josh to be there with Nissy, striding out the front door to sweep Ellie into his arms. But there was no tang of ozone, no electricity in the air. No movement from the house. She could feel Josh's absence like an ache.

She stayed in her car, dabbed her face, and leaned back against her headrest to watch Nissy as the shadows retreated. If she'd believed Josh was there, or if she hadn't seen Nissy in the window, she would have gone inside despite her fear. But he wasn't there. And she didn't need to be reminded not to go creeping in alone after an intruder.

So instead, she waited. It was ironic that she could sit in her car now—the place that had seemed so threatening— and feel sheltered.

The trespasser had broken into her home. He'd made her vulnerable in the one place where she felt safe. But somehow, by bringing his threat right to her door, he'd made everything clear. She'd spent so long worrying about how to make everyone else happy. But in the end, there were only three things in that house that she was desperate to keep safe: Nissy, Josh, and her game. And she was ready to fight for them.

By the time the police arrived—Constable Harrison, a friendly Black woman, and Special Constable Thomas, her slightly younger blond-haired male partner—Ellie had already started a list of what she needed to do.

The constables were empathetic as they walked through the house with her, especially when she ran into the dining room to Nissy, lifting her into her arms to press kisses on her precious, bemused face.

They grew more serious when they found her kitchen

door hanging open to the vegetable garden—the lock apparently picked—and her neatly planted rows of beans and tomatoes smashed into the thick soil, as if the intruder had plowed over them in the darkness.

Ellie ran her gaze over their broken stems and leaves, silently apologizing to the muddy, mangled plants. Almost glad that Josh wasn't there to see what had happened to all their hard work.

The police team dusted for fingerprints and took hers for exclusion—even though she was absolutely certain they wouldn't find anything. They took photographs of her office and gladly accepted a thumb drive with her video of the man at her desk. But, before they left, they also explained that nearly three quarters of thefts were closed without identifying a suspect... and her intruder hadn't damaged anything other than her plants. He hadn't even stolen anything; he'd never made it past her firewall.

Ellie thanked the officers and said goodbye distractedly, promising to call if she needed help. Then, as soon as they were gone, Ellie went through the house again—carrying Nissy with her. Checking if anything was missing. Checking her locks. But mostly checking for Josh. Even though she knew he wasn't there.

Her bed was possibly a little more rumpled than she'd left it, but otherwise, there was no hint that he even existed.

It hurt. The world kept kicking her. And Josh was gone.

She pushed away the ache in her heart—refreshed Nissy's half full food and water—and got on the phone. She bought a new back door, with a diamond-rated lock, to be fitted that day. Then she arranged for a security company to install motion detection, external lights, internal alarm, and panic buttons that afternoon. Most importantly, she included cameras covering both the garden and the main rooms of the house.

She would have plenty of warning if the thief came back. And hopefully enough evidence to identify him. The truth was, she didn't really foresee the police catching the intruder any more than they'd found the driver of the car who'd hit her.

A man in an SUV. Dark hair. Dark glasses. Collar high. Cap low.

The man at her desk. A black ski mask completely covering his head and mouth.

God. What if they weren't two isolated cases of terrible luck? She'd been so busy trying to deal with the break-in, it hadn't occurred to her before. But now she had the horrible feeling they were connected.

Duane called, distracting her from her thoughts, and she spent half an hour updating him and making sure he was ready to step into Vic's role as much as needed. At least that was one thing that didn't feel like a disaster. And by the time she said goodbye, she was feeling more settled. She now had the best security available. She'd locked down her home and her business. She could figure out the rest.

Ellie made herself a cup of coffee and then cleaned her office with bleach, carefully scrubbing anything the intruder might have touched until the air was acrid and her throat burned. She threw open the windows and aired out Nissy's cave, then vacuumed the already clean floor before she finally felt it was hers again. Then she got comfortable at her desk. It was time to thoroughly review her firewall, analyze the hack attempt, and close any gaps she'd missed in the middle of the night.

By the end of the day, her house and her computer system were back under her control. She would need to call

Max at Silver Wolff and decline his offer as soon as possible, but she wanted to do that in person, and it was already well past the end of the business day. Instead she turned to the task she'd *wished* she could have prioritized: finding Josh.

He had no personal items with him when he came to her. He didn't have a phone, or anyone she could call. She tried search engines and read multitudes of heartbreaking missing persons reports. When that didn't help, she tried social media and simply scrolling through everyone called Josh with any kind of profile. There were thousands. None of them were *her* Josh.

She thought about his tattoo—the obvious creative talent in the design, the way the trees wrapped round his bicep and over his shoulder, forming an evocative landscape that was so true to Josh—and spent an hour looking for the artist with no luck.

Eventually, she had to concede defeat and moved on to investigating her accident. She posted notes on every community board and Facebook group she could find, asking for witnesses. Then she read accident reports—another round of heartbreaking insights into loss and other people's grief—and searched for the details of the SUV that hit her.

She briefly considered ways to use her photo of her intruder's eyes to find him... and discarded all of them. The passport office seemed unlikely to be delighted about her hacking their database.

By midnight, Ellie hadn't learned anything new, and she was utterly spent. She showered and crawled into her bed, still jittery from caffeine and wired from days of no sleep, compounded by the anger, vulnerability, and loneliness that had come and gone all day.

There, lying alone in the darkness, dreaming she could

still smell his skin, she finally allowed herself to cry. Her world had fallen apart. Everything she loved, everything she trusted, was crumbling around her.

She missed Josh. Missed his presence in her house. Missed his quiet support. Even his grumpy brooding.

And she had no way of knowing if he was ever coming back.

# Chapter Twenty-Two

THERE WAS DARKNESS. And there was Ellie.

He knew her. He knew her voice. Could hear the tension and the tiredness threaded through her tone. He could hear her working. And working. And working. But he couldn't get back to her.

What if she was alone in the house when the intruder came back? What if a stranger was there now, while Josh was trapped somewhere far away? Unable to help. Unable to reach her.

Had he already used all the time he had with her?

The thought filled him with dread. But as much as he railed and fought, he always slipped back into the mist.

Sometimes the mist parted, forcing him back to the cold, bright place. He hated it there. It was worse than the darkness.

The white lights brought the pain. His head hurt. And his mouth was so dry. His lips cracked, bleeding when he tried—failed—to speak. There was something foreign in his nose, in his throat, but he couldn't move it. He was trapped.

Sometimes a familiar voice spoke from beyond the

lights. Sometimes it whined. Sometimes demanded. It was a male voice. A voice he knew well. And then the voice said, "Fuck, Josh. I'm sorry. It wasn't meant to be like this—" And threw him into a memory.

They were boys. Josh was sixteen, Liam was twelve. Their father was long gone. Their mother worked two jobs, sometimes three. She looked so tired. Sometimes it seemed that only her grit held her together.

She was cleaning a house that day. Josh had gone out to grab some pasta, cheese, and a few wilted vegetables on special at the corner supermarket. He was hungry all the time. But he'd managed to get a part-time job in the local pet store, and he'd just seen his first paycheck hit his account. He wanted to celebrate. And if there was something hot to eat when his mother came home, they could sit together and enjoy it. Maybe they could watch something on the telly. She always helped him with his homework, even when it was late. She always came to say goodnight and listened to his day. But they seldom just sat.

But when he got back to the flat, his brother was gone. Liam hadn't stayed sitting at the small kitchen table doing the math problems Josh had left him, and, infuriatingly, Josh knew exactly where he was. Liam had wanted to play football with friends down at the park. He'd refused to listen to Josh's reasoning that it was nearly dark. That the park was strewn with litter and broken glass on a good day. And that the friends he wanted to meet could make trouble out of air.

Josh dumped the groceries on the faded vinyl counter, pulled his coat back on, and stalked back into the night, mumbling curses. Liam always thought he had a hard life. Always wanted to complain. But he never wanted to do his share of the work. And it didn't help that he was so bloody good-looking. That everyone had always wanted to help the angelic baby with dark curls and blue eyes... even when Liam was a moody preteen and as far from angelic as it was humanly possible to get.

When Josh found him, it was even worse than he'd imagined. Liam—eyes red and face streaked with dirt—was kicking his foot next to a pair of police officers and an enraged motorist. Football had devolved into throwing rocks, and one had hit a passing Mercedes.

The other boys had run, but Liam, for all his faults, always stayed. He'd taken responsibility. And he'd looked up at Josh, looking so young and afraid, and said, "Fuck, Josh. I'm so sorry. It wasn't meant to be like this."

*It wasn't meant to be like this.*

Fuck.

The words churned in his gut, roiling and unsettled. They meant something. Something he knew was awful.

It was a relief when he slipped back into the darkness and the memories—and the words—slowly disappeared into shadow and confusion.

Time passed. And when he finally opened his eyes in Ellie's room once more, the recollections of the bright place and the strange dreams he'd had there were nothing more than mist, slowly evaporating to nothing.

Her cottage was surrounded by the deep, turbulent darkness of late night and a storm lashing against the roof and walls. Rain poured down the windows and gurgled in the gutters as the wind roared through the trees. And the house creaked as it took its beating.

Ellie was lying in her bed, on top of the covers, still wearing a T-shirt and yoga pants. Her legs were curled, but one hand was flung out. As if she'd collapsed, too tired to drag blankets over her body, and fallen asleep still reaching for something she couldn't quite grasp.

She looked cold. The skin beneath her eyes was dark and bruised, even in sleep. He crept closer and risked smoothing a lock of honey-colored hair out of her eyes. She didn't even stir.

God, he'd missed her.

A visceral wave of relief flooded him. She was safe. She hadn't been hurt while he was gone.

In his job—in his life, he suspected—he didn't show emotions. Fear, vulnerability, grief, even hope… they all had to be locked away. He always had to be detached. A little removed. Unbiased. Unemotional. He couldn't let himself get close to an animal that could easily die, and, even if it lived, would soon be gone. His heart could not be allowed to break every time he had a patient on his table, or he would break too.

But standing there, Ellie's silky hair sliding through his fingers, he couldn't deny the truth. He liked her. Far more than he should. He was afraid for her. He needed her. He was *not* detached.

It was the exact opposite of the one moment he'd promised himself.

He couldn't offer her anything at all. He didn't know enough of who he was. He couldn't remember most of his life, let alone share it with her. Soon, their time would be over. He couldn't even promise that, when he left for the last time, he would get the chance to say goodbye.

If he was being rational, he would let her go now before he sank any deeper. He would slip away, back into the darkness or out into the storm, before she meant even more to him. Before he meant more to her, too. Because, however he might try to deny it, he knew their bond went both ways.

If he was sensible, he would wake her, tell her about the intruder, make sure she was safe, and then say goodbye.

But he couldn't do it.

Her passion. Her bravery. Her curiosity and joy. He needed more of it.

And did it really have to end badly? Was it inevitable? Maybe there was a way to figure out why he was there. Maybe there was a way for him to stay for a few days or even weeks.

Ellie never gave up, even when she was afraid. Didn't he owe her the same conviction?

He slipped away and searched through her hall closets until he found a blanket. Then he pulled off his boots and slid onto the bed beside her, throwing the blanket over them both, and closed his eyes.

Beside her, he could drift in warmth. In the scent of her skin, the vanilla and jasmine of her soap. Listening to her small sighs and light snuffles.

She shuffled back in her sleep, fitting herself against his body—her back to his chest—and he wrapped himself around her gladly, safe in their cocoon as the storm raged outside. He didn't sleep. He wanted to have this time holding her, being with her.

She woke before dawn, and he felt the change in her. The tension returning to her body along with awareness. He spoke before she could startle, whispering her name. And she turned to face him over her shoulder, blinking slowly.

"You're here," she said, her voice rough with sleep. "You came back. I didn't think—" She shook her head, a slight movement against his shoulder. "I wasn't sure if you would."

"I'm sorry. I would have come back if I could." He pressed a kiss onto her shoulder. "How long was I gone?"

"Three days." She closed her eyes for a moment, and he could feel the weight of those days pressing down on her.

He tucked a lock of hair behind her ear, wishing he didn't have to say anything. Wishing he didn't have to add to the burdens she already carried. "Ellie, before I... left. There was someone in your house."

She nestled into him, her back pressed even tighter against his front. "I know," she murmured. "I saw him. He was trying to break through my firewall. I think he was going after the game."

She'd told him before about the IP stored on her system. Using Ellie's personal computer to get to it would be a lot easier. But... "That means he knows you." Fuck. "He targeted you specifically."

She hummed her agreement. "I think so too." She swallowed heavily. "I think he knew I'd gone to London. I think he must have been watching my house somehow."

"Why?" He couldn't keep the outrage out of his voice. Ellie loved her game. She'd worked so hard, for so long, and now someone was trying to take it from her. And the thought of someone watching her... Fuck. "What would he do with it?"

"Sell it to our competitors, launch his own version earlier... maybe even blackmail us to have our IP returned. I don't know." Ellie dragged her hand across her eyes. "I've been trying to figure out how best to find him, but where do you even start? I thought maybe some kind of eye scanning, optical recognition. But that means hacking the Home Office, and, well, I don't want to go to jail." She huffed out a self-deprecating laugh. "And to be honest, hacking is harder than it sounds."

"What does that mean?" Hell. He really hoped it wasn't how it sounded.

She turned further, facing him more fully. "I tried to figure it out. But there are no YouTube videos telling you how to break into government databases, can you believe it? Even ChatGPT gave me some useless answer about how it was sorry, but it couldn't assist. Bloody AI." She wrinkled her nose, ignoring the look he gave her. "I decided a better idea would be to look at traffic cam footage... did you know you can put in a request for copies of the videos? But it means driving around, looking for the cameras, figuring out who owns them and then trying to contact them. It's taking hours... and I don't have that many in a day—especially since I have a company to run first, so I'm doing all of that after close of business."

"How is that going?" he asked gently, hoping Vic had done the right thing, but doubting it at the same time.

"It's been tough," Ellie admitted. "I spent most of the day in London yesterday. I had my usual Thursday managers meeting, extra time with Duane, and a review with HR and our security team, which was exactly as much fun as you could image." She yawned tiredly. "The one good thing is I spoke with Max at Silver Wolff, and formally declined the sale."

That was huge. He knew just how hard that step was, and how much it had meant for her to take it. "I'm so proud of you, Ellie."

"Thank you." She smiled. But then her voice fell, and her expression grew more sorrowful, and he knew there was more. He held her tight until she was ready to share the rest, and, voice breaking, she told him what had happened with Victoria. All the things Vic had said and how she'd had to take the horrible decision to lock her friend out of the company. How she'd expected a massive fight—but Vic had walked away and not come back.

Ellie had promoted Duane who'd stepped up massively, but it was still a load of extra work on both their shoulders. And, at the same time, she was single-handedly trying to solve both the hit-and-run that landed her in hospital and the break-in that threatened all her work. All while worrying about her friend. And him.

Had he ever felt so helpless? God, he hoped not.

And it got worse. He didn't want to admit it. Didn't want to open the door. But he had to tell her. "The man that broke into your house; I've seen him before. I felt... Ellie, I think I know him. I made it into the room with him before I faded. I recognized him from somewhere. But—" He let out a harsh breath. "—I don't remember where."

"Okay." She nodded slowly, her quick brain working through what he'd said and, by the look on her face, coming to the same conclusion he had. The knowledge that Josh had recognized her intruder didn't help them at all. Not when he didn't know who he was.

"I'm sorry." He pressed a kiss to her forehead, wishing he could do more. Wishing he could pull the blanket completely over their heads and hide her away in a warm, safe cocoon. "I wish I could fix it for you," he said against her skin.

She tilted her chin to look at him, her eyes full of kindness. "I wish the same. That I could fix everything for you, too."

"And if we can't fix this?" he asked quietly.

"We can," she replied, and she sounded as if she believed it. Or as if she was determined to make herself believe. "I'll just work harder. I'll find a way."

God, he wished that could be true—not that she would

work harder; that was the last thing she needed—but that there was a way to make everything right. And that they would find it.

He pressed another kiss to her forehead, and then another to her temple, and then one over her eye. Down her cheek. The side of her mouth.

Maybe it couldn't be fixed. Maybe nothing could. But for now, she was in his arms. She was warm and soft and full of life. They could live in this one moment. Make it last for as long as possible. And maybe, just maybe, they would find a way.

"Actually, I do have one piece of good news." He smiled down at her. "I remembered that I'm an avian veterinarian —I work with birds of prey. In Scotland, I think."

Her whole face lit up. "That's wonderful!" She kissed him, matching the path he'd taken, kissing his eyes and cheeks. "That makes so much sense! And no wonder we haven't found any missing persons reports for you. We've been looking in the wrong place." The twinkle in her eyes dimmed. "But... why are you down here at the southern coast? It's about as far as you can get from Scotland and still be in the UK."

"I don't know. But we'll work it out. We'll help each other." Together. The idea should have been terrifying, but it wasn't. It was *right*.

Josh ran his fingers down the side of Ellie's face to settle lightly under her chin, tilting her up toward him, and then closed his mouth over hers. He'd been without her for too long. He needed to feel her. To know that she was with him.

Their tongues danced and played, teasing and tasting. And he could feel the tension slowly leaving her body as she met him stroke for stroke.

He skimmed his hand down her shoulder and under the

blanket to drift down her waist and then back up her midriff, under her shirt, to brush the underside of her breasts. She wasn't wearing a bra, and they both sucked in a slow breath at the contact. She was so warm, so real. The scent of her soap surrounded him, her skin was smooth and soft, her hair floating around them both. It was like waking up and finding himself in heaven.

He spread his hand over her thigh, pulling her closer, settling her against his hard length, wishing his jeans were gone, that there was nothing between them.

She broke the kiss, pulling away for a moment to lift her T-shirt over her head—as if she'd heard his thought—and shimmied out of her panties and leggings.

He used the time to pull off his own clothes before dragging her back into the curl of his body. She giggled softly as he arranged her so that her skin was pressed against his—her back to his front, her bottom nestled against his aching cock, her neck open to his lips and tongue—and the soft laughter did something to him. Something profound. It was the first time he'd ever heard her sound so carefree. And it unlocked more than just his memories, it unlocked *him.* "You feel like magic. I want to touch you everywhere. Can I do that, Ellie?"

"Mm-hmm." She lifted her hand to his thigh, dragging her nails over his skin, sending frissons of tingling awareness through his nerves. "Yes. All the touching."

He lowered his head, kissing and nibbling along the slope of her shoulder even as he skimmed his hand higher, up to find her breasts, the puckered nipples and velvety skin. He circled lightly, moving between breasts, dragging his hand away and then returning, until she was arching her back, her breaths coming faster, her hips nudging back, driving him higher with every subtle motion.

"Ellie." His voice was rough and strained. "Do you know what you do to me?" He bit her neck gently. "How do you make me feel like this?"

She turned her head to meet his gaze, and their eyes locked, a deep connection flowing between them. And then she kissed him. Their kiss was open, their bodies twisted, but her tongue found his in a teasing glide, while her body slowly sliding against his drove him even higher.

He closed his thumb and forefinger around her nipple, lightly pinching and tugging until she was squirming and panting into his mouth.

The room was hot, the air around them sultry, even as the storm still battered the house. The rain beat hard against the tiled roof, but nothing could reach them. His cock was nestled between her arse cheeks, her breast was in his hand, her mouth pressed to his. Nothing else was real. Nothing else could touch them.

He slid his hand over her body—dragging the blanket away to reveal her flushed skin—slowly exposing her beauty, stroking all the way down to her swollen clit. God. She was perfect. And already so wet. He slid his first two fingers either side of the heated nub, pinching lightly, gliding back and forth as he rubbed her.

She breathed hard, her body straining toward his, as she turned her face away, offering her neck.

He nuzzled into it, breathing in the scent of her skin. But then she whispered, "Can you see us, Josh? Can you see what *you* do to me?"

The low light of dawn through the storm was dim and gray, and it took him a moment to remember the huge mirror beside the bed. To lift his head and see their bodies, outlined in shadows, the silvery gleam of her skin and the tantalizing valleys of her curves revealed in the soft light.

He licked her neck, scraping his teeth along her tendon, still watching in the mirror. Her eyes never left his as she tilted her hips back, lifting her leg over his to open herself even further, making space for his heavy cock to slide forward, almost to her entrance. She surrounded him even as he surrounded her, and he had never shared anything so erotic.

They ground together, moving in an undulating, intoxicating dance of pleasure. He tapped her clit, then circled it in smooth spirals, and then rubbed slowly, finding the right rhythm, the perfect pressure. He could see every shudder in the mirror, feel every indrawn breath as she gasped out his name, and it was more powerful than magic.

She whimpered, her hips arching, searching. "Josh, I want more. I want to feel you. I want to see you sliding into me."

He pulled his hand away and leaned over her, keeping his body pressed against hers as he grabbed a condom from her side table and rolled it on. And then he kissed her again. He needed her mouth. Needed that closeness. Even as he dropped his hand to her mound, dragging his fingers slowly through her tight curls, tugging lightly, his focus was on kissing her, breathing the air she breathed.

He lifted his head to meet her gaze in the mirror, and then he thrust forward slowly. Driving his cock back into that heated grip between her legs, nudging against her entrance.

She rolled against him, one of her hands sliding down between her legs to help position him. Her pelvis pressed back as she took him into her body, while her other hand found her breasts, tugging and teasing at her nipples.

It took everything he had not to lose control. Watching her hands moving between her legs and over her body while sliding his cock into her heat was almost too much. "That's the hottest thing I've ever seen," he breathed against her neck.

He forced himself to thrust slowly and evenly, driving them higher, building pressure. And when she moved her hand up to grip the back of his neck, his fingers took their place; rubbing her clit at the same, constant speed. The speed that made her whimper, shuddering against him. And God, that sound. He would take it with him for the rest of his life. He would take it with him to his grave.

Ellie moaned, her body writhing against his. Her head fell back, mouth open, her inner muscles gripping him as he stroked into her.

The storm raged on. The gray light showed his body wrapped around hers, both of them climbing toward a shattering peak.

"More, Josh. God. Please. I—" She arched into him relentlessly. Until they were utterly locked together, every shuddering movement another step toward ecstasy. He gently tugged at her clitoral hood, pinching it between two fingers, and she screamed. Her walls clamped down on his cock as her body spasmed, and he couldn't hold back any longer.

He thrust hard into the tightness of her body, a heavy, pounding rhythm, and she screamed again, taking him over the edge.

He emptied himself into the condom, exploding into her in a blinding climax. He lost his rhythm, lost any awareness, except of the pleasure blazing through him and Ellie gripped tight in his arms.

He held her long after their breathing had slowed, even as he softened and slipped from her body. He needed her body and her soul against his. And she must have sensed his need—or perhaps she felt the same—because she turned and draped herself over him, her head tucked under his chin, her arms wrapped tight around his shoulders, her heart beating hard against his.

He quickly removed the condom and then reached down to grab the blanket and pull it over them both, and they lay, hot and sweaty, but neither moving, neither wanting to break the connection between them.

Daylight spread through the room, and the storm slowly abated until just the rain tapped softly on the windows, but still, neither of them moved.

As if they both knew that every moment was precious.

# Chapter Twenty-Three

"Yes, Dad." Ellie walked around her kitchen speaking into her earbud while she made toast.

Josh was sitting at her kitchen table wearing jeans, but no shirt. His hands were wrapped behind his head while he watched her, stretching out his naked torso, showcasing the lines of ink wrapped around his bicep as it flexed.

She could slide onto his lap and run her hands up his chest, through the smattering of hair, circle his nipples. She could bite—

"Ellie! Are you listening to me at all?"

"No." The word blurted out before she could hold it back.

"What did you say?"

Normally that tone, the unbridled censure, would have sent shards of ice through her. She would have already started working to placate and fix. But not this time. This time, she was too relaxed. Too sated. She was finding her feet on the earth.

Josh smirked and leaned back, abdominals rippling as

he ran his hand roughly through his hair. She flushed, and his grin grew. He knew exactly what he was doing.

"All I meant," Ellie spoke into the phone, trying to regain control of the conversation, "was no—my firewall was not breached. Whoever he was, he didn't get access to my system or my IP."

"Good." Warmth returned to Steven's tone. But then he added, "So the sale can go ahead."

And just like that, the old feeling of dread returned. Ellie turned away from Josh and looked out the window at the soaked, wind-battered garden and the gray skies.

She should be used to it by now. Should have known her father hadn't called to check on *her*. And she knew how badly he was going to take her decision—which was why she'd put off telling him that she'd already declined the sale.

And then she felt him. Josh wrapped himself around her, his chest at her back, his hands on her hips, his chin on her shoulder. She could see him reflected in the kitchen window, just as she'd watched him in her bedroom mirror.

Their gazes locked, filling her with that same sense of connection. That same deep knowledge that he saw her. Just as she saw him.

Her work had meaning. Her life had meaning. *She* had meaning.

"Dad." Ellie took a deep breath and injected all the confidence, all the assurance she could muster into her voice. "I've decided not to sell."

"What are you talking about? Of course you'll sell. You wouldn't back out and embarrass me like that. You need to—"

"No, Dad. I won't. I've already called Max to let him know, and we left it on friendly terms. I'm sorry this is embarrassing for you, but that's not a good enough reason for me to give up on everything I've worked for or on this incredible community I've been building." She lifted her chin. "And to be clear, please do not set up any more deals."

Steven spluttered for a moment before falling silent, his stunned disapproval clear even down the phone.

"I would like to move past this," Ellie continued. "We're still a family. We can support each other in better ways."

There was another long moment of icy silence before her father began to speak, hard and cold and vehement. A tirade of how Ellie should do as she was told, how she didn't understand her own business, and how weak this made her look. But he was wrong. Loving something didn't make her weak. And for the first time in her life, Ellie said goodbye while Steven was still speaking and then disconnected the call.

God. She wanted to be sick. Her body was shaking and cold, and she had to drag in slow, shuddering breaths for long moments before she was certain she wasn't going to pass out.

"I'm so proud of you," Josh whispered, and it nearly brought her to her knees. She twisted in his arms and held him, soaking in his strength, his belief in her. And after a moment, a new emotion unfurled inside her. She was proud of *herself*.

Proud and a little terrified. Because it was time to tell Vic. And it was going to hurt.

# Chapter Twenty-Four

Josh put the glass of wine on Ellie's desk and settled his hands on her shoulders. Her neck was a solid mass of knots. How she was even still sitting at her desk, he didn't know. He dug his fingers into the stiff muscles, and she groaned, letting her eyes drift shut.

"Why don't you take a break?" he asked. "You've been in here for hours."

Ever since calling Vic.

He'd listened as she tried to get through several times, and then ultimately left a short message saying that she'd decided not to sell her game and that she'd let Silver Wolff know the deal would not be going ahead. Ellie had explained that she really wanted to help with Vic's house and that she had already spoken to her bank about a loan.

Vic's response, five minutes later, had been her written resignation.

And he'd watched Ellie fold into herself. The brittle way she'd held herself when she showed him the message had made him want to burn the world down.

Ellie gave so much of herself. Her time. Her love. Her

loyalty. It was unfathomable to him that she could be taken for granted and treated so abominably.

The only problem was, the rest of the world couldn't even see him. And even if he could have stormed over to Vic's house to ask her what on earth she was thinking, Ellie would never have wanted that. She was utterly convinced Vic was in trouble and needed help.

Ellie had tucked away her phone, given him history's least believable smile, and then disappeared into her office. He'd seen her a couple of times since then. She'd emerged for coffee and toilet breaks, she'd petted Nissy and checked her food, and came out once to order a pizza —for one, since he still couldn't stomach anything—but she'd always retreated again. And judging by the leftovers on the kitchen counter, she hadn't actually eaten any of it. And now night had fallen, and the day was almost over.

He understood. Her office was her safe place. The place she was in control. But it was a day she would never get back. A day *they* would never get back—although he was trying not to think about how that made him feel—and he wanted more for her.

He kneaded the muscles of her shoulders and up into her neck, finding the knots and points of tension along her skull. "How can I help?"

Her head dropped forward, her shoulders rising and falling on a deep sigh. "I wanted to get some work done. With Vic not there..." She swallowed the rest, and he wanted to scoop her up and take her far away.

But then she straightened and turned to look at him over her shoulder. "Anyway, I think Duane has a good handle on the storylines now and he's done a great job stepping up as head of Development. We're okay." She gave him a small smile. Thankfully, it was slightly more authentic than her earlier attempt. "How did you get on?"

"I can't find anything helpful," Josh admitted.

He'd spent hours looking into wild bird conservation in Scotland. It seemed familiar. But then, so did Ellie's forested paths. He hadn't seen anything that immediately called out to him. Nothing that felt like home. And he hadn't found any record of himself as a missing person. Or even found himself on any staff lists.

Did he not have a home? Were any of the things he thought he remembered real? Did he even want to know?

Ellie spun her chair around to face him, her hands coming up to his waist. "I'm sorry. I really thought we were getting closer." Her hands were warm and reassuring on his hips, even as her brow creased into a concerned frown. "Are you okay?"

*We.* Such a small word, and yet so powerful. And so typical of Ellie; concerned about him even in the middle of her own distress.

For a moment, he almost admitted the truth. That with every day that passed, his foreboding grew. Something in him didn't want to find out who he was. A part of him knew that if—when—he found his past, everything would change. But he didn't want to name it and make it real. And he didn't want to add to her burdens with vague fears and premonitions.

"I'm fine. Frustrated, but fine." Josh bent down and kissed her forehead. "But it's you I'm worried about. You can't do it all, Ellie. Not in one day."

She wrinkled her nose. "Are you doubting me?"

He chuckled and kissed her again. "Not even a little. But I know you can't keep going like this. Not forever. It'll all still be here in the morning. And I—" He left the rest unsaid, but the words still hovered between them. *I might not.*

Ellie winced. "Crap. I've been in here all day. I—"

"No." He stroked his fingers through her hair, pulling it back from the sides of her face as he looked down at her. Her eyes were focused on his, as they had been since that very first day. Green with a silver-gray rim. He could dive into them forever. "That's not what I meant. I know you have to work; there's a lot riding on you. But you've worked all day. You could take a break for a bit without everything falling apart."

He leaned down to kiss her, loving how her hands came up to cradle his face, how she met him in every way.

When they finally broke apart, he pulled up a chair and sat beside her. "Okay, I'm ready."

"For what?"

He nudged her shoulder with his. "Your game. You've suggested it twice—let's play."

"Really?" She tilted her head to look at him.

"Really." He smiled back at her. "I've heard the creator might win some pretty big prizes one day. And that there are spicy sex scenes—I don't remember anything like that in the football game I used to play. I think it's time I saw what all the fuss is about."

She grabbed a couple of controllers and started loading the game before turning one of her screens to face him. But before she clicked start, she leaned over and kissed him on the cheek, whispering, "Thank you."

"For what?"

"You're the first person in my life—outside Dangerous Business—who's ever wanted to play."

Fuck. That was a travesty. He kissed her quickly. "People suck."

She huffed out a chuckle, looking a little lighter. "Most people," she agreed. And then she added softly, "Not you. I'm so grateful for you."

Her quiet words reached into his heart and lanced a wound he hadn't even known he carried. He was important to Ellie. And she was important to him.

It didn't take long for him to get used to the controls, or to become completely immersed. She'd created a stunning world full of shadowy twists and dark humor.

Their characters were so customizable that it was almost like looking at himself beside Ellie on the screen. They were both photojournalists following a story about unexplained disappearances around the Callanish Standing Stones only to discover that people were being sucked into Fae through a shadowy rift that had opened between the stones. And then they were ensnared themselves—dragged into Fae with nothing but the clothes they were wearing and the cameras in their hands.

From the first moment, Ellie took photos in the game, saving them to a shared in-game album. Which meant he now had pinned pictures of his character leaping into the air when the first haggard wraith leaped from a tree, shrieking and wailing in its swirling, tattered cloak... in fairness, he had almost peed himself in real life. There was a whole action sequence from when he was distracted for a moment and a twisting root wrapped itself around him, tightening relentlessly until he realized he could only escape by biting it. And his character's red face when he stumbled on a ring of fairies and stepped closer, thinking they were dancing, before realizing they were all completely naked. And they were definitely not dancing.

Ellie thought it was hilarious.

They eventually found an abandoned cottage in the

middle of the ancient—sentient—forest and made it their home. Ellie showed him how to dig a well for fresh water and saved him from eating the attractive-looking loaf of bread seemingly discarded in the pantry. Although part of him was tempted to experience the weird, distorted visions Ellie promised him eating fae food would guarantee, he did not want to risk the unpredictable symptoms—suddenly turning into a newt or losing the ability to speak at a crucial moment further into the game—she'd also promised.

Probably his favorite was the time they spent sparring with the swords he found shoved into the cottage's thatch roof. Ellie stood under a tree and watched with amusement while he tried to increase his skill level by practicing on a scarecrow in the overgrown garden, until finally she took pity on him and explained that the whole point was for it to be a cooperative game. He could improve his skills alone, but it would take five times longer than if they worked together.

It was so clever. Everything about the game reminded him of her. Thoughtful and quirky. Collaborative. And so very beautiful.

By the time the laptop clock showed midnight, he was just starting to get the hang of the game, and he didn't want to leave it. The deeper they'd trekked into Fae, the more the surrounding shadows seemed to come alive. Strange creatures skittered and chattered in the forest, and he wanted to find another shelter. But Ellie was yawning and rubbing her eyes, and he forced himself to save and quit.

He turned toward her, capturing her knees between his. "I love your game, Ellie. It's dark and magical, and, honestly, even better than I expected."

"Thanks." She smiled, a hint of pink on her cheeks. "I

have a great team. I mean the art alone is magnificent, never mind the score, the coding—"

He leaned forward to press a kiss to her mouth. "I'm sure all of that's true. But you're at the heart. All those little details came from your mind. Where did you get your ideas for the world?"

She answered slowly. "When I went to college, I decided to get help for my panic attacks, and I found a fantastic therapist. She taught me this technique of building a safe place in my mind." She leaned her cheek into his hand, and he moved closer, loving the way she trusted him to hold her when she was vulnerable. "I kept picturing going back to the same cottage in a forest, and then I started to expand it." She huffed out a laugh. "You don't want to know how many lectures, and then boring meetings, I daydreamed my way through, imagining this slightly weird world."

"Weird maybe, but that's what makes it so glorious," he replied before kissing her again. And then again.

She slid toward him, her hands coming up to linger on the back of his neck, pulling him closer as he sipped at her lips, tasting her, wanting even more.

"Let's go to bed," she said between kisses.

He moved before she'd even finished speaking. He wrapped an arm around her back and one under her knees and lifted her as he stood. She giggled, face flushed, and the sound of her laughter sang through him as he carried her up the stairs to her room. He wanted that for her. Laughter and joy, even when the day had been so bleak.

They stripped slowly, kissing and laughing and teasing. And fell into each other gently at first, and then more forcefully. Entirely present. Entirely connected.

He didn't remember the details of his life, but he knew, deep in his soul, he'd never felt so close to anyone before.

When she fell asleep in his arms, he held her close and lay for long hours feeling her chest rise and fall as she breathed. And he listened to the owls outside, calling to each other as they built a home together despite all the dangers of the night forest.

# Chapter Twenty-Five

VICTORIA BRUSHED her hair a hundred strokes before carefully styling it in the way Warren liked best. Another text message from Ellie flashed across her screen, so she turned her phone face down.

She had to look her best for her interview that morning. It didn't matter that she wasn't feeling her best. Or that she didn't really want a new job. Or that leaving Dangerous Business felt like some kind of bereavement. Trying to login from home and realizing that all the passwords were changed was like a punch in the face. And then, yesterday, she'd picked up Ellie's voicemail confirming that she had declined Silver Wolff's offer. God.

Warren had told her a hundred times that Ellie would never listen to her about selling. That Vic would never be appreciated for her hard work. That her colleagues—and Ellie—never trusted her. And he'd been right.

It was time to make a clean break. To look for a role where she would be better appreciated. Where she could make the money they needed to survive but also have more autonomy.

Warren had warned her that Ellie would move on to stalking her when she didn't immediately get her way. And he'd been right about that too.

Hadn't he?

Had she always thought their texts were stalking? Hadn't there been a time when Ellie's interest and support had felt like friendship? She swallowed. Maybe. But things changed.

She leaned closer to the mirror. Her hand was shaking ever so slightly, and she had to concentrate to apply a final flick of perfect eyeliner, then finish with mascara and a dash of lip gloss before packing her makeup bag and tidying the bathroom. Warren liked it gleaming.

She made her way through the house, pausing to appreciate the stunning front room. The gorgeous sash windows let in ample natural light, highlighting the marble fireplace, intricate ceiling rose and the gleaming polished wood floor. God, she loved it. She'd thought it was beautiful when she was a little girl so often left with her beloved granny. And she cherished it even more now her granny was gone.

She'd dreamed of upgrading the cheap rugs to a sumptuous Persian she'd had her eye on. But that wasn't going to happen if she didn't get a job. It wasn't going to happen at all if she lost the house.

She pushed down the nausea that came with that thought. It was going to be okay; she just had to keep telling herself that. She rolled back her shoulders, patted her hair, and knocked quietly on Warren's office door.

He liked her to let him know if she went out, and after the chaos of her childhood—no one knowing where she was, or bothering with what she was doing—having someone to ask after her, someone who cared about her enough to ask, meant the world.

Long ago, Ellie had been that person. Once, when Vic was backpacking, her wallet was stolen in a busy market. Within a few hours of calling Ellie, she had a hotel room to go to and a new credit card waiting at reception. Ellie had cared. Somehow, she'd forgotten that until now.

Warren opened the door and leaned against the frame. He was clean shaven, his dark hair perfectly tousled, his well-defined muscles highlighted by crisp white sleeves rolled up on his forearms. But he was frowning. "Why do you have the look on your face?" he demanded.

Vic made herself smile, improving her expression. It helped to smile, even when things were bad. It might have helped more to have a hug, but she didn't reach for him. He wouldn't like his shirt wrinkled. "I was just thinking of Ellie."

Warren's frown softened. "Sorry, baby. I wish she hadn't betrayed you like that."

Vic stepped closer, wanting his warmth. "I just feel so confused about why she would be like this. She wasn't always." In fact, now that she was thinking about it, Ellie had been working two jobs—as a programmer for a big game publisher as well as developing her own game on the side— when Vic had called her. From a beach.

Warren tilted her chin up with his forefinger. "Ellie's jealous of you, Vic. You have everything she wants."

That was true. Ellie wanted someone to love her, she always had. That was why she was so obsessed with her characters: she saw herself in them. And when she couldn't have what Vic and Warren had, she'd tried to break them up.

Thank God Warren had warned her. He'd known that

Ellie would try anything to keep her control over Vic. So, when Ellie started telling tales of cheating and suggested they split up, Vic was ready. She'd told Ellie she'd broken up with Warren on the day he'd moved into her house.

She'd kept her relationship and her job safe… and slowly started removing herself from Ellie's life. No drama. No hysteria. Just grace under pressure—the exact opposite of her childhood. It hurt, but it was best for everyone.

Vic straightened her shoulders and gave a more genuine smile and Warren rewarded her with a soft kiss on her forehead. "There she is." He stroked her cheek gently. "You look lovely today, Vic. Your hair is perfect."

"Thank you." A soft warmth spread through her chest. "I have that interview today."

Warren nodded slowly. "Good. You did the right thing getting out of Dangerous Business Games. It was toxic for you there." He smiled. "You're better off away from those people with their constant intrusions in your life."

Was it toxic? Maybe it was? She'd liked her job before everything started to go wrong. But they did keep inviting her out when she needed to be home. And they were incessantly asking her about her private life when it was meant to be just that. Private.

The new job she was going for paid better and she could avoid getting entangled in everyone's lives. It was a good thing.

"How about you?" she asked. "Do you have plans for today?"

Warren's hand fell away, and a little ice crept between them. "I'm working on fixing this mess." He paused meaningfully and Vic's heart began to sink. She hadn't made the mess, had she? She wasn't at fault, surely?

"Ellie tried to take us from each other, now she's trying

to take your house," Warren explained with a sad sigh. "That woman will do anything to control you. But don't worry, I'll fix it. Just hang on to your shares for me, baby. We might need them soon."

Vic's relief was immediate and so overwhelming that she didn't even think about why they needed the shares if there wasn't going to be a sale. The mess they were in wasn't her fault; it was Ellie's. And now Ellie had offered to pay for a loan to secure the house. That would have put it in her name, wouldn't it? At the very least she'd owe Ellie a lot of money. And then Ellie would have a whole new way to control her. Thank God Warren was protecting her.

It hurt so much. It was a constant, lonely ache in her heart. Missing her friend and knowing that the one person she'd trusted for so long, the person she'd relied on for so many years, had turned against her.

"Now that frown is back," Warren chided. "Careful, Vic, you don't want wrinkles, do you?"

No. Of course not. She smoothed away the frown, and Warren smiled. She moved forward, tilting her face up, expecting a kiss, but he stepped back and patted her shoulder instead. "Let's not risk that pretty face, shall we?"

# Chapter Twenty-Six

ELLIE AND JOSH fell into a routine. Days spent working side by side—whether online or in the garden—nights spent playing games, talking about the world, and falling into bed together.

Ellie drove up to London to work in her office for a couple of hours twice a week as usual. But she didn't stay overnight, and she was always back before Josh faded—even if he was pale and cold, and usually passed out on the bed when she found him.

She sent several texts to Victoria. The first offered to talk, the second promised her support, and after that she sent funny anecdotes she thought her friend would like. Although she never got a reply.

The more Ellie thought about what Vic had said—and done—the more certain she was that Warren was the cause of Victoria's strange behavior. She spent time reading up on coercive control and how confused and disoriented victims could become. And Ellie wanted Vic to know she wasn't alone. That despite everything, Ellie was on her side.

Every day, she spent some time going through traffic cam footage and updating her requests for accident witnesses. Although she never found anything. And eventually she reached out to a private security company and booked in a meeting with one of their investigators for the next time she was in London.

She tried calling all the avian centers in Scotland, but they refused to hand out employee information—past or present—and became even less helpful when she didn't know Josh's surname. And a thorough search of online staff profiles came up with nothing.

Josh spent his days searching through veterinary services and wildlife conservation websites for anything he felt was familiar, although that was unsuccessful too.

He still brooded on her deck, but he also laughed more every day. He brought her snacks and sat with her while she drank her morning coffee. He played her game and seemed to really love it. And with every touch, every moment when he wrapped his arms around her and nuzzled into her neck, he took more of her heart.

And although she worked hard, for the first time in her life she also rested. Standing up for herself, making the choice to stick to her beliefs, had settled something inside her. She sat in the sun with her feet in Josh's lap. She took long walks. She even went down to the beach alone and swam in the cold sea, shivering and swearing, but emerging full of energy and ideas.

It had been another full day and Ellie was sitting alone in her office, wrapping up her last e-mail when she noticed a new message from an unknown sender. Anything suspicious was immediately flagged by her new security system, but this hadn't been weeded out—even with the vague subject line of "I might be able to help."

She opened it warily to find it was someone responding to a request she'd left on a message board several days before. He apologized for his slow response; his wife had given birth to their first baby, and he'd only just started coming back to his social media. He'd already handed his dashcam video of her accident to the police—who hadn't been able to get anything useful from it—but he attached the video for her anyway, in case it could help.

She called over her shoulder, hoping Josh was in the house and would hear her, and then, not expecting much, she clicked it open and pressed Play.

At first it was fairly boring. The unremarkable road disappeared beneath the car, mumbled conversation from the passengers played in the background, trees flashed past on either side. And then they followed a steep curve before the road straightened, and Ellie knew exactly where she was.

She paused the video as Josh came into her office. He took one glance at the frozen image on the screen—the grainy view of the forested road, time and date stamped on the bottom—and sank onto the seat beside her, one hand coming to settle on her thigh. "Is this from your accident?" he asked.

"I think so." She couldn't keep the tremble out of her voice. The reality of seeing the road sliding away in front of her was worse than she'd expected. She'd lived through it once. She didn't want to see it again.

"Do you want me to look at it for you?" Josh asked. "You can go make a cup of tea and I'll tell you if I see anything that might be helpful."

She threaded her fingers through his, gripping them tightly. "It's okay. I think I need to see it. Just... can you stay with me?"

He shuffled his chair closer, pressing his body against hers. "Of course. I'm here. Whatever you need."

His expression was stoic, as always, but she knew him well enough now to see the signs of stress: the tightness around his eyes, the tension in his jaw. But he hadn't hesitated to offer to take the load entirely on himself.

She leaned a little closer into him and clicked Play. The video restarted. Here were the woods. Here the road grew steeper. And any moment—

Josh's grip on her hand tightened as they approached a group of cyclists flying down the narrow road, helmets gleaming, jerseys in an array of bright colors.

Their car fell back, making space. The cyclists were in a tight, dense group, obscuring the front, but Ellie knew this road. She knew this curve. And she knew this was where she'd pulled ahead.

Beside her, Josh was utterly still. She glanced at him, concerned about how pale he was, how rigid his muscles were.

But then she heard the hooting, and her attention flew back to the screen. The people in their car were swearing at a big, navy blue SUV passing them dangerously close on the narrow road.

A car appeared from the other direction, and the driver with the dashcam braked hard, letting the SUV swerve in at the last moment. The oncoming vehicle roared past them with a shouted curse. But the SUV—now between them and the cyclists—didn't slow down. Within a second, he was moving back out, moving beside the bikes.

Blood thundered in Ellie's ears. Her body was too hot, her hands too cold. Pins and needles stabbed up her back. Beside her, Josh seemed to be having his own crisis. His eyes were too wide, his breaths too shallow, his hand gripped hers tight enough to hurt.

They leaned together, seeking safety, seeking comfort, as if they both knew exactly what was coming.

And then the SUV jerked hard to the side. Was it a response to something on the road? An accident?

Or was it deliberate? Intentional?

*A man wearing dark glasses and a cap pulled low drove the SUV. And he looked right at her.*

God. She wanted to be sick. She hunched over her belly as a cyclist went down: her. And then, almost in slow motion, the entire pack of cyclists crashed into each other. Propelled into a vicious tangle of metal and limbs and pain.

The SUV hovered for a moment—checking he'd got her?—and then took off. The dashcam driver pulled over, someone's voice babbled; high-pitched and panicked, calling 999. People shouted and groaned. But Ellie hardly heard it.

Their car was parked at an angle, the dashcam perfectly positioned to show *her*. Her long-sleeved purple cycling jersey was torn and covered in mud. Her biking tights were shredded and soaked with blood.

She was on her front, reaching out to the nearest cyclist. His hair was matted with blood. His helmet had torn off in the crash.

She pulled herself closer, put out her hand, and just for a moment, their eyes met. And she *remembered*. Clear blue eyes, bracketed by tiny lines, intense and focused utterly on her.

Josh.

Her lips moved, mouthing the words, even as she saw them move on the screen. "Don't leave me."

His eyes fluttered closed on the recording, and she was

filled with the same horror as on that awful day; the terror that he would die there on that broken road.

She watched herself take his hand. And she remembered begging. "Stay. Please. God. Please stay."

# Chapter Twenty-Seven

Josh gripped the railing on Ellie's deck, letting his head drop as the shadows over the forest thickened and darkened into night.

He was Josh *Taylor*. He remembered his name. He remembered...

Living in Scotland, far from everything. And everyone. But then the call came from home, and he'd left his job. He'd taken a long sabbatical and traveled all the way back down to Dorset. Back to the village where he grew up, about twenty miles inland from Ellie's cottage.

His mother was worried. And when his mum—the woman who'd raised him and Liam by herself, who'd loved them, cared for them, and hauled their small family out of the rough council block they'd lived in and all the way to a neat little semi-detached home in a pretty village—was worried, Josh dropped everything.

Liam had fallen into a crowd she didn't like. He'd abandoned his dreams of becoming a sports physiotherapist. Ignored his years of education—that Josh had paid for—choosing instead to stay at home and trade stock from his laptop. Liam was spending his days playing football with the lads, and his evenings turning himself into some kind of rich-kid-wannabe; spending money he didn't have on flashy cars, designer suits, and enough overpriced alcohol to leave him utterly useless most mornings. And he took every chance to pressure their mum to invest in things she didn't know enough about—but then he never seemed able to give her the details when she asked for them.

When Josh arrived home, Liam had seemed glad to see him. Only too happy to have him around the house, taking their mum out, helping with chores. And he'd promised that he was doing well. His career was taking off. He'd hit a slight snag on an investment he'd made, but it didn't matter because he had a way to make it all back. All he had to do was help his good friend Warren out with something easy, and then he'd be back on top.

Josh had been home for about a week when he asked Liam to come over to help with some work in the garden. But Liam couldn't make it... he was going out for a cycle ride with the local club.

It had irritated Josh immensely. Liam was yet again unavailable to do chores, blowing them off to head out with his friends instead. And Liam knew how much Josh loved mountain biking. It was part of why he'd taken the secondment to Scotland.

Of course, the main reason he'd gone so far away was that after decades of taking care of everyone—especially Liam—and battling with everyone—especially Liam—Josh had wanted to go somewhere with as few people as humanly possible.

He'd wanted a break from being responsible for everyone else. A break from the constant churn of work and more work, broken only by a string of meaningless one-night stands. He'd reached a point where he knew he didn't want more than one night but didn't want so little either. Getting away had seemed ideal.

But then his mother had called, and he'd put all his things in storage and gone back to stay with her. And then Liam had planned to go cycling while Josh stayed at home and pulled weeds.

No. He wasn't having it. He'd insisted that he join the ride, and Liam could come back with him to help with chores afterward. He hadn't given Liam the option of refusing. He'd borrowed some gear from a friend and met his cranky brother at the start of the ride.

It was a club Josh didn't know. Liam had signed up only the week before and—under duress—brought him along as a guest. They didn't bother to sign him in, Liam signed in for both of them. He was an unnamed guest, riding a friend's bicycle, wearing an ancient helmet.

And Josh certainly wasn't supposed to see Liam checking the names on the sign-in list, or the quick thumbs-up he gave to the SUV parked across the road.

But he had seen it. And he'd recognized the car immediately when it drew up behind him. And he'd known something was very, very wrong when Liam fell back, encouraging the other riders back, and let one particular cyclist—Ellie—go ahead.

Fuck. Darkness swirled at the edges of his vision, and he gripped the rail even tighter, letting the wood cut into his hands. Using the pain.

He'd sped up. He'd tried to reach her. Legs pumping, chest burning. He didn't know her. He didn't know what Liam wanted with her. But he'd known it was wrong.

But he couldn't get there in time. He couldn't match the speed of the accelerating SUV. He'd watched the front bumper hit her, watched her flying over her handlebars, through the air, heard the sickening crunch.

He braked hard, too late to stop. He'd glanced off the side of the SUV, crashed into Ellie's mangled bicycle, tipped over the handlebars and landed hard on his head, his helmet cracking and falling away.

For a few seconds, he felt nothing. And then a tidal wave of pain slammed into him like nothing he had ever known.

He remembered her clear eyes locked on his, her hand reaching, her voice telling him to stay. Demanding that he didn't leave. Sirens in the background.... And then nothing but darkness.

Darkness, and a woman. Ellie.

Warm arms wrapped around his waist and held him tightly, dragging him back to the present. Her body pressed against his back. Full of life. She was here with him, right now.

And he *knew* he should have walked away weeks ago. Knew he should have kept his emotions cold and hard. But it was too late. "I'm sorry." He whispered the words, but they still tore at his throat.

Her grip around him tightened as she spoke against his shoulder blades. "You have nothing to be sorry for."

"I know—" He swallowed heavily. "I think I know who did this."

She was utterly still, but she didn't let him go. If anything, she held him closer. "Who is he?" she whispered.

Josh wrapped his hands over hers, holding them tight against his chest for a moment before releasing them. He would tell the truth and take the pain when she understood that his brother was deeply involved in all the terrible things that had happened to her. That his family was responsible for the pain and fear she'd suffered. She wouldn't blame him—not Ellie—but how could she possibly look at him the same as before?

He didn't want to face her while he did it. It was easier this way; looking out over the dark woods, her body against his for one last, precious moment.

"Liam. He was the cyclist in the Manchester City football colors, the one who pushed you to the front. He's my brother...." Josh choked on the words, forcing them out. "I saw him signaling to the SUV before we started the ride. He set you up. And it was him in your house the other day."

Fuck. Admitting it out loud made it sound even worse. She would hate him now, and she would be right. Then she would walk away. Like his father. Like Liam. Like *him*.

"But... *why?*" Her voice was so small and sad and confused. So devastated and betrayed. And God help him, if Liam had been standing in front of him, Josh would have killed him with his bare hands.

"I came back from Scotland because of the trouble Liam was getting into. Because he had fallen into a crowd my mother didn't like. And there was one man, a particularly bad influence. Always encouraging Liam to spend more, drink more, party more... and invest in things he should have stayed a million miles away from. Warren Bailey."

She shuddered, her hands gripping his shirt, and suddenly he couldn't bear looking away from her for one more second. He turned in her arms and pulled her into his embrace.

She must have heard what he'd said, must have heard his confession, but she didn't hesitate. She wrapped herself around him so tightly that he could feel her heart beating, her chest rising and falling with each trembling breath.

"I'm sorry, Ellie. So very sorry."

She looked up at him and he knew, this was it. He'd only wanted a moment, but now, when it was over, it hadn't been enough.

But she still didn't let him go. She nuzzled even closer. "No. Don't do that. Nothing that happened was your fault."

"But my brother—"

Ellie gave him a small, tired smile. "You are not responsible for his mistakes."

*You are not responsible.* God. All his life he'd been responsible: for his father, for his brother. He'd carried the weight like an albatross. But Ellie lifted it so easily. She didn't blame him, or hold him accountable, at all.

He nearly went to his knees. Only Ellie's body against his kept him standing. Ellie's strength. But she didn't seem to realize how her words had rocked him. She was distracted, working through what they'd learned.

"This was Warren," she said slowly. "He got them all involved in something that lost millions. Hell. He took Vic's house, whatever Liam gave him, maybe even money from the kind of people who take physical exception to delays in being paid back. He thought that Vic could pressure me into selling, and they'd get a big payday. When that wasn't quick enough, he thought that if they hurt me, I'd have to sell. And if he killed me, it would work out even better for them: then Vic would get the business. She's my principal beneficiary. She could sell, and they'd get the money."

Ellie shivered, her tension ratcheting up. Her eyes were wide and horrified. "Do you think... God. Do you think Vic did this to me?"

He stroked her hair, wishing he could take this pain from her. "I don't know. Fuck. I wish I could say she wasn't involved, but I can't."

She slumped against him, and suddenly he was holding

her. "It's terrible either way," she whispered against his chest. "Either Vic knows, or she's in danger." She lifted her eyes to his. "We have to do something. We can't wait for the investigators now."

He murmured his agreement, tightening his arms around her. She was right, there was a lot to do. But first there was more to face. And before they did that, he needed to hold her. She smelled of sunlight, and she felt like a dream. He wanted to remember this feeling forever.

But then he took her arms and gently guided her back so he could meet her eyes. "Ellie..." He didn't want to say it. Didn't want to rip off this last, awful bandage. But he had to, and he had to do it now. "You were right all along. None of this—" He grunted, the words thick and bitter in his throat. "None of this is real."

"It is though." She pushed forward, back into his arms, and he didn't have the strength to hold her away. "It feels real to me. You feel real."

"I'm not here. I landed badly. I'm lying in a hospital somewhere." The bright white lights. The harsh smells. "This... I don't know what this is."

Her arms tightened around his waist as she laid her head on his chest. Her voice was low but determined. "I don't care what this is. I don't care if no one believes it or it doesn't make sense."

"You must care, Ellie." He didn't want her to care about making sense: he wanted *her*. He wanted her to hold on to him exactly as she was. But how could he expect that of her? Now, when he finally found the one woman he could imagine a life with, his life was already over. And he wanted more for her. "How can we have any kind of future? How can we ever be together?"

She leaned back, then, and looked up at him, and there

was nothing but determination and strength in her gaze. "We're together *now*. I'm not letting you go because I'm scared about the future. We'll find a way."

"Will we? Ellie... this..." Fuck. He'd known the truth would hurt.

But Ellie didn't let him go. Her hands on his waist held him tethered to the ground. Her determination tethered her to him. He had learned to walk away—she had the strength to stay.

"I *don't* care about any of that. We have to wake you up, and then you'll... I don't know—" She gave him a tiny smile. "You'll float back together somehow."

He barked out a rough laugh. A laugh of combined misery and joy. How did she do this to him? "I want to believe you," he murmured.

"Believe, Josh." Her smile grew more confident as she gave his words back to him. "*I* believe in *you*."

He tucked her hair behind her ears before cradling her cheeks gently, looking into her eyes. Seeing her resilience, her trust, the truth of just how much she cared for him.

God. He could fall for her. He could fall all the way and never even care about the landing. He could love her forever.

"Okay," he agreed softly. "I can believe in magic. Because I believe in you."

She stood up on her toes to press a quick kiss to his lips. "Good. Because now we have to find Vic, and figure out exactly how involved she is—and just how much danger we're all in."

# Chapter Twenty-Eight

Ellie called Vic again and again. Left messages. Tried her DMs. Called her home… and got nothing. She didn't want to believe her closest friend in the world, the woman she saw as her sister, could have been actively working to hurt her all this time. She had to listen to Vic's voice. Give her a chance to explain. And then she would know what to do.

Eventually, just as she was climbing in her car to drive there in person, Vic answered. "Hello, Ellie."

"Thank God, Vic. I—"

"I can't speak to you now, Ellie, I'm busy," Vic said. Her tone was distant, threaded through with irritation. "I just answered to tell you to stop calling me. I don't want to speak to you."

The words hurt, and, for the first time, Ellie didn't hold back. "Did you try to kill me, Victoria?"

"Did I *what*?"

"Did you try to kill me?" Ellie's voice cracked. "I want the truth."

"What? God! How can you…? Are you insane?"

Victoria's words were fast and high pitched. "Wait. When did someone try to kill you?"

"I'm talking about my cycling accident, Vic. It was intentional."

"It was... what? I don't understand."

The shock, confusion, and horror in Vic's voice was undeniable. And despite everything, Ellie had known her for enough years to know it wasn't an act. Vic wasn't pretending to be surprised. She was genuinely appalled. And that meant she was in danger.

"Just listen, okay. You're my best friend. I love you. And I need you to listen." Ellie paced through her cottage to stand at the living room doors, looking out at the garden. "I don't know how to say this. Don't put down the phone. Just let me finish. Please." Ellie looked back at Josh where he'd settled onto the sofa to watch her with undisguised concern and tried to give him a reassuring smile. "Someone broke into my house while I was in London."

Vic sucked in a shuddering breath. "God. Sorry, Ellie. Are you okay? Yes, of course you are. You just said you weren't there. You should... I..." Vi's voice trailed off, and when she spoke again her tone was firmer. "What does that have to do with your accident?"

"The intruder's name is Liam Taylor. He came into my house. He used my name to try to hack my computer. And Vic, he was part of my accident. He was the one who pushed me to the front so the SUV could drive into me"— her gut tightened painfully as she told the story, but Vic needed to know the truth—"and he was working with Warren."

"Warren?" Vic said roughly. "No. That's just... No."

"Where are you now?" Ellie asked. "Are you with him?"

"I..." Ellie could hear Vic breathing, the sound rough and unsteady.

"You need to leave, Vic. Right now. Please. It's not safe for you there."

"I'm not... I mean. He's out at the moment." Victoria took a longer, slower breath and seemed to gather her thoughts. "How do you even know this? Did the police catch the intruder? Did he say that he was working with Warren?"

Hell. How was she going to explain? "A witness sent me a video of the crash. Liam's brother, Josh, was with me when I watched it, and he identified Liam." Damn, this was hard. "Liam admitted that he was working with Warren just before I got hurt. Liam pushed me forward so the SUV could knock into me.... I think Warren was driving. I think he tried to kill me."

There was a long silence before Vic spoke, the ice back, her tone even more cutting than before. "So, basically some guy you've never even mentioned until now says he recognized his brother and magically knows all of this. But the police aren't involved at all. You've never actually spoken to this mythical Liam. And you have no real evidence Warren was anywhere near there or involved in any way. Damn it, Ellie, this is going too far."

"It's complicated—"

"Is it though?" Vic spat. "You've always been against Warren. You've always been jealous of me—of us—and you've done everything possible to keep us apart. And now you're accusing me of trying to kill you! You really are insane."

Blood pounded in her ears, but Ellie forced herself to stay calm, to stay reasonable. "I suggested you split up after your birthday party because I saw Warren kissing a stranger outside the club toilets. I told you at the time."

"No." Victoria's denial was instant and absolute. "Warren warned me about how controlling you were becoming. He warned me that you would try to split us up *before* you came up with that story. And that's what you do, Ellie; you make up stories."

Ellie swallowed against the tension in her throat. "None of that is true, Vic. Warren is trying to drive a wedge between us because he knows that I care for you and want you safe."

"Warren wants what's best for me. He's protecting me from you."

God. How was this happening? "Vic, we've been friends for years. I would never lie to you about something like that. You *know* this."

"I don't know anything." Vic's voice was full of tears. "I feel so betrayed."

Josh stood up and walked over to wrap his arms around her and Ellie leaned heavily against him, letting his solid strength support her.

Shouting wouldn't help anything. She had to find another way to solve this. She took a deep breath. "Let's sort it out together. Just please, get away from him for a couple of days."

"I can't—"

"You can always come here, always. Or if you can't come here, go north and see your cousins. Is your mum in the country? Go to her. Or stay in a hotel. Just please, get out of there."

"No, Ellie. You don't know what you're talking about."

"Can I come up and help? I can show you—"

"No. You accuse me of this, and then you want to visit? Absolutely not."

"But—"

"I said no. If you come here, you'll make everything worse."

Hell. She was certain now that Vic wasn't involved, but even more convinced that Warren was. The problem was, Vic was right: she had no proof. And in the meantime, Vic was still with Warren. "If you change your mind, just call me. Please. Vic—" Victoria disconnected the call before Ellie could finish.

She'd thought everything was crumbling around her before. But now... What was she going to do? Ellie looked out at the dark garden and the forest beyond. The sound of the night whispered in through the open doors. Leaves rustled, the breeze murmured. And somewhere out there, a pair of owls were working to keep each other safe.

They knew who Josh was now. They could start calling hospitals looking for him, although merely finding his unconscious body wouldn't do much good. They needed a witness. Someone who could speak to the police. Someone who could help her save Josh at the same time as helping Vic.

She turned to Josh, knowing he was not going to like her next suggestion. "How do you feel about visiting your brother?"

# Chapter Twenty-Nine

Victoria put down the phone, breathing hard.

Why would Ellie do this to her? Warren was right; Ellie was spiraling. Her behavior was becoming less and less rational. And now, to accuse Warren... and *her*! It was a horrible thing to do.

And yet... *I love you. You're my best friend. I want you safe.* Ellie had sounded so genuine, so horrified—and hurt—by Vic's accusations. And in the past, Vic wouldn't have doubted her at all. It was only recently, only since Warren...

Vic shivered. He wanted what was best for her. Because he loved her. Didn't he?

Had he ever actually said the words? He often wanted her to do things *because* he loved her. He regularly told her other people *did not* love her like she deserved. But had he ever said, "I love you, Victoria"?

He must have. Surely.

She pulled on a tight black sheath dress and held her breath until the zipper closed smoothly. Warren did not believe in making poor diet choices, and not fitting into her dress would have been a problem. She'd run for hours after the apple pie at Ellie's house. God. Leftovers for breakfast would have been a disaster.

This was all a disaster—a devastating, infuriating, horrible disaster—but she didn't have time to think about it now. First, she would host this party, and then she would think about it.

She finished her makeup and checked herself in the mirror—she looked acceptable—and made her way into the kitchen to serve up trays of delicate hors d'oeuvres. Warren was entertaining investors who should be arriving any moment.

And there he was. Warren strode into the kitchen in a perfectly fitted Savile Row suit and glanced over the trays of cut-crystal glasses and elegantly presented canapés. He was always on time. Always calm, refined, and utterly reliable.

He glanced over the preparations for a moment before frowning and moving closer to one of the trays. "This glass is chipped." His voice was like ice.

God. How could she have missed something like that? She hurried closer and lifted the offending glass. Was it chipped? "I think it's just a mark—"

He grabbed her arm and yanked it closer, holding it so he could see the glass in the light.

She tried to pull back, but she was trapped, and she didn't dare let go of the crystal. They were her granny's glasses, and if she lost the house, these were the only things she would have left. "Warren, you're hurting me."

He released her immediately. "Sorry, baby." He took the glass and settled it safely on the tray before lifting her hand far more gently and pressing a series of soft kisses to her wrist. "I would never hurt you, Vic. I just want to help you. You could be truly magnificent."

She swallowed and made herself smile. Her arm hurt.

And maybe she was seeing things that weren't there. Maybe Ellie had rattled her, made her doubt everything. But Warren hadn't done any of the work. None of the glasses were his. He hadn't paid for the canapés. It was all hers. So how was he helping?

Warren pressed another kiss to her arm, but it didn't take away the sting. "Can you pop out and get us some more champagne?" Warren asked gently. "The guests are arriving soon, and I'd like to be here to greet them."

Without her? In the past, they'd always stood side by side. It had made her feel like a princess standing beside Prince Charming.

She didn't want to go out, not in what she was wearing. And she had no idea how they were going to afford the champagne. But she nodded anyway, and he rewarded her with a proud smile. "You're the best, Vic."

She rubbed her arm as she made her way down to the car. He'd hurt her. He *had hurt her*. She hadn't imagined it.

What was happening to her?

Victoria sat in the driver seat and forced her shoulders down and spine straight. What she needed was proof. She needed to show Ellie that she was wrong about everything. Then she could finally let go of any stupid doubts and just be happy. She'd worked hard for this perfect life with Warren, and she deserved it unsullied.

Her gaze fell to the satnav. It was so easy—all she had to do was prove that Warren had been miles away when Ellie had her accident. And she knew exactly how to do it.

# Chapter Thirty

WHAT THE FUCK was wrong with people? Why the hell didn't they just answer their bloody phones?

Josh wanted to kill Liam—and Warren, but that would be a slower, more painful death—*not* visit him. And now they couldn't even get hold of the bastard.

Liam's phone just rang and went to voicemail every time Ellie called. He also wasn't at his flat, despite it being nearly 10:00 p.m. He wasn't at the pub, the gym, or any of the places Josh thought he could be. He wasn't even at their mother's house; all the lights were off when they crept slowly past.

Which was a problem. Because with every mile Ellie drove—every time he looked across at her as she piloted them back and forth, navigating the night-time roads—he remembered how easily she could've been lost. He remembered how badly hurt she'd been. How hard it was for her to get back into a car and out onto the road. And his rage grew.

Finally, there was only one place left to look. The one place Josh *really* didn't want to go. He folded his arms over his chest, glaring at the night as he admitted, "He might be at the hospital."

"Good idea." Ellie glanced at him, a quick appraisal. "Do you want me to drop you at home before I try there?"

Yes and no. He wanted them to both go home and never leave—and when did he start thinking of her cottage as home?—but he wanted to stick close to her side far more. And if they did find Liam... well, that would be the perfect time to explain to his brother exactly how he felt about what had happened to Ellie. "I'd rather go together."

"Okay, then." Ellie turned a corner and pointed them toward the hospital.

There was only one local hospital large enough to take long-term patients with brain injuries, and Ellie had been there enough over the last few weeks; she probably knew the way in her sleep. Hell. They'd probably been there together, just a few floors apart.

She found a parking bay and turned off the engine before twisting in her seat to face him. "How are we going to do this?"

"We're going to go in and find Liam." And explain to him the consequences of bad choices.

Ellie laid her hand on his arm. "Do you really want to see yourself?"

Josh leaned back against his headrest. God, he was tired. Truthfully, he didn't think he could see himself. He had no logical explanation. Not even a quip about the Upside Down. Just the same dread he'd had when he was looking for evidence of who he was. And a bone-deep knowledge that he absolutely could not go into that room.

"I can't go into my room but—" He caught a glimpse of a tall man with dark hair and swallowed the rest. "Never mind. He's here!"

They jumped out and jogged over to where Liam was making his way between rows of parked cars. "Liam!" Josh called. "Stop!"

His brother didn't even pause.

"Liam!" Josh roared. But his brother didn't respond at all.

Fuck. Shit. Damn it all. Liam couldn't hear him.

Josh glanced at Ellie, already knowing she would understand.

"Liam! Liam Taylor!" she shouted.

Liam stopped and turned to face them, grimacing in confusion. "Who the—" He flinched bodily, stepping back. And then he turned away as if to run.

Ellie darted forward and got in his path before he could escape, just as Josh growled, reaching out to grab his arm. His hand went straight through Liam's bicep with a spike of cold, and he flinched back at the same time Liam gasped out, "What the hell?"

Liam rubbed his arm roughly, trying to step around Ellie. But at least something of their childhood lessons had stuck, because he did it almost politely and completely ineffectively, before finally giving up and stopping in front of her.

At first glance, Liam looked largely the same as when Josh had seen him last. He had the same slightly too-long, dark, wavy hair. The same lean muscles. They were about the same height, but Liam had always come across as less intimidating than Josh. Liam was more charming. More friendly. More attractive.

Maybe that was part of the problem? Liam had always been a little too good-looking; cute enough to get away with hell as a child, and then handsome enough to continue getting away with it long past the age when he should have started to grow up. Long past the age when he should have stopped constantly looking for the easy way out of everything.

Liam sighed, his shoulders slumping. And, for the first time, Josh looked properly at his face, and then he couldn't miss the changes. Liam looked as if he'd aged ten years overnight. He looked as if he was grieving. Guilt and shame warred in his expression.

"You were in my house," Ellie said softly.

She didn't say, "*And you tried to kill me*," which was where Josh would have started. But Liam couldn't hear him.

Liam dragged his hand slowly down his face, his shoulders curling even more. "I'm sorry."

"You're not even going to deny it!" Josh muttered. How was he going to kill his brother when he couldn't even touch him?

Ellie must have heard him, but she ignored his grumbling and focused on Liam. "Warren blackmailed you, didn't he?"

Liam blinked at her. He clearly hadn't expected her to know about Warren. But he didn't pretend not to know what she was talking about. "He didn't *exactly* blackmail me."

"Then what the fuck did you do it for?" Josh demanded as Ellie raised her eyebrow.

"Warren said no one would get hurt. He guaranteed you would be in London overnight. He gave me a key to the back door; I didn't even have to break anything. We could get what we needed to—" Liam cleared his throat, eyes darting away from her before coming back guiltily. "We needed you to sell the game. His girlfriend would get her share, and we would all get our money back. And you would walk away with a load of cash too. It would have been best for you too."

"But I did get hurt! *We* were hurt," Ellie snapped. "You broke into my house! How could you possibly convince yourself I wanted that?"

"I know. I'm sorry," Liam replied. "It was just... I needed that cash. I thought there was a way for everyone to come out better off."

"Cash! Money! What *you* need!" Josh stalked around his brother, wishing he could punch him in the fucking face. Wishing he wasn't so bloody helpless.

"You did it all for money?" Ellie asked, echoing him, horror in her voice.

"Yes... no... none of this was supposed to happen." Liam glanced back at the hospital, misery written in the red blotches staining his neck and face. "I *am* sorry. But my brother's in there. He's not waking up. And I need another opinion. We're going to need private healthcare. Therapy... It's so expensive!" The sheen of unshed tears caught the hospital lights. "I lost ten thousand pounds of my mother's savings," Liam admitted in a rough voice. "Warren said he'd give me the full amount back if I helped him."

Fuck it all. His mum hadn't mentioned the missing money. Probably because she knew what Josh would have said. "You arsehole!" He strode in front of Liam and gripped his shoulders, trying to shake him but failing. "You already helped him! You helped him to run Ellie off the road! And you'd already lost Mum's savings!"

Liam blanched, his body wracked by a violent shiver. "What are you doing to me?" he croaked, stepping back. "Don't do that."

Josh wanted to follow and shake harder. Finally, he was doing something. Finally, Liam could feel him. But Ellie put her hand on his arm and steered him away. "You forced me off the road!" Ellie snapped at Liam. "I broke two ribs and punctured a lung! I nearly died. And Josh—" Her voice broke. "Josh was hurt even more."

"I know," Liam whispered. "I'm so sorry. Warren said he wanted you alone at the front so he could speak to you. I thought he was going to tell you to pull over. Like you had a puncture or something. He said you wouldn't speak to him otherwise, no matter how hard he tried. That he just needed this chance to convince you to do the right thing for your friend. For everyone."

"You didn't think at all," Josh spat, staying back. The temptation to strangle him was too high. And maybe Liam would feel it. Maybe it would actually make an impact.

"What do you want me to do?" Liam asked in a broken voice. "I'll do it. Honestly. All I want is Josh back."

Ellie sighed, softening. "Me too."

Liam stared at her long enough—his gaze troubled enough—that Josh wrapped his arm around her and glared.

He needed to have his real body back, damn it. He needed to be able to hold her and kiss her and claim her so that everyone could see. So that Liam and the rest of the bloody world knew he was with her. So that they didn't fuck with her ever again.

She leaned into his side, taking the support he offered. But to anyone else it would have just looked like she was standing slightly off-balance.

"How do you know my brother?" Liam asked.

Ellie narrowed her eyes. "We met cycling," she said.

Josh huffed out a half chuckle at the dark joke. But then she continued and took the breath right out of his lungs. "He's important to me."

Josh tightened his hold on her and looked down to meet

her eyes. "You're important to me too," he admitted softly, wishing he could have said it anywhere else than in a windy, gray hospital car park, two feet from his increasingly disturbed-looking brother, and a few thin walls away from his own unconscious body.

# Chapter Thirty-One

Everything was wrong. Warren had tried to take everything from her. Vic was still with him. They were standing in the cold wind outside the hospital where Josh's body lay, unconscious and locked in darkness. Liam was staring at them—her—like she was insane. And Josh looked like he was going to finally tip over the edge and kill his own brother. Except... it also felt right.

All her life, she'd battled to be perfect. Battled and tried, and worked, until the pressure had almost crushed her. Now, nothing about his situation was perfect. But for the first time, it didn't matter. Josh was beside her. They would figure it all out. Together.

"Did you mean it?" she asked Liam. "That you'll help?"

Liam shoved his hands into his pockets, looking even more dejected. But he didn't try to weasel away. "Yes, I'll help."

"Warren started all of this," Ellie said. "It'll never be over until we're rid of him. That has to be our priority."

"Absolutely," Josh agreed, far too quickly. Just by

looking at his face, she knew he was already imagining several scenarios for how that could be achieved.

She scowled back at him. "Not by killing him."

Liam's eyes widened, and he took a step back. "I don't want anything to do with killing him!"

"You didn't seem to have a problem with attacking Ellie —" Josh started, turning his glare onto glare at his brother.

She cut him off. "None of that is helpful now." She stepped between them, focusing on Liam. "Nobody is killing anybody. We need to do this properly, which means getting the police back and making a statement."

Liam chewed the inside of his cheek. He looked like he wanted to be sick. "What kind of statement?"

"The kind that—" Josh started, but Ellie spoke over him.

"I'll keep you out of it as much as I can. I promise."

Josh growled, and Ellie ignored it. Liam was his brother; she wasn't sending him to jail for being selfish and naïve— especially when she needed him to help her. Her priority had to be Josh and Vic.

"Can you follow me back to my house?" she asked. "Actually, you already know—" She caught sight of the muscles tightening in Josh's jaw and stopped herself with a strangled cough. "Never mind. Can you follow me?"

"Ah... no," Liam admitted. "I don't have a car."

"Where's your BMW?" Josh asked, but Ellie shushed him with a look.

"That's okay, you can come with us... ah, me." She started walking, but Josh didn't move.

"Ask him where his car is. Please." It took everything she had not to roll her eyes, but then Josh continued, "He loved that car."

"Where's your car, Liam?" Ellie asked, unlocking hers and pulling the seat forward so he could climb in the back.

"I sold it. Last week."

She raised an eyebrow. "After you broke into my house?"

"Yeah." Liam looked at his feet. "It was awful. I didn't want to do it, and then you caught me and... Hell." He swallowed. "The truth is, I knew it was wrong. Even before I got there. The next day, I sold my car, and I used the money to pay my mother back."

"Oh. Well. That's...." She didn't really know what that was. But he was trying. And Josh's eyes had gone from arctic to somewhere more like the Irish Sea: cold and dangerous, but slightly less deadly.

And then something Liam had said earlier caught up with her. "You had a key to my kitchen door. How? Where did you get the key?"

Liam looked away, suddenly even more interested in the stones at his feet. "Warren got it from his girlfriend."

"Victoria gave him my key?" Her voice broke on the question. She'd been so sure, and now—

"No, he made a copy when he borrowed her car," Liam explained.

Josh took hold of her hand and squeezed it gently. "Given everything we've learned about him, it sounds true."

She squeezed back. It made sense. And Vic wouldn't have done that to her. She had to believe that. No matter what else had happened.

"I'm really sorry," Liam said again. And for the first time, she started to believe him. Even Josh looked like he might not kill him in the next few minutes.

"Okay," she sighed. "Let's get Warren out of our lives, and then we'll take it from there." She nodded to the back seat. "Jump in."

"But that's tiny!" Liam protested. "Can't I sit in the front?"

"No!" Ellie and Josh both growled at the same time, and she couldn't help but look at him and laugh. Josh's lips turned up and he almost smiled, and it just made her want to laugh harder.

"Tell him 'nix,'" Josh said. She rolled her eyes at him, and he shrugged.

"Fine." She looked at Liam. "Nix."

Liam stared at her. "What did you say?"

"Nix," she repeated, while Josh muttered, "Follow the fucking rules," under his breath.

She chuckled, grinning across at Josh. "He can't hear you."

"Obviously," Liam grumbled, "since he's unconscious." He stared at Ellie, his expression full of confused suspicion. And she couldn't blame him. From his perspective, her behavior must have been weird at best. Especially when she walked around to open the door for Josh—Liam would definitely not have been happy with the door opening by itself—and made a show of putting her bag in the footwell.

In the end, he climbed into the back seat without complaining, and Ellie took the reprieve.

The drive home was weird. Josh was silent, occasionally glaring at Liam as if plotting something dire. While Liam spent the time looking out his window as if he was imagining climbing out and making a run for it. It was a relief to turn down the single track to her cottage and pull onto her own driveway.

Until she saw the familiar car already parked there, and her adrenaline spiked all the way back up.

Victoria lifted her head from where she'd rested it on

her steering wheel, watched Ellie park, and then slowly climbed out. She was wearing a tight black sheath dress that showed off her unusually prominent collarbones, and stilettos that must have made the drive a nightmare.

Ellie made her way across to Victoria, meeting her in the middle of the drive just as two doors slammed behind her. She winced, wondering what Vic and Liam would say, but they didn't seem to have noticed. They were too busy staring at each other. Vic with confusion, Liam with guilt.

"What are you doing here, Lee?" Vic asked.

Ellie stopped, frozen by the words. "You know Liam." It wasn't a question. "You straight-up told me he didn't exist."

Victoria brushed her hands down her skirt, trying—and failing—to smooth the wrinkles. "Not Liam. *Lee*. He's—" She blanched. "He's one of Warren's friends."

Liam stepped up beside her. "It's Liam," he admitted. "A bunch of the football lads shortened it to Lee, and it stuck."

"And you've met before?" Ellie asked.

Vic shook her head, mouth opening and closing as if she had no idea what to say.

"A few times," Liam answered for them both. "I think I've been to at least four parties at Victoria's house over the last few months. Everyone was there."

It was worse than a slap. All those times she'd invited Vic to get together and she'd been too tired or working late. All those missed calls.

Victoria grimaced. "I—"

"How many times did you fob me off and push me away?" Ellie whispered as Josh came up beside her, his expression going back to a deathly glower. "Why, Vic?"

"I just thought... maybe if we had some time apart, you would get over your... jealousy." Victoria had the grace to look ashamed as she said it. But then she lifted her chin, a gleam of stubbornness returning. "I didn't want to fight. I wanted to keep my job. And I *was* busy. Warren had a lot of entertaining. He tried to protect me from you..." Her voice trailed away.

"I hate Warren!" Ellie spluttered. "I detest him. But I have only ever tried to look after you."

"He said—"

Ellie cut her off. "I don't want to hear what Warren said." Her eyes felt hot, and her cheeks were burning. She had never been so angry in her life. And she had the horrible feeling she was going to cry—not because she was sad, but because she was so furious.

Josh took one look at her and wrapped his arm around her. He pulled her close into his side and pressed a kiss to the top of her head. "I've got you," he said softly.

He was warm and safe, and he felt more like home than anywhere she'd ever lived—even her cottage. She let him hold her, no longer caring what it looked like to anyone else.

A part of her wanted to rage at her friend, but she couldn't, not when Victoria looked so fragile. "Why are you here, Vic?" she asked instead.

"After I spoke to you, I wanted to prove you wrong. I wanted—" Vic shook her head as if clearing a disagreeable thought. "I remembered that Warren borrowed my car on the day of your accident. I wanted to show you that he was far away from you." She bit her lip. "I wanted to prove that everything you said was a lie, so it could just be over."

Victoria rubbed her wrist distractedly. "I checked the satnav for recent destinations. I probably wouldn't have thought anything of it, but the SUV that hit you was stolen from Duncton. It stuck in my mind. *Duncton Wood* was one of my granny's favorite books and—" She swallowed heavily. "None of that matters. The point is, Warren borrowed my car to go to a meeting in Guildford. That's where I thought he was on the day you were hit." Her voice dropped to a rough whisper. "But he actually went to Duncton."

# Chapter Thirty-Two

DINNER WAS AWKWARD. So awkward that even Ellie's best cottage pie couldn't save it.

After the shock of Victoria's revelations, Ellie had herded them all into the house and made tea. It had seemed like the most sensible next step while they figured out how to deal with Liam's misery and Vic's silent, mechanical behavior.

Ellie had taken them through to the living room and pretended that it was normal to tell her guests they couldn't sit on the armchair—which she left free for Josh—and then for them to perch as far away from each other as humanly possible while sharing a sofa.

She'd made everyone hot drinks and tried to smile reassuringly at Josh, even though no one could see or hear him—except for Nissy, who decided to lie stretched out on the back of his chair, one paw on his shoulder, purring loudly. And then she'd called Constable Harrison, who thankfully was still on duty.

The constable listened carefully as she took Ellie's statement—that Warren had been pushing for her to sell her game, that he had grown angry when she hadn't, that he'd known she would be cycling that day, and that he had been in the village where the SUV was stolen—taking notes and asking questions.

It was exhausting, watching every word she said. Trying to ensure that her claims about Warren were taken seriously, but that she didn't involve Vic any more than she had to, or incriminate Liam. Both of them looked withdrawn and ashamed enough without making it worse.

Josh had other ideas. He'd stood up and stalked over to hover beside Liam, glaring, while stridently suggesting fifty years of community service, and once she thought he might have muttered something about haunting his brother until the end of time.

Liam must have felt something uneasy in the air, because he looked behind himself more than once and eventually asked Vic to swap places with him.

And after all that, their evidence wasn't anywhere near enough to arrest Warren. It was circumstantial at best. But Constable Harrison promised to get a detective involved immediately, and reminded Ellie that she could call her anytime.

"I'll make a statement," Liam offered quietly when Ellie put down the phone. "I'll tell them what happened and hopefully it won't be too bad."

Josh muttered his agreement, while Ellie replied, "Thank you. I have an investigator lined up and I'll call them in the morning. Waiting for a face-to-face meeting doesn't make sense now. Maybe they can find something that helps. And if not... then yes. It might come to that. But I think it would be helpful to speak to a lawyer first."

"Okay." Liam dragged his hand down his face tiredly. "Whatever you need."

Vic was utterly silent throughout, and she didn't say anything while Ellie bustled around making up the spare bedrooms for her and Liam—by some unspoken agreement, it seemed that everyone was staying—she simply disappeared into her room and closed the door.

Ellie stared at the door uncertainly before finally giving up and going downstairs to warm up the pie.

It was too late for dinner, but no one had eaten. Everyone was exhausted and pale. And no one looked like they could sleep. It was hard to wrap her head around how much had happened in the few hours since she'd opened the dashcam video. And, in the end, she wanted everyone taken care of, even if it was just by eating something warm.

But damn, dinner was painful.

Victoria emerged from her room looking rumpled and red-eyed, sat at the end of the table as far away from everyone as she could get, and silently pushed her food around her plate. Her phone was conspicuously absent, and Ellie could only imagine Warren had been blowing it up for hours. Liam sat between Vic and Ellie, devouring the food as if he hadn't seen a meal in days. While Josh sat on Ellie's other side, with his hands linked behind his head and a vicious glare trained on Liam.

"So, Liam, Josh mentioned you trained as a sports physio," Ellie said after a particularly torturous few minutes of listening to cutlery scrape along the porcelain. "Did you enjoy it?"

Liam finished chewing and put down his fork. "I did. I was really happy at uni." He tilted his head to the side, smiling softly, as he remembered.

Josh grunted. "Of course you were happy. I was paying your fees while you were playing football and drinking beer."

Ellie kept her focus on Liam. "Do you think you might go back to it now? Or do you like being a stock trader?" she asked.

"I like—"

"Sitting around in your pajamas with your dick in your hands," Josh grumbled.

Ellie glared at him and then turned back to Liam. "Sorry, what were you saying?"

"I liked the idea of making lots of money," Liam admitted. "My friends who went into management were making much bigger salaries than I could earn." He looked away. "I just wanted it to be easy. Easier, anyway. And"—he scraped his hand through his hair in a gesture that looked just like Josh—"I thought if I could make enough, I could help my mum more, you know? Maybe even pay my brother back. I thought I could go back to being a physio later." He gave her a lopsided grin. "I also wanted a BMW."

She couldn't help but chuckle, and then when Josh turned his brooding glare on her, she snorted and had to look away, swallowing the urge to laugh at him.

"Josh said you loved that car," she said sympathetically. Selling it was obviously a big step for Liam. And wanting to pay Josh back meant something too. Maybe he really would turn things around.

"Hmm." Liam put down his knife and fork and leaned back, watching her. There was confusion in his gaze, but also intelligence as he eyed the chair beside her. "How exactly did you meet Josh?" he asked. "You said you met while cycling, but he's been away for a long time. And he's never said anything about you. In fact, the first time he went cycling after he came back to stay with mum was when..." He swallowed the rest of the sentence, but they all knew what he meant.

Ellie glanced at Josh uncertainly. How much should she try to explain? Liam looked even more suspicious, while Josh was back to looking a little stabby.

And then Vic looked up and made it worse. "Who even is Josh?"

"My brother," Liam replied. But Victoria didn't let it go. She pushed her plate away and focused directly on Ellie.

"No, who is Josh to *you*?"

God. There was no way she would deny him, especially after how vulnerable he'd looked, how bereft, when he'd said they had no future. Josh needed to know that she saw him. But what was she going to say? He's my lover? He's haunting me? I'm haunting him?

She looked across at Josh and told the truth. "We're together."

"Since when?" Vic demanded, at the same time as Liam frowned and said, "You haven't visited him in the hospital even once."

"I was at the hospital today," Ellie argued weakly, but Liam wasn't listening. "It's been weeks," he muttered, "you haven't visited him at all."

"Hey," Victoria turned on him, high streaks of color burning on her pale cheeks. "She's hardly left her house. She was in the same accident. An accident *you* helped cause."

"I still think—" Liam started.

"That's not important now." Vic cut him off. Liam responded with a mocking laugh, and in seconds, they were sniping viciously at each other across the table. Both blaming the other for not stopping Warren, both claiming the other should have done more, seen more, cared more.

God, Ellie hated conflict.

Josh grunted and held out his hand. She took it without

thinking and wrinkled her nose at him. "This is going well," she murmured.

Josh shrugged. "Maybe we should put them on the naughty step?"

Just like that the tension that had been building in her fizzled out, and she giggled.

Which cut Liam off mid-tirade. He waved his hand pointedly toward her. "See, that. What the hell is that?"

Ellie guiltily moved their clasped hands onto Josh's thigh.

"No. No." Liam shook his head, a vein beating visibly in his throat. "It's too late. You think I don't know? You think I'm stupid, but I'm not." He leaned forward, nostrils flaring. "I listened to all the old stories Mum used to tell. About her Celtic granddad who read the cards and was always uncannily accurate in his predictions. And her grand-aunt who knew the minute her son died on the battlefield because she spoke to him *after he was dead*." His fists clenched on the surface of the table. "And I've been watching you talk to air since the moment we met."

Josh's eyes widened, the muscles in his jaw ticking in a way she hadn't seen since he first started appearing. "I forgot about that," he whispered. "I forgot about the cards and the soldier. I guess I thought they were just stories."

He started to pull his hand away, but she held tight. The worry and distress rising in his eyes was too much to bear. She leaned into him, no longer caring what Liam and Vic saw. "I believe in you, Josh. You *are* real. This is just more proof."

"No." His voice rasped. "It means I'm dead... or as good as."

No. That couldn't be true. She wouldn't let it. "You're

not dead. You're in the hospital." She turned to Liam. "Tell him he's alive. Tell him!"

But Liam didn't tell Josh anything. He stormed out of his chair and around the table, reaching out toward the space where Josh was sitting as if he would strangle him with his bare hands. "He *is* here! You've been here the whole time. You fucking bastard!"

Josh stood, and the chair fell back with a crash, which only seemed to incite Liam further. He thrashed through the air, hands stretched out toward where Josh had been, roaring, "How could you do this to me?"

Josh stepped out of Liam's reach even as his brother flailed more wildly, his face going dangerously blank. "*You* did this, Liam."

Liam turned the wrong way, still searching. "How could you? Fuck you, Josh! Fuck you!"

Josh clenched his fists, bringing them up in a fighter's stance. But Ellie could see what Josh had missed: tears were streaming down Liam's face.

She grabbed Josh's arm, drawing his attention. "Wait, he's hurting. Look at him."

Josh growled, but his face was already softening, already taking on the protective air she recognized. "He's... what?"

Liam turned, and they could all see his distress. "Why?" he asked brokenly. "Do you know how many hours I've spent sitting beside your bed—Mum too? Do you know how much we've cried?" He dragged in a sobbing half breath. "She asked me so many times if she would ever see you again. And I had to sit there. Knowing it was all my fault. Knowing you might be gone forever. And you never once... you never... you were *here*."

Josh lurched back, stunned, and Ellie stood for a moment, torn between the two brothers. But then she stumbled forward—she could help them both, she could be their voice—and rested her hands on Liam's arms, turning him to face her. "Josh didn't know. He would have wanted to see you, but he didn't know."

Liam scraped a hand over his cheek, dashing away the tears. "I don't understand."

She shook her head. "I don't either. But when he came here, he didn't remember anything. We only figured out who he is today, and we started looking for you straight away."

"But you didn't tell me!" Liam sniffed, scrubbing at his damp cheeks.

Ellie snorted sadly. "How would that have gone? Hey, Liam, I've only known you for three seconds, but I think your friend tried to kill me... which you helped him with. I also know you broke into my house to steal the only thing I have of value. Oh, and by the way, I'm sleeping with your brother who is a... ghost? Maybe?"

Liam winced, but the tension in his frame softened slightly. "Okay, that's fair, I guess." He wiped his nose with the back of his hand. "He's here? He's with us now?"

"He's with us," Ellie agreed.

"Right," Liam said shakily. "Right. Can I... Can you tell him I'm sorry?"

"I can hear you, arsehole," Josh muttered. "It's Ellie you should be down on your knees begging for forgiveness, not me."

Ellie huffed an amused breath. "He can hear you, Liam. Just speak to him, and I'll tell you what he says. He's standing next to me."

Liam stared intently at a spot at her side—the opposite side to where Josh was standing—which made Josh growl and Ellie want to laugh hysterically. She took pity on them both and told Liam where Josh was, then wrapped her arm around his waist, linking her fingers into his belt. It probably looked bizarre, but she was fine with it.

"I'm sorry, Josh," Liam said earnestly. "I'm going to do better, I promise. You remember that time I ran away from home? Mum was working such long hours, and I guess you were busy. When I think about it now, you were sixteen years old, working hard at school and carrying two part-time jobs to help with the bills. But I was eleven, and I hated being alone, and I wanted you to pay me some attention." Liam gave a small, wry smile. "You realized I was gone pretty quickly, and you came looking for me. You found me down at the bus station buying a ticket. I was going to London to look for Dad. Hell. That would have been a disaster, right?"

Josh let out a rough breath. "It would have been a disaster," he agreed.

"You didn't even shout at me," Liam continued. "I thought I'd get a blistering lecture, but you took me for ice cream and apologized for ignoring me. You said you wished I'd stay because you and Mum loved me. But, if I really felt I had to go, I should have told you where I was going, should have made plans for who I'd stay with. And then you took a bunch of ten-pound notes from your wallet and gave them to me. It was everything you had. You said the most important thing to you was my safety." A fresh set of tears dripped down Liam's cheek, but he didn't seem to notice. "You've always looked out for me. Always protected me. But now, *you* aren't safe. And it's all my fault."

"God, Liam." Josh rubbed the back of his neck with his free hand. "It'll be okay. We'll figure it out."

"No," Liam replied. "It's really not okay." And then he jerked violently. "I heard you! Fuck me. Say it again."

"It's okay," Josh said again. His face was pale, a deep frown carving a groove down his forehead, and the tendons in his neck stood out in harsh lines. The air around him seemed to grow even more charged, the metallic tang of ozone even sharper. "We're going to be okay," Josh said roughly.

"I can see you!" Liam whispered. And then he flung himself forward into Josh's arms.

Ellie stepped back, giving the brothers space as they held each other. Liam wept, and Josh supported him—they supported each other—as they found some peace. Some forgiveness. And as Liam's tears slowly ebbed.

Ellie gave a watery smile to Vic, who, after her initial gasp of shock, had settled into a wide-eyed stillness as the brothers embraced. She had the look of someone who had been through too much in one day to truly process a response. But, after a few moments, Vic dipped her chin and returned a small, shaky smile.

For the first time, Ellie felt like there was hope for their family. That they might make it through the damage that Warren had done.

Eventually Liam stepped back, looking tired but far more settled.

But Josh... Josh looked exhausted. Somehow making himself solid had utterly drained him, and even as she watched, he seemed to grow a little less distinct, a little more translucent.

"There's still something I don't understand," Vic said, looking between them all as Ellie made her way back to hold Josh as he leaned heavily against her. "Why did Josh come here to Ellie?"

"Something happened between us during the accident,"

Ellie answered slowly. "I can't explain it, but it linked us somehow."

"*Don't leave me*," Josh murmured, the words twisting through her like an oath. "That day, lying there on that rough tarmac, I was broken. I was going to close my eyes and let it all go. I was so tired. So cold. The pain was so excruciating. But you said, 'Please don't leave me.' And maybe something in me recognized you, because I stayed."

She stared at him, words frozen in her mouth. He'd stayed for her. He'd come back for her.

She wrapped her arms around him, tucking her head under his chin. He was so cold, his skin like ice, and she tightened her grip, pouring all her own heat, all the love growing in her heart, back into him.

She felt him press a kiss to the top of her head just as Liam gasped, and she knew no one else could see him now.

"I won't leave you, Ellie. Not if I can help it," Josh whispered, just for her.

She believed him. But she also knew the world. Knew how difficult it would be for him to keep that promise.

# Chapter Thirty-Three

Josh looked up from where he leaned on the rails of her decking as Ellie stepped outside.

The vicious cold that had gripped him earlier had eased. The tingling in his hands and at the back of his neck had slowly faded. And the feeling of warmth grew as Ellie came closer.

Her hair was up in a ponytail, her T-shirt slipping off one shoulder, and he wanted to scoop her up and carry her back to their soft, safe bubble. And then strip the offending T-shirt away completely and convince her to stay there with him.

"Hey, honey." She smiled tiredly. "The kids are asleep."

He snorted. "Are they really?"

She stepped into his arms, looking up at him with shining eyes and a widening grin. "I honestly don't know," she admitted. "I said goodnight and ran."

A laugh rose through his chest. It was one of his favorite things about her: the way she had of always finding humor. No matter how dark, no matter how difficult, the situation.

"What have you been doing out here?" she asked.

Josh shrugged, rocking gently just to feel her body moving with his. He'd been thinking of how to find Warren and end the threat hovering over Ellie. He also needed to work out how to help his brother... and whether Liam deserved help in the first place. And he needed to visit his mother. He wanted to introduce Ellie to her—which was unsettling enough—but it also reminded him to worry about what kind of future they could possibly have together.

But he didn't want to talk about any of that with the moon rising over the trees, the fresh night air smelling of the forest, and Ellie in his arms.

"I was thinking about the best way to start haunting my brother," he said instead. "I used to make slime for him to play with when he was little. I reckon it would make an amazing ectoplasm."

Ellie chuckled and he smiled down at her. What was the point in thinking about Liam when he had Ellie pressed against his body? "Or... we could take a walk together." He kissed her cheek and then the side of her mouth, right on top of her smile. "Let's go see if we can hear the owls."

She let out a low laugh. "Is that what we're calling it now?"

"What do you mean?" He widened his eyes innocently.

"I remember what happened the last time we took a walk in the forest. And the last time we heard the owls. Also, it's a bit too dark."

He kissed her again, just below her jaw, along the soft smoothness of her neck. "What would you suggest then?"

She turned her face to catch his earlobe gently in her teeth, tugging it slowly before pressing a scorching kiss to the tingling flesh. "I thought we could have a dip in the hot tub."

He groaned. "Fuck, yes."

"I'll just go and get my swim—" She broke off with a low gasp as he slid his fingers under her shirt and started dragging it up.

"Do you really need to?" He tugged a little higher. And then, when she lifted her arms, he pulled her shirt over her head and off, revealing a black lace bra that sent even more blood to his rapidly lengthening cock.

"Or we could just swim like this," Ellie agreed, kicking off her jeans to stand in front of him almost naked, her skin glowing in the dim light. He hauled her closer once more, needing to kiss her and touch her and hold her. Needing everything about her.

He broke the kiss to look down between them, watching himself as he skimmed his fingers over the smooth fabric of her black silk panties, feeling her heat, the dips and valleys of her pussy. God, he loved the way she widened her legs, giving him better access, even as her hands wound around his neck and pulled him back to her mouth for another kiss.

Fuck, he wanted her. He wanted his aching cock inside her. He wanted to cover her, and take her, and know that she would always be his.

Ellie whimpered as he pulled his hand away and pressed a hard kiss to her mouth. It physically hurt to let her go, but he had to step away for a moment to strip off his own clothes. She watched him unashamedly and then led him across the deck to lift away the lid of the hot tub. A billow of steam filled the air, clouding the twinkle of the fairy lights that decorated the privacy wall.

He climbed into the hot water and turned on the bubbles, then held out his hand to help her in. She took it with a smile, her fingers linking with his as she stepped elegantly into the tub.

It was his fantasy come to life. The dark night

surrounding them, the light breeze raising goose bumps, and Ellie, beautiful and magical in the soft light.

Josh turned and sank onto the submerged seat, still holding her hand. And she lifted their clasped hands to press a kiss to his fingers before releasing him. She reached behind her back to unclasp her bra and then lowered it slowly, removing one strap at a time before dropping it outside the tub.

God, she was beautiful. Lit from behind by the glittering lights, her hair like a soft halo falling loose to her shoulders. He reached for her hips and guided her forward to stand in the V of his legs as he lowered his head and took a long, slow taste of her flushed breasts. He ran his tongue over the soft flesh, around the darkness of her nipples again and again before sucking one puckered tip into his mouth and laving it with his tongue as she squirmed and panted.

The bubbles churned around them, surrounding them with heated mist. Creating a tiny world, enveloped in fairy lights and enclosed by darkness, just for them.

He pulled her even closer, and she settled onto his lap, legs straddling his, nothing between them but a slip of soaked silk as he savored her. He kissed her breasts, her chest, her neck, her shoulders, her cheeks, her mouth, everywhere he could find her skin and taste it, luxuriating in the soft glide of Ellie moving against him.

His body ached with need for her, but he ignored it. He took his time. Adoring her. Reaching every part of her. As if they had forever to kiss and touch each other.

She pulled away, and he drew her nipple between his teeth, making her shudder, but she was determined. "I want you," she panted. "Come up."

He couldn't deny her. Or resist her. He left her skin with a last lingering kiss and then lifted himself to sit on the edge of the tub, while Ellie sank to her knees among the bubbles on the seat he'd just left. Looking up at him from between his legs.

He tucked a damp strand of hair behind her ear. "You're a siren. Enchanting. Utterly irresistible."

A smile spread over her face and he traced it, rubbing his thumb slowly across her lips. She nipped the flesh and grinned. "I promise not to sing," she said against his hand, "but pleasure... that I can give." And then she lowered her head and took his cock in her mouth.

Josh closed his eyes, shuddering. Her tongue tortured him, feathering over him so gently at first, it was almost painful. His balls were tight and heavy, drawn up against his body, and his cock pulsed with every pass she made.

Slowly she built pressure, drawing the head into her mouth and sucking gently, one hand coming to wrap around the stalk, just tight enough to drive him wild, while her other hand found his balls and tugged. And God. Fuck. He wasn't going to last.

He hauled her up and dragged her out of the water into his arms and carried her to the furthest lounger, hidden in the darkest part of the deck.

He lowered her gently and climbed over her. Her body was flushed and pink, her eyes sparkling. "I need you, Ellie," he whispered roughly. "I've never... I don't...."

She pressed her soft hands against his cheeks, and the emotion in her eyes nearly felled him. "I need you too. I know we said we can't let emotions get involved. But I have." She lifted her head to kiss him softly. "I'm falling for you, Josh."

"I'm falling for you, too," he admitted. He'd been terrified to acknowledge it. But it was the truth. And it felt like freedom.

He kissed her again, slowly and thoroughly, letting her sink into his skin. Letting himself sink into her. He kissed down her throat, over her clavicles, into the notch at their center. He kissed down her breasts, over her puckered nipples, and across her softly rounded stomach. Then he dragged her wet panties away and kissed her *everywhere*—reveling in her taste, her scent, everything about her—while she trembled and arched and eventually begged.

It still wasn't enough. He could never have enough of her. But he wanted her to have everything.

He lifted his head, ready to carry her up to her bed, but she dragged him back up her body to kiss once more. "Let's stay here," she whispered.

He blinked slowly, brain fogged and thundering with desire. "I don't have a condom."

Ellie smiled. "That's okay. I'm on the pill."

"Are you certain?"

"Completely."

"And your ribs?" he asked roughly.

Ellie let out an amused breath. "I had completely forgotten about them," she whispered.

And then she wrapped her legs around his waist and dragged him closer, until he could feel her body surrounding his, until he was fully joined with her and they began to move together. Powerful and primal and utterly connected.

Perhaps the stars wheeled across the sky. Perhaps the earth spun. He didn't know. All he knew was Ellie.

And when she found her ecstasy, he was right there with her. Their fingers wove together and gripped tightly. Their bodies clenched and spasmed around each other. And he knew the truth. He wasn't falling for her: he'd already fallen.

Afterward, he found some fluffy towels in the nearby closet and dried her carefully before wrapping one around his waist. Then he lay down behind her on the lounger, pulling her to sit with her back against his chest, her head resting on his shoulder, looking up at the stars as they drifted together.

His skin slowly cooled, and his worries rose once more. Ellie was strong and brave and smart, but she was also human. Vulnerable.

Warren had escalated from coercion to actively trying to hurt—maybe kill—Ellie. What would he do when he discovered she'd taken her accusations to the police? What would he do when Vic didn't go home?

In the distance, the tawny owls called to each other. The male's *hoo-hoo* and the female's *kee-wit* resonated eerily over the nighttime woodland.

The hair rose over the back of his neck, and he held Ellie tighter, reminding himself that the owls were beautiful. Magnificent. And mated for life.

They were not the harbingers of death—the guides to the underworld—his great-granddad had believed.

# Chapter Thirty-Four

Ellie knocked on the door nervously.

It had all happened so fast. She'd hardly had a sip of her morning coffee when Liam declared that he'd spoken to his mum and it was all arranged for her and Josh to go and visit.

A million excuses had swarmed through her mind, but one look at the guarded hope in Josh's eyes had pushed them away. He needed to see his mum. Of course. He needed to see her as soon as possible, just in case. And Ellie could help him do it.

She'd called her investigator and arranged a virtual meeting for the afternoon. Then they'd dropped Liam back at his flat and made the short drive to Donna's snug little terraced cottage. And now, here they were... and the excuses had mutated to miniature hounds, taking part in their own Wild Hunt through her belly.

She laced her fingers through Josh's and gripped them tightly, trying to remember to breathe.

It wasn't as if she'd never met parents before; of course she had. But this was Josh's mum. Josh, who always tried to hide—or perhaps not even feel—his emotions. And yet his face lit up when he talked about his mum. He'd rearranged his whole life when she needed him—and clearly there wasn't anything Donna wouldn't do for her sons either.

The thought of making a mistake was terrifying. Who was Ellie to this family, anyway? God, she wished she'd asked Liam what he'd said about her. She wasn't prepared. She needed more time. What was she going to say?

There was no time to find an answer. The door flew open to reveal a pretty, middle-aged woman with bright blue eyes and silver streaking through her dark hair. She was obviously Josh's mum—from the intensity of her gaze to the way she held her chin, she looked just like him.

"Hello, Ellie?" Donna asked, her eyes darting across her face and around the space behind her, her hands fluttering as if she didn't quite know where to put herself. "I'm so glad you're here."

"It's lovely to meet you too." Ellie tried to smile but couldn't quite manage. Hell. Was that the right thing to say? *Was* it lovely for Donna? Probably not. Nothing about this was lovely. She nudged Josh forward. "Um... He's here."

Donna took a nervous step forward, her hands stretched out, and Ellie moved out of the way. Beside her, Josh grunted out a tight breath, his face growing pale and strained as he concentrated. The sweet, metallic taste of ozone filled the room. And she knew from the awed grief and love on Donna's face that he was growing clearer. "Hi, Mum," he said quietly.

Donna flung herself forward, her arms coming up to enfold him. Tears ran down her face as she rocked him. "Josh," she murmured, "Joshy. My beautiful boy."

Josh—so tall and strong and brooding—seemed to melt. He held on to his mother, whispering, "I love you, Mum. I'm here," again and again while Donna cried quietly. And

Ellie thought her heart would break for this beautiful family, who'd been through so much and who obviously loved each other so deeply.

She wiped her eyes and left them to have a private moment. She wandered through the front room, enjoying the proud display of photographs. Josh holding a swaddled baby and looking down with astonished adoration. Josh and Liam with scraped knees and rosy cheeks standing side by side. Josh's arm around his younger brother's shoulder, a football in his other hand. Josh graduating. Liam grinning, holding a gleaming trophy. The house was full of their love for each other.

Ellie explored until she found a kitchen where she made cups of strong tea for herself and Donna and a small glass of ice water for Josh. Then she let herself into the small conservatory and sat looking out at a tiny garden. The space was wild with spring abundance. There were dog violets and flowering blackthorn covered in tiny white buds. Bumblebees visited the bluebells. And everywhere she looked, there were bird boxes and birdbaths.

Donna and Josh found her there, watching a pair of house sparrows carrying twigs and pieces of grass up toward the roof. Donna's face was damp and tear-streaked, and Josh was glassy-eyed and quiet, but they both seemed at peace.

Ellie looked around for something to say, but before she found it, Donna pulled her up and into her arms, squeezing her tight. "Thank you, Ellie. For bringing my son home."

Ellie closed her arms slowly around the older woman, wishing she deserved the gratitude. "I don't—"

Donna shushed her. "You kept him here. You gave him this chance," she whispered in her ear. "Thank you."

They held each other for a minute before settling at the table to drink their tea. But even as they sat, Donna's eyes filled with worry, her attention focused on Josh—who looked increasingly strained and grim.

"Sorry, Mum," Josh said roughly, "I can't hold this... I can't stay solid enough."

Donna leaned across the table to press a kiss to her son's forehead. "It was perfect. Seeing you. I couldn't ask for anything more."

Josh sighed, a long breath of relief. Donna blinked, and then blinked again before turning away to subtly wipe her eyes, and Ellie knew he'd faded. Only she could still see him. But even to her, he looked a little less substantial than usual.

Donna asked a question, and Ellie laced her fingers through Josh's as she replied, passing on his comments from time to time when he interjected. They chatted easily, Donna sharing stories until she hopped up and grabbed a much-loved album bulging with photographs of Josh and Liam.

Donna ran her finger slowly over a picture of her and the two boys sitting side by side on a sofa wearing Christmas jumpers and grinning. "I love your smile so much, Josh," Donna said, mostly to Ellie. "You stopped smiling for so long. I mean, you loved your animals—those magnificent birds—I know you did." Donna's head was down, her focus on the photo, but there was a new kind of sadness, an element of regret, in her tone. "I always felt that maybe they were easier for you than dealing with people. You never really trusted anyone again after your dad left."

"No, Mum, I always—" Josh started, but Donna waved his words away almost as if she'd heard them.

"I know you trusted me and Liam," she continued. "That was it. And when Liam fought you more and more, when he pushed you away... it hurt you." She sighed. "I often wondered if that was why you needed to go so far. All the way to Scotland. So you could help your birds—creatures you always let go—and never have to trust anyone again. Never get close to anyone or anything again."

"Mum," Josh rasped as Ellie wrapped her arm around him, looking for the right response and failing.

Donna looked at the air beside Ellie where Josh sat, although she couldn't see him. "I'm so glad you came back so I could tell you how much I love you." She smiled even as she dabbed her eyes. "I'm glad I get this chance to tell you that you don't have to shut yourself away for the rest of your life. I should have said something before, but I didn't want to hold you here. I didn't want to add to that heavy burden of responsibility you've shouldered for so long. And now, look"—Donna turned her soft gaze to Ellie—"you're figuring it out for yourself."

Ellie swallowed heavily. Josh had been so alone for so long. Just like she had. She leaned against him, offering her support. Offering herself. And her love.

Donna closed the album, and they moved on to lighter subjects, talking quietly and drinking their tea. But Josh looked increasingly exhausted. The stress of seeing Liam, the emotion of the morning, and straining to make himself visible was clearly pressing on him. She held his hand, feeling the cold grow within him, knowing that soon he would fade, and wishing there was something—anything—she could do.

"Do you know anything that can help?" she asked Donna. "Anything at all? Maybe something passed down in your family?"

Donna shook her head sadly. "I don't. I'm sorry. My granddad always claimed that the sight ran in our family, but I don't know that any of us grandchildren really believed it. My mother certainly never claimed to have any special abilities." She looked across to the chair where Josh was sitting. "Except... maybe Josh does, after all?"

They all chuckled. And Ellie snorted when Josh added quietly, "*Now* you tell me."

Donna raised one eyebrow. "There's always true love's kiss—" She paused dramatically. "—but I'm guessing you already tried that."

Ellie coughed, and Josh spluttered a choked, "Mum!" but Donna just hummed quietly, amused at her own joke.

Ellie adored her. What would it be like to have a family like this? To meet Donna for lunches or Sunday dinners. To be embraced with so much love.

It would be a dream. A dream she'd never even dared to truly dream before.

# Chapter Thirty-Five

THEY PULLED up outside the cottage in the warm afternoon sunlight. Josh let out a slow breath as his body finally released the tension he'd held all day. They were home.

*Home.*

Somehow, this hidden cottage had become his home. It was the place he wanted to come back to at the end of the day. To the peaceful garden, the lush vegetable patch, the steamy art, and the curious, bright-eyed friendship from Nissy. But mostly, it was Ellie he wanted to come back to.

They climbed out of the car, stretching tiredly. The last few days—especially the effort he'd poured into making himself solid enough for his family to see—had utterly drained him, and Ellie looked just as wiped. She had her video call to make, and then they were done. Then they could finally rest for a few moments. Thank fuck.

And yet... a frisson of something traveled up his spine. A strange spike of awareness.

Victoria's car was still parked on the drive. The cottage still looked like something out of a fairy tale, with its aged stone walls covered in flowering clematis, all surrounded by forest. But with every step they took toward the door, his hackles rose.

Perhaps it was exhaustion. Perhaps it was all the hours of stress. But something wasn't right.

Ellie must have felt it too. Her shoulders tightened, and her steps slowed. She pulled her phone out and double checked her new alarms. "Nothing has been triggered," she said quietly.

But then why did it still feel so wrong? Josh ran his eye over the cottage again, looking for anything out of place. "Where's Nissy?" he asked. Usually, she'd be sitting on the windowsill enjoying the sunbeam. But she wasn't there.

"I don't know." Ellie looked around them before shaking her head. "Maybe's she's out the back."

Maybe. Hopefully. But she didn't sound convinced. And neither was he.

They let themselves inside. Ellie dropped her keys in the bowl in the hallway before lifting her eyes to meet his in the mirror. It was so much like the first moment he'd seen her, and yet so different. Because now he would give anything—everything—to stay with her.

He stepped forward, wrapped his arms around her waist, and dropped his chin to her shoulder so they could watch each other in their reflection.

Ellie closed her eyes, leaning back into him, and he used the time to watch her face, to memorize it. They held each other, resting together. And he very nearly started to relax. Until a rough sound—a strange, hushed scraping noise—cut into the silence, and her eyes flew back open.

"Vic?" Ellie called. "Is that you?"

Nobody answered.

"Nissy?" Ellie squeezed his arm and then pulled away to stride toward the kitchen. "Victoria?"

Her hand was on the door, just pushing it open, when Josh heard the whimper. And then he knew.

Alarms didn't work if they weren't set. No security system in the world could keep out an intruder who'd been invited in.

He flew forward, desperately reaching for her. "Ellie! Stop!"

But it was too late. The door was already open, and Ellie was already frozen in the doorway, her face draining of color as she stared, horrified, inside.

Josh grabbed her shoulder, ready to pull her back from whatever was in that room, but she dug her heels in and refused to move. And he could immediately see why.

Victoria was sitting at Ellie's beautiful polished wood table. Her hands were tied in front of her with rope, her mouth was stuffed full of navy fabric—a tie perhaps—and a scowling man sat beside her playing with a wicked-looking carving knife.

A quick glance at the wall showed a gap on Ellie's magnetic knife holder where it used to be.

The man looked athletic, with perfectly styled dark hair, a short, well-groomed beard, and the coldest eyes Josh had ever seen.

"Warren," Ellie hissed. "What the hell are you doing?"

"Come in, Ellie-belly." Warren gestured her inside with the blade. "We were just talking about you, weren't we, darling?"

Victoria shook her head frantically, and Ellie's eyes narrowed. "Don't call me that."

But Warren only sneered. "Come in," he demanded. "Right now."

Ellie glanced back toward the door, and Warren immediately shifted the knife to Victoria's throat. "Don't even think about it. In fact, *Ellie-belly*"—he stressed the words—"let's see those hands while you take a nice big step forward."

Ellie slowly raised her hands and stepped closer. Her fingers were trembling, but she held her chin high. God, he was so proud of her. So proud, and so fucking terrified.

"And another. And just to be clear, if I hear an alarm, or an unusual noise, or even sense that you've triggered the fancy new security system I noticed at the front door, I will slit her lovely throat." Warren shifted his grip on the knife's handle, and Victoria swallowed heavily, her eyes brimming with tears.

What the hell was he going to do? Josh stalked through the door just behind Ellie, sticking as close to her as possible as she walked into the kitchen and up to the table.

The only thing on their side—the only glimmer of hope to hold on to—was at least Warren couldn't see him.

For the first time since he'd woken up and realized that everything was wrong, he was grateful that he wasn't truly a part of the world. That he wasn't real. He was grateful that only Ellie could see him, and that Warren had no idea he was there.

Ellie's phone taunted him from her back pocket, but there was no point in calling anyone—they wouldn't be able to hear him anyway. And he didn't dare to trigger a panic button and endanger Vic. Watching Warren murder her friend would kill Ellie—and she would risk everything if she thought it might happen.

He had to make sure that it *didn't* happen. There was nothing he wouldn't do to protect Ellie, and that meant protecting the family she had created.

Josh inched around Ellie, stepping carefully so that he didn't jostle her on the way past. He couldn't leap over the table and risk Warren shoving the blade into Victoria's throat—not yet—but he could stand beside Ellie. He could let her know he was with her. And he could wait for the perfect moment.

"What are you doing here, Warren?" Ellie asked again.

"Well, let's see." Warren shifted his chair even closer to Victoria. "It seems that the police have been looking for me. I've had several calls. Even an officer waiting for me outside my house. I'm supposed to go down to the station to *help with inquiries*." He spat the words, injecting them with scorn. "And as soon as I saw them, I knew exactly where my missing lover had disappeared to." He pressed a kiss to Vic's ashen cheek, but his eyes were open and on Ellie the whole time.

"It's *not* your house," Ellie said quietly.

Warren's eyebrows shot up. "What did you say?"

"It's not your house," Ellie said louder. "It's Victoria's."

Warren barked out a laugh, loud and abrasive in the tense silence. "Oh, Ellie, Victoria's mine. What's hers is mine. Surely you know that by now?"

A slow tear tracked down Victoria's face, but when Warren glared at her, shifting his grip to dig the blade deeper into her skin, she carefully gave a tiny nod.

"So... what?" Ellie prompted. "You realized Vic was here and decided to visit?"

She sounded so confident. So cool and collected. But Josh could feel the way her body trembled at his side. Could see the short, strained breaths she was taking. She was holding it together, but only just.

And then he saw Nissy. She was lying in the corner of the room, blood on her fur. And he almost vomited. His heart thundered in his ears and his palms grew clammy. He couldn't let Ellie see her, he couldn't—

Nissy lifted her head and looked at him. Fuck. What a time to realize that Nissy had always seen him. She blinked, and then lowered her head tiredly. She was alive. She would be okay. And it was time for Warren to pay.

"I caught a cab," Warren said as Josh dragged his attention back to him. "You owe me two-hundred and twenty pounds for that, by the way."

"I don't owe you anything," Ellie replied, stalking forward. "You're insane."

A mottled flush spread over Warren's face, but he stayed seated. Kept his blade pressed to Vic's throat. "You'd think you'd be more polite to the man with all the power here," Warren said as tilted his head toward the empty chair across the table. "Sit down, Ellie. I'm tired of looking up at you."

Ellie sank into the seat, her voice shaking as she argued, "What's the point of this? Surely you can see that this ends badly for you. If you hurt either of us, you'll go to prison for the rest of your life."

Josh disagreed. Warren didn't think it was going to end badly for him. He was a narcissist, convinced he would always get his way. It was clear from the look on his face. But Ellie always tried to fix things. She would try to fix this, too. Unless he fixed it first.

Josh squeezed her shoulder, and she tilted her chin, caught his eye, and held it for a second, recognizing him. Seeing him. Even in the middle of this terrible nightmare. God. He loved her. "I'm here," he murmured, knowing only she could hear him. "I'm with you, Ellie."

Warren sneered. "I'm not going to jail. I promise you that."

Ellie leaned forward, her hands spread over the table as she glared at Warren. "I'm not giving you my game or my company, and I don't have anything else of value. Even if I did give them to you—even if I promised you the whole world and everything in it—as soon as we stepped out of here, it would all be over anyway. No court in the world would uphold a contract signed under duress."

"That may be...." Warren shrugged. "But that's not at all what happened."

Here it was. Josh let go of Ellie's shoulder and slowly started to step around the table.

The silence stretched until Ellie eventually capitulated. "What did happen, then?"

Warren grinned. "Everyone knows how jealous you've been, Ellie. How you would do anything to have Vic's life. We tried to keep away, tried to stay out of your path, but you couldn't let go. Everyone knows you're a geeky loner, stuck down in your basement playing violent games. Everyone knows about your mental health problems."

Ellie flinched, and Victoria hung her head, sobbing quietly. And Josh stepped forward. He was going to kill this fucker, and he was going to feel a lot better. And since no one could see him, he genuinely wouldn't be going to jail.

Ellie must have seen the violence in his face, because she grabbed his hand and whispered, "Please don't. I don't want Victoria to get hurt."

Warren must have assumed he was finally breaking her; his eyes shone even brighter. "It all came to a head when you accused me of a crime—with no evidence, no reason other than to harm me." Warren gestured with his free hand, the movement jarring his hand holding the knife and digging the blade deeper into her friend's delicate skin. "Victoria confronted you. And you were so enraged that you attacked her with a kitchen knife. You fought, but she managed to defend herself. Unfortunately for you, the knife turned. You'll die of your injuries before the ambulance can get here."

"No one will believe you," Ellie whispered. "I already gave a statement to the police. Victoria will tell the truth."

"Victoria will explain that as soon as she found out you'd called the police, she came here to try to talk reason into you. She'll weep over the loss of her friend. And then she'll get the game, the company, her grandmother's house, the man, and the wedding of the year," Warren said smugly, nostrils flaring. "She'll do as she's told."

"I trust her." Ellie looked across at Victoria and gave her a reassuring smile that nearly broke Josh's heart. "Vic is one of the best people I know. She'll do the right thing." Ellie's hand was shaking in his, but she didn't back down. "And she won't be alone. Liam knows the truth."

Warren laughed. "No one will believe the drop-out who broke into your house. In fact, I think you'll find he was even cycling behind you on the day of your 'accident.' Victoria mentioned some photographs of his eyes from when he tried to break into your system and steal your IP... I'm sure your constable would love to take a look at those."

Josh had heard enough. He let go of Ellie's hand and stalked forward, rounding the table just as Ellie stood, her fists clenching into tight balls of fury. "No. You don't threaten Liam. You don't threaten Vic. You don't threaten *my family*! You pointless, useless, incompetent arsehole!"

The mottled flush on Warren's face turned crimson as he roared. "Don't ever speak to me like that!"

And maybe she'd been waiting for that moment. Or maybe Victoria had borne too much and finally snapped, but she launched up, crashing into Warren with a muffled scream.

Everything happened in slow motion.

Victoria hit Warren in the chest, but he didn't lose his grip on the knife. He surged to his feet, dragging Vic up with him by her hair. And, in the uncontrolled fury of the moment, the knife slid along her throat, slicing a vicious gash. Victoria fell, bleeding, choking, and screaming into the gag in her mouth, but still kicking out at Warren.

Ellie let out a wail of fury and terror and leaped. But Warren had already pulled his hand back, already wound up, and then his arm was swinging forward, wrist snapping as he released the knife and threw it straight at Ellie.

Josh didn't hesitate. There was nothing in his mind except his need to protect her. He would sacrifice *everything* to keep her safe.

He flung himself into the path of the blade, willing himself solid—pouring every ounce, every iota of energy, all the warmth Ellie had given him, all the trust, all the hope, all the love—into taking the knife.

It embedded in his chest as he flew over the table, slid across the smooth surface, and crashed brokenly on the other side.

Ellie screamed; a horrified wail of utter despair. And the sound pierced him all the way to his heart.

Somewhere in the distance, Warren howled and Victoria sobbed brokenly. Nissy met his gaze and then dropped her small head.

The world faded and flickered. Black mist swirled around his vision. There was only pain. Agony.

Josh closed his eyes. Opened them in a white hospital room. The ceiling spun as nausea churned, and he retched around the tube in his throat. An alarm rang discordantly. Fuck. *Fuck.*

He closed his eyes.

Opened them in Ellie's kitchen. He was crumpled on the floor and she... she was a goddess of vengeance. She picked up a chair and smashed it over Warren's head where he stood staring at Josh in abject horror. Warren lifted an arm to defend himself too late, and the wooden legs caught him with vicious strength. She was magnificent.

Warren crashed to the floor beside Victoria, tried to crawl, and then slumped unconscious. Vic spat out the gag and pressed her bound hands to her throat, dark blood running slowly down them.

Not arterial. The thought filtered in through the haze.

Thank God. Because Ellie was going to be alone. She would need her friend. They would need each other.

Josh blinked. A white light blazed. Someone called for a crash cart. "I'm losing him!"

He blinked again. Ellie spun back to him. She threw herself down beside him, pulling out her phone to click the panic button. "Hold on, hold on." She found his hand and gripped it tight, even as she dialed 999 with her other hand.

She shouted something, begged for help, gave her address. He wasn't really listening. The blaring sirens had followed him. His soul was untethered. Drifting. Only she held him.

There was only Ellie, and the growing darkness.

"I love you," he whispered. "I'm glad, so glad we had this time. I wouldn't take it back." He lifted his hand to her precious face, streaked with tears and wracked with desperation. "I'm sorry I couldn't stay. I wanted to. I would have, if I could."

"Don't leave me," she sobbed. "Please. Please, Josh."

He shuddered, body spasming. The words unraveled through him. They couldn't hold him this time. He'd had his moment. His precious, shining, magical moment.

Ellie must have felt it too, because her tears poured harder. Her hands cradling his face were almost as cold as he was. "I love you. Do you hear me?" She kissed him frantically. "I don't want to be without you. I can't do it."

"You're the strongest person I ever met." He coughed, the taste of iron filling his mouth. "You can do anything. Tell them I said goodbye."

There was Ellie.

And then there was only darkness.

# Chapter Thirty-Six

ELLIE MOVED through the world as if she was a phantom herself. The paramedics came and bustled around Victoria while Ellie held her hand and tried to explain what had happened.

She found Nissy and cradled her small body while she rang the emergency vet and tried to talk through her sobs.

The police came and dragged Warren away as he cursed and stumbled, pausing to vomit all over her driveway before being shoved into the back of a police car. Blue lights swirled. People shouted. But all she could hear was Josh saying goodbye. All she could feel was Nissy's panted breaths.

She called Liam. She said something, tried to explain. Or maybe she didn't. Maybe she just cried, and he knew what she couldn't say.

Somehow—she didn't know how, she couldn't remember giving her address—a vet came and took Nissy, promising to care for her as if she was his own. It physically hurt to part with her, but there was nothing more Ellie could do to help her. She had to trust. Even so, she clung to Nissy's precious body, wishing she could somehow imprint her with her love before she reluctantly handed her over.

Then she climbed into the ambulance with Vic. They rode to the hospital together, both crying, their hands gripped tightly even as the paramedics worked around them.

She called Vic's mum and then sat beside her bed until she was taken away for surgery.

She called her dad and left a message when he didn't answer.

Everything was a blur.

She found Josh's ward and stumbled there, begging to see him. She had to see him. The nurse said something, but she couldn't hear what it was, only the gist. She couldn't go in. She wasn't family. Oh God.

She couldn't breathe. Her lungs were trapped in a vise. Her entire body trembled, panic clawing at her. Ellie doubled over, wrapping her arms around her waist, trying to suck in air. The panic was back, and this time it wasn't a familiar demon; it was a vast and terrifying monster. It was right on top of her, tearing at her skin, suffocating her, overwhelming her.

Josh needed her. She didn't know if he was still alive. Didn't know if the knife had destroyed him. Didn't know if he was lost in the darkness. And she couldn't reach him. She couldn't even breathe.

And then, suddenly she wasn't alone. Soft, warm arms came around her and Donna was there. And then Liam too. Donna held her like a mother would. Whispering and shushing. And she clung to her, weeping with her, finding her path back through the panic, as Donna's words slowly penetrated. "He's alive."

Ellie scrubbed shaking hands over her cheeks. "He's alive?"

"He's still unconscious. And there was—" Donna took her hands and gripped them in her own. "There was a scare. His heart stopped. But they got him back."

"Is he...? Did he wake up at all?" Ellie whispered.

Donna shook her head, a tiny, tired motion. "No. He's still in a coma."

God. Ellie didn't want to tell them. Didn't think she could bear it. But she forced the words out. "He was... hurt. There was a knife." She swallowed against the heavy ache in her throat. "He said goodbye."

Donna flinched, blinking against her tears. "I think I knew."

"I'm sorry," Ellie whispered, despair and grief, guilt and fear twisting through her. "I'm so sorry. This is all my fault."

Donna tugged her to sit in one of the plastic chairs, Liam on her other side, and waited until Ellie looked up and met her eyes. "None of this is your fault, Ellie. None of it. You brought my son *back*." She leaned forward, still gripping Ellie's hands. "Do you know how seldom he smiled? After his father left, it was like he had to save everyone, all the time. But with you—he laughed again. He was happy. You gave him that." Fresh tears flooded over and slid down Donna's face. "He loved you, and I'm glad."

"I'm glad too," Liam agreed brokenly. And they clung to each other, three strangers brought together by their love for Josh, supporting and holding one another.

Eventually, Donna wiped her face and stood. "Come. We've cried enough." She pulled Ellie with her as she explained to the nurse that Ellie was Josh's fiancée.

They made their way into his room hand in hand. It was so white. So cold. And Josh looked so fragile, so alone.

He had a drip in his arm, a feeding tube taped to his face and inserted into his nose. He was so pale, the bruises under his eyes so dark, that it almost took her to her knees. But it was her turn to hold on to Donna, to support her as they made their way closer.

And she did it. One aching step, one wavering breath at a time, they held each other. And when they sat beside Josh, they sat together, the three of them.

An hour later, a nurse came to tell her that Victoria was out of surgery. Donna and Liam promised to stay with Josh —and call her if there was any change—so she made her way down to the women's ward and waited for Vic.

She called the vet, who assured her that Nissy would be fine and even let her FaceTime to tell Nissy how much she loved her. It looked like Warren had kicked her, but with time and care, she would be okay.

Vic came back with a nurse who explained that the cut in her neck was shallow enough that they could clean and stitch the wound closed without major surgery. Warren had missed her artery and her esophagus. Thank God. But the trauma would be another question.

Ellie sat quietly as Vic came out of the anesthetic, offering her ice chips when she needed them.

"Ellie," Vic croaked eventually, "I have to tell you how sorry I am. I have to tell you—"

Ellie shushed her. "Please don't be sorry. It was all Warren. All of it." She pressed a kiss to her friend's forehead. "I only wish I'd realized just how bad things were for you."

Vic shook her head gingerly, wincing as the moment tugged her wound. "I wouldn't have listened. I—" She looked away. "I wanted him to love me."

God. Ellie hadn't realized it was possible to hurt any

more that day than she already had. But it was. "I know you did," she whispered. "That's okay."

"It's not okay," Vic rasped, her eyes heavy with exhaustion and red from crying.

"It will be," Ellie replied, stroking her hair. "We all want to be loved, Vic. It's going to take time, but Warren's gone now. And we can do it together."

"How's Josh?" Vic asked carefully. "Is he... okay?"

Ellie tried to smile, but all it did was make her tears spill over. "His heart stopped when the knife..." She swiped at her eyes with her sleeve. "They got him back. But he's still in a coma. There's no change."

Vic leaned against the raised back of the hospital bed and closed her eyes. "I'm sorry."

"No more apologies," Ellie whispered. "Focus on getting better." She pulled up a blanket and tucked it carefully around Vic's shoulders and then sat with her until her mother bustled in and took over, crying dramatically and demanding to see her baby.

Victoria looked more horrified about her mum's theatrics than the news that she would have to stay for a night to make sure there were no complications—but it was the first spark Ellie had seen in her friend, and it gave her hope.

She hugged Vic gently and promised to come back in the morning—or sooner if Vic needed her. Neither of them mentioned that her own father hadn't come at all.

It stung, but in a strange way, it didn't hurt as much as before. Ellie didn't need Steven's approval. She was creating a new family. A family who loved and supported each other, even when things were bad.

She gave Vic one last careful squeeze and made her way back up to Josh's room. Donna and Liam were where she'd left them. She settled in between them and took Josh's hand.

They didn't talk. There was nothing to say. But just being there, together, was enough.

The sun set, and Donna and Liam got ready to leave, but Ellie couldn't do it. Maybe tomorrow. Maybe next week, she would have the strength, but not yet. Liam took her keys and promised to see what he could do to clean up at her house, and she thanked him gratefully. And then she pulled the plastic chair close to Josh's bed and told him stories—about her life, about the future she wanted, about the future they could have—but he didn't stir.

She reminded him of the owls, mated for life, creating a home just outside their window. But he stayed just as still as ever.

She threaded her fingers through his and leaned her forehead against their clasped hands and told him the story of the orcs she was going to write into a game. With a brooding orc rebel who climbed the ranks young, trusting no-one, and the witch who escaped with him from the cruel king's dungeons. How they fell in love, and their love was powerful and true. How their love was enough to save them.

But he didn't wake.

She kissed his hand, whispering, "It's you, Josh. It's you I love." But he never moved.

And then she put her head down and wept, her tears soaking the crisp hospital sheet.

There was no work she could do. No effort she could make. No way to save him. But she didn't let him go. Even when she closed her eyes and finally drifted into a strange and shadowed sleep. She held on.

# Chapter Thirty-Seven

THERE WAS DARKNESS. And there was a woman.

She spoke to him. A rambling dialogue interspersed with the occasional huff of irritation or snort of quiet laughter.

The melody of her voice rising and falling unsettled him as much as it soothed him. It held him in the darkness, and it beckoned him toward the light. It was the voice of a siren, dragging him to the rocks. Beautiful and otherworldly, bathed in soft light, the ocean bubbling and roiling around her. She was a fantasy and a dream, both utterly intoxicating and utterly impossible.

Sometimes she cried. Those were the worst times. He could hear the desolation of her grief. The misery that gripped her. But he couldn't see her or touch her. And she didn't hear him when he called.

He swam through the darkness for a time, floating in the currents that tugged at him and tried to drag him down. But he never sank. Something gripped him. Held him. And ever so slowly, he drifted toward the surface.

There was pain there. Sharp and bright. And there was... Ellie.

God. There was Ellie. And she was in danger.

He flew into consciousness, choking on the tubes in his throat, fighting to escape the needle taped to his arm. Machines blared alarms, and bright lights burned his vision. Someone pushed him back, but he bucked against them. He had to get to her.

Someone tugged the tube, pulling the tape off his cheek and then drawing it out, and he gagged as it scraped his throat, choking and swallowing hard. Panic shoved his heart rate up until it thundered in his ears as he flailed for purchase.

"Ellie!" he rasped. Fuck. His muscles were so weak. The astringent smell of hospital disinfectant assaulted him. But then she was there, pushing through the nurses, grabbing his hand and forcing herself closer. And he could hear her precious voice over all the noise, or perhaps despite it. Perhaps he would have heard her all the way from hell.

"Josh! Josh, I'm here." Her hand grasped his and her beloved, tear-streaked face was beside him, and then she was cradling him, her arms around him as she rocked him.

"I heard you." His voice grated over his raw throat, but he had to tell her. "I heard you, and I came back."

She wrapped herself tighter around him. "I love you. God. I love you so much. I thought I'd lost you."

"I love you, too," he croaked. "I *was* lost, but you found me. I'll always come back to you, Ellie." He swallowed against the ache in his throat. He almost didn't want to ask, but he had to know. "Nissy?"

"She'll be fine." Ellie pulled out her phone and showed him a video from the vet: Nissy with a bandaged chest, lying in a basket, paw dangling, her favorite toys around her, looking into the camera with amber eyes.

And somehow, that was what broke him. He sobbed helplessly, clinging to Ellie as they wept and then laughed and then wept again. And then she called for Donna and Liam, and everyone was there. He was surrounded by love. *They* were surrounded by love.

She was real and he was real. She loved him and he loved her. And nothing else in the world mattered.

# Epilogue

There were a thousand glittering lights. Purple and red spotlights flashed, a huge monitor array blazed with car chases, sword fights, gun battles, and magic, and gleaming champagne bubbles rose and popped. But Josh only saw Ellie.

He leaned back in his chair and watched as she strode across the stage wearing a floor-length shimmering silver dress held up by two tiny straps he was looking forward to sliding down her smooth shoulders later, a stunning silver-and-diamond pendant shaped like Arwen's Evenstar around her neck, and combat boots. She would have gone barefoot and brought Nissy if she could.

She looked out across the room to meet his eyes and grinned. God, he loved her.

And then she held out her hand and called Victoria and Duane to the stage to stand with her, to share the spotlight and the accolades.

From the moment they got the news, she'd been sharing the glory. She'd told everyone that they won Game of the

Year together, and they would collect their awards together too. Because that was Ellie's way.

He knew her acceptance speech well enough that he could concentrate on watching her as the words rose and fell.

She was everything—the courageous warrior battling the shadowy fae to save her lover, the wild and brilliant witch seducing her orc and uniting a kingdom, the siren surrounded by the frothing ocean, and so much more. She was his friend. Her mind was so full of curiosity and ideas that it never failed to challenge and delight him. She had glued his family together. She was the woman who had pulled him back from the darkness and given him hope. She was his lover. She was the other half of his soul.

On the stage, Ellie flung her arm around Vic, and the two women rocked together, beaming and laughing.

Victoria still flinched at loud noises and sometimes seemed oddly fearful of dark corners and shadowy nooks, even with Warren in jail far away. The investigators Ellie hired had found enough evidence to help the police put him away for years. But Vic was slowly starting to smile again and even graciously accepted Ellie's help with putting a deposit down to secure her house.

Josh took a sip of his champagne as Liam caught his eye from across the table where he sat with their mum. Liam was wearing a wool and silk twill tuxedo—Josh had no idea what that meant, but Liam had told him at least three times —and his mum was in sky-high heels and a plum velvet dress embroidered with hundreds of tiny beads. They'd gone all out with their sparkling evening wear, even though Ellie had told them several times that most people would be wearing jeans and leather jackets.

Ellie still hadn't heard from her father. He never called

again after she'd decided not to sell her game. And Josh knew it still hurt her. But it didn't stop her from loving freely and openheartedly. And she adored his mum just as much as Donna adored her.

His mum looked happier and more relaxed than he remembered ever seeing her. Liam had gone back to live at home while he built his physiotherapy practice, and they enjoyed needling and teasing each other, looking after each other, and spending time together in a way they never had before. And Josh's relationship with his brother had never been better. For the first time ever, they were becoming true friends.

True friends who sometimes wanted to strangle each other, but who never forgot how much they loved each other.

On the stage, Ellie thanked the rest of her amazing team at Dangerous Business Games, calling on them to stand and share the applause as she, Vic, and Duane lifted their trophies. They had won best design, best narrative, and overall game of the year.

And given the excitement already building for *Strong Hold*—the first game ever to center entirely around an orc romance—it wouldn't be more than a couple of years before Ellie was back to accept another award.

Fans were already clamoring for the release date. And the art they sent to Ellie... Josh had never seen art so evocative, so primal, or so erotic in his life. It had already inspired several nights of orc games, and he was looking forward to many more.

He shifted in his seat, and Ellie's grin widened. Of course she was looking at him just at that moment. Their eyes met and held. And by the pink rising on her cheeks, she was thinking something very similar.

The speeches finished, and the food was served while Ellie moved slowly through the room, accepting congratulations and well wishes before settling in beside him. Lobster bisque shots with a swirl of truffle oil were followed by a beef Wellington with buttery flaky pastry, rich mushrooms, and tender beef, and to finish, the creamiest, airiest honey cheesecake he'd ever tasted. He still —even all these months later—appreciated every bite. And it tasted even better with her at his side.

They laughed and chatted and told jokes. And when the dance floor opened, Josh pulled Ellie to the floor just so that he could hold her in his arms.

They swayed together as the music rose and fell around them. Other people danced in wild, joyful circles, but he kept her close. Her body was warm and fitted against his perfectly. The darkness didn't threaten him; not with her light shining in the world.

He lifted her hand and spun her out and back, loving how she tilted her head up, eyes sparkling and full of joy as she rested her palm against his chest.

"You look magical," he whispered against her ear, and her smile grew even wider.

"I feel magical," she replied, looping her hands around his neck as they danced. "I'm so glad you're here." She chuckled. "And tomorrow, we can take a day off and just sleep."

"Mm-hmm," he agreed noncommittally. Ellie had stuck to her decision to take more time to relax. She went for walks now. She'd started swimming in the morning even when the sea was freezing. And he distracted her whenever he could.

He'd also found a balance. He'd joined a birds of prey sanctuary as the consultant veterinarian, and, for the first time, he was there when the birds stayed. They took in other animals too—hedgehogs and little roe deer—and sometimes those stayed too. And every day, he went home to Ellie. And sometimes they did take a day off and just sleep.

But not tomorrow. The fridge was full of strawberries, champagne, and the pancake batter he'd prepared while she was getting dressed earlier. He'd spent an hour setting soft towels, organic massage oils, and plenty of snacks ready beside the hot tub. There was even a luxury tin of chicken and salmon in gravy for Nissy—her favorite. And a gorgeous vintage leaf-and-vine diamond-and-sapphire engagement ring was hidden in his sock drawer. There wouldn't be much sleeping if he could help it.

But not yet. Tonight was for celebrating her team, her achievement, the family she'd made. For dancing and laughing. For remembering how close he'd come to the darkness, and how grateful he was for the light.

He bent and pressed a kiss to her cheek. "I love you, Ellie."

She smiled up at him. "I love you, too."

There were glittering lights and smiling faces, and joyful music in the air, but all of it faded into the background. Because there, in his arms, was Ellie.

# Thank you!

Thank you for reading Ellie and Josh's story. I hope you love them as much as I do. And I'm sorry if you cried as much as I did!

I write stories about strong women, brooding heroes, and found family. Sometimes they're contemporary paranormal or supernatural, sometimes they're high fantasy set in other worlds, but they're always romance first, full of suspense and spice, and touched with magic. And they always end with a HEA.

Find out more here:
https://jennielynnroberts.com/

You can also visit to sign up for my newsletter and receive the prequel to my completed medieval fantasy romance series—The Hawks—for free.

Or if you're reading an e-book, simply click here: and get Kaden right away!

I hope to see you there,
    Jennie x

# The Hawks

Steamy medieval, adult fantasy romance filled with brooding warriors, courageous heroines, swords, shifters (kind of) and tons of action. Expect court intrigue, betrayals, found family, and a band of loyal brothers.

This series is complete.

Kaden

**He has to leave. He can't take her with him. And he needs to go now.**

**(Only for newsletter subscribers)**

Tristan

**His redemption might be her downfall…**

Val

**He'll do anything to save her. And then he'll say goodbye…**

Mathos

**All he has to do is find the princess, help her claim the throne, and not fall in love with her. Easy…right?**

Tor

**What is it about her that makes him lose his mind? Every. Damn. Time.**

Reece

*She's everything he doesn't want.*

*Honorable. Beautiful. Strong... wait, what?*

# The Blood Shadows

Three couples rise to battle a deadly foe threatening London—and the world—in this paranormal romance trilogy.

Expect shadow magic, supernatural danger, found family, plenty of spice, fated soulmates, and a villain corrupted by an ancient evil.

This series is complete.

### Shadow Guardian

**Not all Shadows are what they seem.**

*Shadows are growing over London. Their enemy is powerful—and closer than anyone realizes. Can Kay and Ethan claim their happily ever after? Or will the darkness take them first?*

### Shadow Seer

**Their Shadows recognize each other immediately. Their hearts need a little more time…**

*Zach and Emma will need to trust each other if they want to overcome the danger ahead. Will they take a chance on love, or walk away and face the darkness alone?*

### Shadow Healer

**To reach the light, first they have to face the Shadows….**

*There's nowhere left to hide and time is up. Can Riley give James a second chance? Or will they stand apart, divided, while everything they love crumbles?*

# About the Author

Jennie Lynn Roberts believes that every kickass heroine should have control of her own story, a swoony hero to fight beside her, and a guaranteed happily ever after. Because that doesn't always happen in real life, she began creating her own worlds that work just the way they should. And she hasn't looked back since.

Jennie would rather be writing than doing (almost) anything else. But when she isn't building vibrant new worlds to get lost in, she can be found nattering with friends, baking up a storm, or strolling in the woods around her home in England.

If you want to talk about books, romance, movies, or reluctant heroes with Jennie, feel free to contact her.